SACRIFICE

Also by Laura J. Burns and Melinda Metz

CRAVE

SACRIFICE

o o o o o o o o o o o o o o o o

LAURA J. BURNS &
MELINDA METZ

SIMON & SCHUSTER BFYR

NEW YORK   LONDON   TORONTO   SYDNEY

SIMON & SCHUSTER BFYR

An imprint of Simon & Schuster Children's Publishing Division
1230 Avenue of the Americas, New York, New York 10020
Copyright © 2011 by Laura J. Burns and Melinda Metz
SIMON & SCHUSTER BFYR is a trademark of Simon & Schuster, Inc.
For information about special discounts for bulk purchases, please contact Simon &
Schuster Special Sales at 1-866-506-1949 or business@simonandschuster.com.
The Simon & Schuster Speakers Bureau can bring authors to your live event. For more
information or to book an event, contact the Simon & Schuster Speakers Bureau at
1-866-248-3049 or visit our website at www.simonspeakers.com.
Also available in a SIMON & SCHUSTER BFYR paperback edition
Book design by Chloë Foglia
The text for this book is set in Jenson.
Manufactured in the United States of America
2 4 6 8 10 9 7 5 3 1
The Library of Congress has cataloged the paperback edition as follows:
Burns, Laura J.
Sacrifice / Laura J. Burns and Melinda Metz. — 1st ed.
p. cm.
Summary: Vampire Gabriel and half-vampire Shay, convinced that
they can make their relationship work, run away to Gabriel's coven expecting
them to embrace her as one of their own, but instead they view her as an
abomination and a threat, not belonging in either world.
ISBN 978-1-4424-0818-0 (pbk.)
[1. Vampires—Fiction. 2. Love—Fiction. 3. Interpersonal relations—Fiction.
4. Identity—Fiction. 5. Supernatural—Fiction.] I. Metz, Melinda. II. Title.
PZ7.B937367Sac 2011
[Fic]—dc22
2011005044
ISBN 978-1-4424-3900-9 (hc)
ISBN 978-1-4424-0819-7 (eBook)

For our mothers, Grace Burns and Jan Metz
"Always choose love and forgiveness"

SACRIFICE

PROLOGUE

EMMA

ONCE UPON A TIME . . .

That is the way my story must begin, because mine is a strange and magical story. Once upon a time, I fell in love. Yes, it begins there, with love, but not a simple, ordinary love, because once upon a time, my beloved revealed a secret to me. He revealed he was a vampire.

And that only made me love him more. I loved him for the compassion and knowledge his hundreds of years of walking the earth had given him. And he loved me for exactly who I was, although he had seen many women more beautiful, more gifted, more *everything* in all those years.

Soon I had a secret to tell him—I was carrying his child. Again, a secret made our love grow deeper. We decided we would begin our happily ever after. We would marry, and our child would bring our two worlds together. Our child wouldn't be human. Our child wouldn't be vampire. She—for some reason, we both felt our baby was a girl—would be something new, something special. Throughout history, once in a great while, such children had been born, but none had survived. We were sure ours would be different, because our love was so strong.

We had many dreams for our little girl, my beloved Sam and I. We decided we would call her Shay, because the name means "a gift" and that's what she would be to us. We hoped she would be a gift to all humans and all vampires as well, a gift that would unite them, that would take them the first step toward living in peace.

Sam gave me a beautiful necklace engraved with two birds flying through a sky that held a sun and a moon both. He said it had belonged to the woman who was his mother in everything but birth. He said that one day we would give the necklace as a gift to our gift, our Shay, and that it would symbolize the two worlds that had been brought together in her. Day and night. Human and vampire.

In that moment, I thought nothing could be more perfect than our love.

And then he abandoned me. I never saw Sam again.

When we think about fairy tales, we think about happily ever afters, forgetting the darkness that stories beginning with "once upon a time" so often contain.

I tried to protect Shay from that darkness. But there was no way to shield her from the truth: Life is not a fairy tale.

○ ○ ○ ○ ○ ○ ○ ○ ○ ○ ○ ○ ○ ○ ○ ○

"GABRIEL!" SHAY MCGUIRE YELLED. "Gabriel, help!"

He can still hear me. With his vampire senses, he could probably hear me from a mile away, she thought frantically. But the thick glass doors of the research center had closed between them.

"Why are you doing this?" Shay gasped. "Where are we going?"

The guy on her left didn't answer, his mouth set in a grim line as he dragged her through the lobby. Shay's mind whirled, unable to match the ultra-ordinary room—tall, long reception counter; waiting area with magazines just like every other waiting area in the world—with the horror of strong hands on her arms, cold eyes regarding her as if she were some kind of vermin. Two men, just to keep hold of her? She was small. She was human. She was weak. It didn't take two vampire men to subdue one sick girl.

"Let go!" she shrieked. Shay dug the heels of her boots into the pale gray carpet and twisted her body, trying to pull away. She still had the strength that Gabriel's vampire blood had given her, and maybe they wouldn't expect her to fight. It worked with the guy on the right—he jumped in surprise at her loud cry, and his grip loosened. The one on the left just tightened his fingers around her wrist like a vise.

"Shut up," he said, and then he jerked her so hard that she would've fallen if the other guy didn't reach out to steady her.

"Where are we putting her?" the second guy asked. "Ernst said the cellar, but there's only the storeroom, and that lock is wonky."

"I'll tie her hands, then." The first guy, the worse one, kept pulling her forward while he spoke. As if he couldn't wait to get rid of her. As if he couldn't stand to be in her presence.

They're afraid of humans, Shay reminded herself. She had a fast impression of a lab—stainless-steel tables, glass cabinets filled with vials and beakers, an industrial-size fridge, a centrifuge—then she was yanked through another door and down a long set of metal steps. The temperature dropped and the air took on a metallic tang.

Shay took a deep breath, trying desperately to get her thoughts under control. Gabriel had brought her here, to his family. He'd told her all about the place and about the people she would meet here. She hadn't expected them to haul her around like a sack of trash, but maybe if she kept herself calm and just talked to them, they'd see she was no threat.

They were taking her down a long corridor now. Through a

half-open door, she spotted a broom closet. It seemed so . . . normal. And normal was weird, in this case. Although she'd known that they didn't live in some Gothic castle, somehow she hadn't pictured it being so bland. Gabriel's family ran this entire research center. They were scientists, all of them, including both of these men. Scientists and vampires.

"You're Richard, right?" she said to the one dragging her. The mean one.

He didn't answer, but his gray eyes narrowed.

"And you're Luis." She took in the darker skin of the other guy, his thick black hair, his Latino features. There were only two other men in the family besides Gabriel and Ernst, their leader. And Ernst had stayed outside with Gabriel. Shay knew that Richard was serious— that's how Gabriel had described him. The guy with the death grip on her arm was definitely serious. Hence, Richard.

"Don't talk to her," he said.

But Luis was staring at Shay now, and he looked a little spooked. "Luis, I know all about you," she said in a rush. "I know that you came from Texas and that Sam and Gabriel found you there when your parents were killed. I know you like *Iron Chef* even though you can't eat—"

"Shut. The hell. Up." Richard jerked her arm up behind her back, and Shay cried out in pain.

"Richard! What's going on?" A pale, blond woman had come down the stairs behind them and stood staring at them open-mouthed. "I thought I smelled Gabriel. I ran back from the caves as fast as I could."

Tamara, Shay thought. The only one of the family she hadn't met yet. If you could consider being taken captive "meeting." Shay tried to remember what Gabriel had told her. Tamara was with Richard. She was the only one who hadn't been brought into the family as a child.

"Gabriel showed up with this human," Richard said, a sneer in his voice. "Ernst wants her locked away."

"I'm Sam's daughter," Shay cried, her eyes pleading with the woman. Gabriel hadn't told her many details about Tamara, but Shay wasn't getting anywhere with the other two. "I'm your family. Gabriel said I'd be safe here."

Tamara gasped, her eyes widening. "Sam's daughter? The baby with the human woman?"

"Yes." Richard's voice was like a knife.

"She's an abomination," Tamara breathed, backing away as if Shay were contagious.

"I'm your family," Shay repeated desperately. "Gabriel said I would be welcome here, he said—"

But Tamara was already gone, racing back up the metal steps.

"Get the duct tape," Richard said, pushing open a door. He shoved Shay inside, his eyes searching the room. *Searching for an escape route*, Shay realized. *Making sure there isn't one.*

Luis appeared in the doorway with a roll of tape. Richard pushed Shay down on a wooden chair—the only piece of furniture in the small room, which was mostly filled with shelves—and yanked Shay's arms behind her back. Luis wrapped the tape around her wrists, binding them together.

"That hurts," Shay said, her voice coming out barely louder than a whisper. Her pulse was pounding in her ears, and her breath came fast. Shock was robbing her body of the strength she'd gotten from drinking Gabriel's blood. Five minutes ago she'd been sitting in a car with Gabriel, talking about these people—Richard and Luis and Ernst—as if they were friends. Family. Safety. She'd been looking forward to meeting them.

Luis reached over to loosen the tape, but Richard knocked his hand away. "Let's get back to Ernst."

"But I'm one of you," Shay said, fighting down her fear. "I'm like you. I'm half vampire. I'm not a regular human."

"You're a thing that should never have been born," Richard told her. "And that's worse than a human."

"Gabriel said you'd accept me," Shay stammered. "He said . . . because I'm Sam's daughter, and Sam was your brother . . ."

"Sam was a traitor," Richard cut her off. "He betrayed us all."

He turned and stalked out of the room. Luis followed, not looking at Shay. The door slammed shut, and the lock snapped into place, and Shay was left alone in the dark.

"Gabriel," she whispered. "Help me."

I've got to get to Shay. I've got to get to Shay. The thought spun through Gabriel's mind in a frantic loop. Where was she? Had they hurt her, his brothers? He stared at the glass doors to the research center as if he could will them to open and return Shay to him.

She needed their protection. Didn't they understand that? The human world would be no more accepting of a half vampire than a full one. Humans would be as much a danger to Shay as they were to his family.

"We should go inside," Millie said softly. But she wasn't talking to him, she was talking to Ernst.

"Whose car is that?" Ernst asked, his voice sharp and grating. It took Gabriel a moment to realize that the question was directed at him. His gaze strayed to the Escalade ten feet away, but he couldn't really comprehend what Ernst had said. His mind was filled with a fog of fear.

"We . . . I stole it," Gabriel said slowly. *I've got to get to Shay. Got to.* "We had her stepfather's car at first, but he had it traced and came after us. When we ran from him, we had to steal another one. There was no choice."

"How much more trouble have you brought to our door?" Ernst spat.

Gabriel just stared at him, the words making no more sense than the tone of voice. Ernst was his father, the one who had taught him everything about the life they led, everything about being a vampire and about the importance of family. But his voice was that of a stranger.

"Ernst." Millie's voice was sharp. "Gabriel's home, that's what matters."

I've got to get to Shay. "I'm sorry," Gabriel said out loud. "It's been a difficult time. I . . . did what I thought I had to." Was that what Ernst wanted to hear? Gabriel would say anything he had to if it would help him get to Shay.

Ernst ran a hand through his silvery hair—he was the only one of them old enough to have gone gray before he gave up the sun. "I ought to be the one apologizing. You've been through an ordeal," he said. "It's simply that you startled me with the human, my son. The vehicle isn't a problem."

"Gabriel!" Tamara pushed through the front doors of the research center and stopped, gazing at Gabriel suspiciously. "I could smell you even from the caves."

"Sister," Gabriel murmured, forcing a smile. "How are the bats?"

"Surviving. The white nose syndrome appeared in one colony since you left," she told him. "Where were you? What happened?"

"There will be time for explaining later," Ernst cut in. "Tamara, take this SUV to the cliff and drive it off. It can't be found."

Her eyes flicked over to the Escalade. "I won't have time to dump it and get back before dawn."

"You'll have to take to the caves," Ernst told her. "Find one of the entrances back by the cliffs and hide there for the death sleep. We cannot risk someone tracking a stolen car here while we're all vulnerable."

"Of course." Tamara went straight to the SUV and backed out of the tiny parking lot—there weren't many visitors to the remote research center, so they didn't need more than a few spaces. Gabriel felt a stab of worry as she drove off. He'd never felt close to Tamara— she'd joined their family as a vampire, rather than being raised with them from childhood the way Millie had, and Richard and Luis. It didn't seem fair to ask Tamara to take a risk to cover for him, but Gabriel couldn't offer to do it instead. *I've got to get to Shay.*

"Come." Millie took his arm and gently steered him toward the building. "Ernst, come."

She led the way inside, through the seldom-used lobby, Gabriel beside her and Ernst behind them. Gabriel's gaze went straight to the stairwell door. His brothers had taken Shay through there and downstairs, to lock her up at Ernst's command. He could smell her panic.

I promised her she'd be safe here, he thought, his stomach twisting with worry. He wanted to shove through that door and run down to Shay, to let her out, to get her away from his family. How could he have been so wrong about them? Didn't matter. He'd find a way to make them understand that this was the place Shay belonged. They were shocked, frightened, the way they were of all humans. They needed time. Gabriel had needed time too. At first he'd only been able to see Shay as a human like all other humans, like the humans who had slaughtered almost his entire family so long ago.

Gabriel forced his eyes away from the stairwell and followed Millie around the reception counter. She led the way past a small conference room and a bathroom. When they reached the thick steel door at the end of the hall, she punched in the code that unlocked it, and she, Ernst, and Gabriel headed down the windowless corridor that led to the lodge where the family lived. The labs and reception area were in the main building, on the outside of the mountain. The lodge where their true lives were lived—the common room and sleeping quarters—was behind it, in a structure carved out of the rock, as if it were a part of the Tennessee mountain itself. There was no possibility of sunlight leaking inside.

Only when they reached the common room in the lodge did Millie stop and turn to Gabriel. "Sit down," she said. "You must be exhausted."

"Yes." He sank onto the leather couch, so familiar. When he'd been chained to an exam table in the office of Dr. Martin Kuffner—Shay's stepfather—he had pictured this room a thousand times, trying to remind himself of home. He'd imagined every detail again and again to escape from his prison, at least in his mind. The plasma

TV, the racks of DVDs and CDs, the pool table, and the foosball table—Richard, strangely, loved foosball, even though he was so serious most of the time. He'd tried to re-create Tamara's huge abstract paintings in detail and to remember every title in Millie's collection of travel guides crammed on the bookshelves. She read and reread them as if they were novels.

He'd wanted to bring Shay here and give her the comfort he always found in this room.

But it offered no comfort now. *I've got to get to Shay.*

"Tell me," Ernst said, sitting next to him. "What happened to you?"

"It was my own fault," Gabriel said. "I went online, to one of those vampire sites."

Millie snorted. "Wannabe vampire sites."

"Usually, that's all it is," Gabriel agreed. "But this was different. Well, this one message, anyway. It was about Sam."

Millie sucked in a sharp breath, pain and guilt clouding her green eyes. But Ernst didn't react at all.

"This person was looking for Sam. Knew his name and his description. All kinds of details about him. I e-mailed back and forth for three hours, trying to figure it out. I thought it must be some kind of hoax."

"By who? Nobody knows about Sam but us," Millie whispered.

"The human woman," Ernst said coldly. "The one he betrayed us for."

"Yes." Cold fear seeped into Gabriel's belly. They were getting too close to Shay's mother, and he had promised Shay that he wouldn't let them hurt her mother. Shay had trusted him, but all his promises seemed empty right now. "The woman had known the details." He wouldn't say her name. He wouldn't tell Ernst anything about Emma McGuire. He'd find a way around that truth.

"We should have taken care of this years ago." Ernst shook his head. "Why didn't you tell me?"

"I don't know." He *didn't* know. Usually, he told Ernst everything, but when he'd seen Sam's name in print, read descriptions of Sam's wiry dark hair, his olive skin, his donkeylike laugh . . . it had felt private. Like getting a glimpse of his friend—his brother—again. And he missed Sam. It was a constant ache in his soul. Ernst wouldn't have understood that.

"What happened then?" Ernst went on, all business. "You didn't tell this woman anything about us, did you?"

"Of course not," Gabriel said. "It wasn't the woman, anyway. It was a man, a doctor. They were married, but . . . something happened to her. I'm not sure."

Can he tell I'm lying? Gabriel wondered. It wasn't possible to lie to his family, not when things were normal. Not when their communion was in place. Family members felt one another's emotions like their own. But his own communion with his family had been severed when he was captured by Shay's mother and stepfather.

Ernst was frowning, as if he didn't quite buy the story. Gabriel rushed on before his father could think through it any further.

"Dr. Martin Kuffner, he's the one who took me. He's famous. He studies leukemia, or he did. Then he met Shay." Gabriel's voice wavered when he said her name, he couldn't help it. Shay, who he'd held in his arms only yesterday. Shay, who had changed every opinion he held about humans. Shay, who he loved.

"The girl?" Millie asked.

Ernst made a sound in his throat. Disgust. Revulsion.

"Yes. She was sick and no one knew why. Martin married her mother, and he began researching a cure for her blood disease, but of course it wasn't really a disease. She's Sam's daughter. She's half vampire, half human. It made her weak. Actually, it almost killed her."

"It should have died at birth," Ernst spat. "If I'd had any idea that *thing* could live, I would've hunted down the woman myself."

"Modern medicine," Gabriel replied. It was what Sam had said to him, back when he first found out about Emma's pregnancy. Modern medicine would keep the baby from dying the way half bloods always died. And it had—it had kept her alive, but always on the brink of death. "Anyway, Martin knew the truth about Shay's father."

"Because the woman couldn't keep her mouth shut," Ernst said. "No surprise there."

"She only told him—a doctor she thought could save her daughter. She never even told Shay," Gabriel protested. "The mother was gone by the time I met Shay, and Shay still didn't know who her dad was. Think about it. This girl just found out what she truly is a few days ago. She needs a place . . ."

Ernst's expression had clouded over, and Millie's eyebrows drew together in confusion. Gabriel let his words trail off. He shouldn't be defending Shay. They weren't ready to hear it yet. He couldn't let them see how attached he was to her, not any more than he already had. He had to stay calm, act rational . . . and keep them from suspecting that he planned to rescue her if he couldn't find a way to convince them to let her stay.

I've got to get to Shay. He planned to take her out of here if his family wouldn't accept her. He was willing to leave his home, to anger and betray his father. Just like Sam had done when he'd fallen in love with a human. The realization stunned Gabriel. The thought made him sick. But if that's what it took to keep Shay safe, that's what he would do.

"This Martin, he's a monster," Gabriel went on, the words coming quickly. That part was true, and it was easy to let his fury and hatred show. "He's almost pathologically ambitious. He never cared about Shay's sick blood, he only wanted to find out what characteristics were vampiric, so he could use them in his science. Create medicines with the blood, isolate what makes us strong, what makes us immortal. It's the fountain of youth, and he wanted to discover it."

Ernst leaned forward, his long fingers steepled in front of him as he listened. "I shouldn't be surprised," he said. "They know everything about blood now, about DNA, about life itself. I should have seen this threat coming."

"It's very recent science," Millie pointed out. "Barely the blink of an eye to you. You spent centuries in a world where people believed in dragons and demons."

"All the more reason to keep them from believing in vampires," Ernst shot back. "I shouldn't have let Sam's woman live."

"It's Martin you have to worry about," Gabriel said. "He's obsessed. When Shay's blood proved useless, he went looking for her father."

"And he found you online. What then?" Ernst asked.

"I agreed to a meeting. I know I shouldn't have," Gabriel said before the others could. "I wasn't thinking. I wanted to find out how he could know about Sam. I didn't think there was any danger."

"And?" Millie asked.

"And he had hawthorn," Gabriel said. "He injected it before I even knew he was there." It wasn't true, or at least not the whole truth. A human could never have snuck up on him unless he was distracted . . . and he had been, by Shay's mother. She was talking to him, proving to him that she knew about Sam. And Martin had come from behind while he was focused on Emma.

"He knew how hawthorn would affect you?" Ernst asked.

"I guess maybe Sam had told . . . the woman," Gabriel admitted. "Maybe he didn't really believe it, who knows? None of us had ever actually experienced hawthorn before. I always thought the danger was a myth myself."

"It didn't kill you," Millie said.

"It paralyzed me. I could see everything, hear everything . . . but I couldn't move." Gabriel wrapped his arms around himself, a feeling of nausea overtaking him at the memory. "It didn't dull my senses at all, or my thoughts. I was entirely awake, in the prison of my own body. I had to watch while they dragged me into a van, while they chained me to a lab table. I was a rat to be experimented on. I had to listen to Martin describing his plans for glory while he drained my blood day after day, and I couldn't so much as spit at him."

"The hawthorn must have severed our communion," Ernst said. "If I'd felt you in such distress, I could have followed your emotions to you. I would have rescued you."

"The link was cut immediately," Gabriel agreed. "As soon as the paralysis set in, I reached for the comfort of my family. But you were gone, all of you." It had been the worst part, in fact. Since the day he gave up the sun, centuries ago, Gabriel had been able to feel his family's emotions, to know where they were and that they were with him. The communion was a gift that the blood ritual gave to them . . . and that the hawthorn had taken away.

"Gabriel, you were gone for almost a month," Millie said. "Were you—How long did the paralysis from the hawthorn last?"

"I'm not sure. I tried to count the death sleeps, but at the beginning I was panicked and then I was weak from hunger. I think it was only a matter of days. But he had me chained fast, and he took huge amounts of blood. Even after the paralysis wore off, I couldn't escape. And I couldn't feel any of you."

"Do you think the communion will ever come back?" Millie asked, turning her eyes to Ernst. He was the oldest of them and the one who'd raised almost all of them. Any question a family member had always went to Ernst.

"No," he said.

It felt like a slap. Even though his family was holding Shay now, Gabriel missed the connection to them. Its absence was a nagging pain.

"But we can restore it," Ernst added quickly. "Once broken, it won't come back on its own. We'll do a blood ritual, like we did when Tamara joined the family."

Gabriel nodded. Tamara had been a vampire already when Richard brought her to them. He loved her, so they all agreed she would join them. And Ernst had devised a ritual to let Tamara join their communion. *That's how easy it is when you fall in love with another vampire*, Gabriel thought. *If only Sam's love for Emma had been so simple. Or mine for Shay.*

"I'll gather the others." Millie stood up.

"Not now," Ernst told her. "Gabriel, you said this Martin would come for the girl. Why?"

"She's his test subject," Gabriel replied. Shay was also his stepdaughter, but he knew Martin didn't care about that. The way Martin had backhanded her across the face when she'd tried to keep him away from Gabriel had proved it. "He'd been giving her transfusions of my blood, and it made her stronger. He thought it was a breakthrough."

"That's why he drained your blood? But she isn't a full human. He had no real breakthrough," Ernst said.

"He was trying to figure out how the two could work together, vampire and human," Gabriel replied. "He told me that even for long life, no one would buy a drug that made them need to drink blood. No one would want to actually become a vampire. People would only want the strength and longevity, not the 'undesirable' aspects."

"He talked to you?" Millie wrinkled her nose.

"More like talked *at* me. He was thrilled with his own brilliance, he couldn't keep it to himself," Gabriel said. "I never said a single word back."

"That thing is in the supply room," Richard announced, coming into the common room with Luis on his heels. "The door's locked and we bound its hands."

"She's not a *thing*," Gabriel protested before he could stop himself.

They all looked at him, and he felt a rush of fear. He had to act reasonably if he wanted them to trust him. He had to pretend he wasn't horrified by everything his brother had just said. Shay, with her hands bound?

As if you didn't tie her hands yourself, a voice inside his head whispered. He'd kept Shay prisoner and bound her during the day while he fell into the death sleep. He'd treated her like a thing too. How could he blame his family for doing the same?

"What are we supposed to do with her?" Luis asked. "It's dangerous just to have a human here."

"She's here as bait," Ernst said. "Gabriel planned to use her as a lure for the people who took him. Dr. Martin Kuffner. And that human woman Sam left us for. They'll come for her, and then we'll kill them all."

"I told you Shay's mother wasn't involved," Gabriel protested.

"You told us more than one person abducted you," Ernst countered. "You said *they* put you in a van, *they* chained you to a table. Maybe the woman didn't interact with you, but she was there, my son."

Gabriel's mind was spinning. *I've got to get to Shay.* He had tried to keep her mother out of it, but had he slipped up? He was still so enraged every time he thought about Martin and those weeks held captive in his office that it was hard to think straight. And his own feelings for Shay were overwhelming—the gratitude for saving his life, the love, and now the fear. Was she all right?

". . . too risky drawing them here," Richard was saying. "Gabriel knows where Martin lives. We should go and kill him there instead."

"He's right. What if they bring other humans with them?" Millie asked.

"No. I'm not going back there," Gabriel snapped. "Don't you think Martin would expect that?" Besides, Shay's mother lived at Martin's house. He wasn't going to let his family attack her.

"We're safer here anyway," Ernst said. "We don't want to give Martin the advantage of fighting on his home turf."

"He doesn't want publicity. He wants to study vampires, and he wants a monopoly on it," Gabriel said. "He won't bring anyone else— he doesn't want anyone else to know."

"Well, how long is it going to take?" Luis asked. "We don't have any human food for the girl."

Ernst waved his hand dismissively. "There's no need to feed her."

Millie made a small sound of protest, but she didn't contradict him. Gabriel swallowed down his anger and tried to make his voice sound reasonable. "You want to starve her and keep her tied up? You're treating her as badly as Martin treated me."

"That seems only fair," Ernst said.

"She needs blood at least," Gabriel insisted. "She's sick, like I told you. She can't live without vampire blood."

"There's no sickness, there is only abomination," Ernst spat. "We're not going to waste our blood on that creature. We only need her alive long enough to be bait for the trap."

○ ○ ○ ○ ○ ○ ○ ○ ○ ○ ○ ○ ○ ○ ○

TWO

GABRIEL CAN SEE IN THE DARK, Shay thought. *My father—Sam—
he could too. Why can't I?*

She stared at the tiny sliver of fluorescent light that marked the
bottom of the door. It was all she could see. The rest of the room was
nothing but blackness. *Why did I have to inherit only the bad parts of
being a vampire?*

Shay chewed on her lip, trying to make herself think so that
she wouldn't go crazy with fear. She hadn't actually spent much
time thinking about her father since she'd discovered who he
was. She'd been too busy reeling from her new understanding of
why she was sick, of why nobody had ever been able to diagnose

her illness. Of why she had to live on other people's blood.

Well, that and being with Gabriel.

He'll come for me. He'll get me out of here, Shay told herself. But it wasn't comforting. She couldn't even imagine what they were doing to Gabriel. Would he be in huge trouble for bringing her here? He had told her how much they hated humans. Humans had massacred their family, a long time ago, back in Greece. Only Gabriel and her father had survived. And Ernst.

But I'm not human, Shay thought. That was supposed to matter. She was Sam's daughter, and Sam was part of the family. Gabriel had said that family was the most important thing to Ernst . . . but Gabriel had been just as shocked as she was by Ernst's reaction to her. Abomination. That's what he had said. Tamara said the same thing.

Half vampire, half human. Maybe she *was* an abomination. But she still felt like herself.

A loud humming sound startled her, making her heart slam against her rib cage. "Get a grip," she said out loud. "It's the heat coming on." Here in the dark, her hands bound behind her, in the lair of a gang of vampires, it was easy to feel like she was being held in some kind of nightmare world. Things like temperature control didn't really fit in.

Shay's heartbeat wasn't slowing down. She took a deep breath, but it didn't help.

"Self-check," she whispered. Her stepfather, Martin, had made her do self-checks every few hours back when he was still acting like a responsible doctor instead of like a mad scientist. And he was a good doctor, a famous and well-respected one. Not everything he had told her was a lie. The self-checks were important.

She couldn't take her pulse with her hands bound together by duct tape, but the pounding heartbeat told her that her pulse was too fast. Not good. But she didn't feel dizzy at all, and her extremities weren't cold. Well, no colder than the rest of her body. She did feel a little nauseous, though, and there was a monster headache building behind her eyes.

The effect of the blood is wearing off, Shay thought. She'd drunk from Gabriel before they stole the Escalade and set off for Tennessee. But she'd only taken a little. They had a long drive and wanted to get started. And she'd thought—they had both thought—that there would be plenty of time for her to have more when they got here.

They hadn't planned on Gabriel's family roughing her up and tossing her in the basement. But it had taken its toll on her, clearly. She didn't feel exactly weak yet, but she definitely wasn't as strong as she had been at the beginning of this interminable night.

What time was it, anyway? They'd arrived around midnight. It had to be at least three in the morning by now. Or maybe the darkness of the room and her terror just made it seem like more time had passed. Maybe upstairs, Gabriel was still explaining it all and once his family heard the whole story, they would let her out and she'd be able to feed from Gabriel.

I can pretend to write in my journal again, Shay thought desperately. That's what she had done during the day that Gabriel had tied her up, back when she was his prisoner. Before they'd realized that she was Sam's child. Before they'd made love.

Okay. Mind journal. Um . . . hi, I'm Shay and I'm an abomination. She let out a short, hysterical laugh. "Abomination." *That's what I'll call my autobiography.*

"Oh, for God's sake," a voice muttered at the door. The sliver of light grew to a rectangle as the door swung open, and a figure stood silhouetted against it. "They didn't even turn on the light?"

Suddenly, the room flooded with fluorescent light that seemed unbearably bright. Shay blinked back the tears of protest that sprang to her eyes.

"Sorry about that." It was a woman's voice. Shay tried to focus on her. Red hair, an elfin face.

"Millie," she croaked.

"Yeah. I'm on guard duty." Millie stepped into the room and let the door close behind her. She frowned at Shay. "Are you all right? I promised Gabriel I would check on you, not just stand out in the hall."

"Has someone been standing guard out there all this time?" Shay asked. "But my hands are tied. And any one of you could snap me like a twig."

Millie's eyes widened in surprise. "Well, yes. But you're human."

"Half," Shay muttered.

"Are you all right?" Millie asked again.

"No. My arms are aching from this," Shay admitted. "Why do I have to be tied?"

Millie hesitated. "I don't really know. It seems pointless to me." She glanced around the room—which was a storage room for things like office supplies and paper towels, Shay now saw—and picked up a letter opener from one of the shelves. She stabbed it through the duct tape that bound Shay's wrists, breaking the bond in about a tenth of a second.

"Thank you." Automatically, Shay reached for the locket around her neck, the locket that had come from her father, Sam. It was what she always did when she was upset, but this time the movement sent pain shooting from her shoulders down both arms. She winced. "Where's Gabriel? Is he okay?"

Millie's eyebrows drew together. "Why do you care?"

"I care about him," Shay said. "Just like you do. I know you . . . did he tell you that?"

The vampire girl took a step backward, toward the door, wary. "He told us your father kidnapped him and used his blood to feed you."

"Stepfather," Shay corrected her. "And I had no idea where the blood was coming from. But it gave me visions—during my transfusions—and I saw you in them."

"Okay, now you're freaking me out," Millie said, twisting the beaded bracelet she wore.

"I'm sorry. Sorry. I just don't understand." To her horror, Shay felt herself beginning to cry. She swiped angrily at the tears, the motion sending pinpricks through her hands. They'd gotten numb when they were tied behind her. "I saw your family in my visions, and there wasn't any evil or . . . Look, I liked you. I liked Ernst. I don't know why you're all treating me this way."

"Because you shouldn't be here. You shouldn't even exist," Millie said.

"Everyone keeps saying that!" Shay burst out, her breath coming fast. "But I *do* exist. I'm right here in front of you." She held her arms out wide. "And I didn't ask to have a vampire father and a human mother. I didn't ask to be sick all my life."

Millie didn't reply, just continued twisting her bracelet around and around.

"Now I need a place to be safe, because of what I am. You're Sam's family and Sam was my father," Shay continued. She wasn't sure why she kept saying that to these people. They obviously didn't care. "That meant something to Gabriel," she murmured. "He loved Sam."

"I loved him too," Millie said, taking her by surprise. "I miss him."

Shay stared at her, stunned by this simple kindness.

"But what he did was wrong. To breed with a human—it's . . ."

"Verboten," Shay finished for her. Gabriel had told her that, had tried to make her understand what a big deal it was. And Shay had thought he was being bigoted. Why hadn't she listened better?

"Yes." Millie gazed at her for a long moment. There didn't seem to be anything else to say.

"Can you get me some water?" Shay asked. "Or food?"

"We don't have any food," Millie told her.

Shay's heart sank. If she didn't eat, the weakness would take hold even sooner. "Water, then?"

"Okay. I'll find some." Millie left, and Shay heard the lock turn in the door behind her.

Luis had said that lock was wonky. Should she try to get out?

Sure, why not? Get out into the nest of vampires so they can kill me for trying to escape, she thought. Shay took a deep breath. It wasn't a good time to try. The vampires were still awake, so it wasn't dawn yet. When the sun came up, they would fall into the death sleep. She'd seen Gabriel like that many times now, and she knew that almost nothing could wake him up. If she could last until morning, she'd have the whole day to figure out how to leave.

And what then? a voice inside her head whispered. *I can't live without Gabriel's blood. The amount of time the strength lasts is getting shorter. Even one day without feeding from him might be too long.*

"Cross that bridge later," she murmured. For now she needed to try to rest, and to drink the water that Millie brought back, and to preserve whatever strength she had for the daytime.

And to call for help.

Shay gasped, yanking her cell phone from the pocket of her cords. With her hands free, she could call someone!

Mom, she thought immediately, reaching to dial. Then she froze, her finger hovering over the keypad. Her mother had helped Martin capture Gabriel, had helped him steal Gabriel's blood and give it to Shay—all without telling her. Shay knew that Mom had only done such terrible things out of desperation, to keep her sick daughter from dying. Well, and maybe out of anger at Sam, the vampire who'd abandoned her when she was pregnant with Shay. She didn't know how much Sam had really loved her.

Mom still thinks Martin was trying to help me too, Shay thought. *She doesn't know he only cares about how his vampire research will land him in the history books. She doesn't know he backhanded me across the face when I got in his way.*

Shay's heart sank. She loved her mother, but there was no time now to explain the reality of the situation. She needed help, not a family feud.

"Olivia," Shay whispered. She hit speed dial 2.

Her best friend, Olivia, knew what was going on—well, not the part about Gabriel being a vampire. Or Shay being half vampire. Or them being in Tennessee. But she knew that Shay had taken off with a guy, and that they were running from Martin, and that Martin was a bastard. And Olivia would help. She'd proven that already.

"Oh my God, what's wrong?" Olivia barked into the phone a second later. "It's the middle of the night."

"Oh. Sorry. I didn't even think about that," Shay said, trying to keep her voice low. Vampires had incredibly sensitive hearing. "Liv, I'm in trouble."

"Why? What happened?" Olivia asked. "Did Martin find you? Kaz drove by your house, and he said Martin's car was back. I figured it meant he gave up on looking for you."

"No, it's not him. It's—" Shay stopped talking. What could she say? *I'm being held captive by a bunch of vampires.* Nobody would believe that, no matter how good a friend they were.

"Is it that guy? Gabriel? Did you have a fight or something?" Olivia yawned as she spoke. "Where are you, Shay?"

"I'm with Gabriel. We didn't fight or anything. But his family . . ." *His family thinks I'm an abomination. Oh, and they'd hate you, too, for being human.*

"Shay. What do you need? Should I come get you? What?" An edge of annoyance crept into Olivia's tone.

"No! You can't come here," Shay said, realizing it was true. If Olivia came, Ernst would kill her. And if she sent the cops instead, then the authorities would find out about the vampires. And they'd kill them, or study them, or lock them away. Which, frankly, would be fine with Shay right about now, but the police wouldn't know that Gabriel was special. And they also wouldn't know that Shay needed his blood to live.

"Do you need help?" Olivia asked, frustrated.

"Yes," Shay whispered. She desperately needed help, but there wasn't any. If anyone discovered the vampires, it was a death sentence for Gabriel—and for Shay.

"What about your mom? Should I call her? She calls me all the time. And, not that you asked, but she's on her way home from Miami. She said she talked to you and you made it clear that even if you were there, you weren't going to meet up with her. She's losing it, Shay."

Shay bit her lip, feeling a stab of guilt. After she took off with Gabriel, Shay had sent her mom on a wild-goose chase, searching for Shay in the wrong place. "I know. But she can't help me. God, she definitely can't come here. If they hate me, they *really* hate her." Shay felt a chill run up her spine. She hadn't even thought about that. It was a good thing she hadn't called Mom.

"Who hates you? What the hell is going on?" Olivia sounded completely awake now, and pissed off.

"It's Gabriel's family. They're, um . . ."

"Shay."

"Sorry. They're just . . . Can you tell my mom that Gabriel's family knows what she did?"

"*What?* His family knows your mother? I don't get this at all."

"Just call her and tell her that. Tell her she's in danger. They know what she did and she's not safe. Okay, Liv? Please just tell my mom that."

"Shay—"

"Crap!" Millie's voice cut through the air like a knife. Before Shay could even turn toward the door, her cell phone was gone from her hand, snatched by Millie so fast that Shay's brain couldn't even process it. "Who did you call? Who?"

As bad as the two vampire guys had been, this was worse. Millie was an inch from Shay, grabbing her neck, face twisted with anger and fear.

"No one!" Shay gasped. "It's not the police! I didn't tell anyone, I swear. I just called my friend. Check the call log."

Millie just stood there, breathing hard, staring at Shay. Her green eyes glittered with anger.

Shay swallowed hard. The girl's hand on her neck was like a cement collar—hard, cold, immovable. Vampires were strong. Millie really could snap her like a twig. "Look, I was calling for help. But then I realized that I couldn't tell anyone to come because you would kill whoever showed up. Or else they would kill you. Either way, I lose."

"You don't lose if they kill us," Millie said.

"Yes, I do. I can't live without vampire blood," Shay told her. "You die, I die. And, anyway, if Gabriel dies, what's the point of anything? I ended up here because I wanted to save his life."

Millie's grip relaxed a tiny bit, and Shay suddenly realized how weak her own knees were. "I swear. It was just my friend. I didn't tell her anything. She wouldn't have believed me."

Millie's eyes narrowed. "Was it your stepfather?"

"No!" Shay said quickly. "I hate him. I'm the one who got Gabriel away from him. Didn't he tell you that?"

"Yes," Millie said after a moment. She let go of Shay's neck, and Shay slid down to the floor, trying to calm her racing pulse. "He told me that you unchained him and helped him escape from Martin. And that you stole blood from a hospital to nurse him back to health," Millie added. "Why would you do that?"

"I cared about him," Shay said. "And I felt responsible. Martin had him there because of me—he gave me Gabriel's blood, and I didn't even know it. I owed it to Gabriel to make sure he recovered."

"None of that makes any sense," Millie said, but she sounded as confused as Shay felt.

"I know it doesn't." Shay drew in a long breath. "You expect humans to act like Martin, not like me. But we're not all bad."

Millie looked doubtful.

"You probably haven't seen a human in eighty years," Shay said. "Ernst never lets you interact with the university people who provide the lab's funding. He keeps you away from humans."

"I see the people I feed from," Millie told her.

"But you don't talk to them. And you don't feed from people very often. You order your bags of blood on the Internet," Shay said. "Gabriel told me all about it."

Millie handed Shay a bottle of water. "He told you way too much."

"He knew I wouldn't spill your secret, and I won't. It's my secret too," Shay said, trying to get the cap off. Her hands felt useless. "My point is, Ernst taught you we're all a threat, but I for one am not."

Millie grabbed the bottle and opened it. "I do watch TV, you know," she said. "I see how humans are."

"TV reality isn't actual reality," Shay said. "Anyway, you probably think that if any of those TV people found out you were a vampire, they'd kill you. Maybe a lot of them would. But I wouldn't." Shay raised the water to her lips with trembling fingers.

"It's not my decision. I have to tell Ernst about your phone," Millie said.

"Please, Millie. I'm sorry. I did call my friend for help, but as soon as I started talking, I realized there was nothing she could do." Shay sighed. "What is Ernst going to do about it now, anyway? Kill me?"

Millie stared at her for a long, silent moment.

"I need vampire blood," Shay whispered. "I won't live without it. Why would I send anyone to hurt your family when I need them?"

"Do I have to bind your hands again?" Millie asked.

"No." Shay sighed. "I didn't mean to take advantage of your kindness. I just panicked."

Millie's eyes narrowed as if she were trying to figure out Shay's angle. Then she turned abruptly and left, turning the wonky lock behind her.

"I need to talk to Ernst," Millie said, pushing into the common room. Her face was pinched, as if she was worried, and when Gabriel tried to meet her eyes, she looked away.

"He's in the caves," Richard replied.

"But it's almost sunrise," Millie grumbled.

"He wanted to check on the Crag Five Colony before the death sleep," Luis said.

Millie sighed in frustration. Gabriel frowned. He'd assumed that Ernst had simply gone back out to the lobby, to lock up for the day. It was disorienting to not know where his family was, how they felt. Everyone here shared the communion. Everyone except him. "Why?" he asked.

"There were three infected bats," Richard told him. "The disease spreads rapidly. If more of our colonies become ill, we'll lose our reason for studying here. We'll have to find another cave, secure new funding."

"Or refocus our research on finding a cure for the white-nose syndrome," Gabriel said. "We can—"

"I've already been discussing it with the Duke people," Richard said, cutting him off.

Gabriel froze, surprised more by the fact that Richard had spoken with their university colleagues than by the spread of white-nose syndrome to their bats. Since they'd come to the Tennessee facility, more than a decade ago, it had always been Gabriel's job to handle the human contact necessary to keep up their masquerade as scientists. Not that it was a lie—they all had advanced degrees, and they all had more experience than most humans ever would. But their identities changed from time to time, so people wouldn't notice their eternal youth. The research on bats and sonar was really only an excuse to live in dark caves and isolation. And Gabriel was the one who spoke to the professors who funded their research. He was the only one Ernst trusted around humans. Until now.

"That's a big step for you," Gabriel said quietly.

Richard was watching him with a mixture of worry and triumph, as if he himself couldn't decide which to feel. "It didn't bother me."

"You only had to talk on the phone. Face-to-face, you would've had trouble," Luis said.

"We don't know that for sure," Millie cut in. "None of us know how we'd handle interacting with humans. Gabriel's the only one who's had to deal with them in person."

"And look how well *that* turned out," Richard muttered.

"What is that supposed to mean?" Gabriel demanded.

"You courted this disaster! You went looking for humans," Richard growled. "Did you think it was a good idea, visiting those websites? Agreeing to a secret meeting?"

"They knew about Sam." Gabriel sighed, collapsing back onto the couch. He was exhausted. Outside, dawn approached. He could feel the coming of the sun like a weight around his neck, dragging him down to the earth. When the sun rose, the vampires slept like the dead.

But not Gabriel. Not today. He had to fight the death sleep. *I've got to get to Shay.*

"You should have told us. We would've gone with you to the meeting, and we would've killed them." Luis sounded more sympathetic than Richard, but only a little.

"How many times must I apologize?" Gabriel asked. "It was a mistake." A mistake that had led him to Shay. Could he really regret that? Even the awful weeks of being chained to that table, held captive by Martin, seemed a small price to pay. He'd never been in love through all the centuries he'd lived. And now that he was, nothing else mattered.

"What's wrong?" Richard asked Millie.

Gabriel's attention snapped back to his family. Millie's expression was worried, but he couldn't feel her emotions. Richard could.

Millie's gaze flicked to Gabriel, then back to Richard. "Nothing," she said. "I mean . . . I checked on the girl. It upset me."

Gabriel nodded his thanks. He'd asked her to make sure Shay was all right. Of all the new family that he'd made with Ernst and Sam, Millie was the one he felt closest to. He'd been like a big brother to her as she grew from a small girl to the twenty-year-old who gave up the sun, the same way Sam had been his big brother. He knew Millie recognized his worry for Shay. He only hoped she would forgive him for what he was about to do.

"What about daytime?" Luis was asking. "None of us can watch her. We're vulnerable during the death sleep."

Ernst could keep watch, Gabriel thought. *But that would be a disaster for me.* With Ernst's great age had come the power to fight the death sleep, though it wasn't easy even for him. "Haven't any of you noticed how weak Shay is?" Gabriel asked. He had to make sure none of them thought it necessary to have Ernst stand guard. "She hasn't had any food. Any blood. She probably wouldn't be able to walk out of here even if every door was unlocked."

"We should just kill her," Richard said. "It's insane to keep a human in our midst."

"She's locked in and she's weak," Millie said. "And, anyway, she needs our blood to live. If she leaves, she dies. She knows that."

"I knew it—you talked to her," Richard spat. "I can smell her scent on you. Tomorrow you won't be on guard duty again."

"That's not up to you," Millie said.

"Then I'll tell Ernst," Richard replied. He shot an imperious look at Gabriel, and it felt like a slap. Other than their father, it had always been Gabriel in charge. Well, at least since Sam. Gabriel was the eldest, the second-in-command. No one had ever said it, but no one had ever had to.

"You took my place while I was gone," he said softly, looking his brother in the eye. "You're not happy to see me, Richard."

Richard had the decency to look embarrassed, but only for a split second. "I'm not happy that you chose to expose us all to danger of the worst kind, no," he said. "And I don't understand how you can stand it—either of you." He glanced at Millie. "The stink of that thing repels me."

Gabriel fought the urge to breathe in deep, to revel in Shay's scent on Millie. The smell of her was intoxicating to him, as it had always been. Enticing, almost unbearably so . . . and deadly. He'd drunk from

Shay once, and it had almost killed him. The blood of a vampire was poisonous to another vampire. And his own blood had been pumping through Shay's veins when he drank.

"It doesn't smell human," Luis commented. "I didn't smell it when you arrived, or at least I couldn't tell it was human."

"*She*," Gabriel put in. "Why do you all need to use such hateful terms? Shay is a she, not an it. She's Sam's daughter. She's a part of all of us."

"He's right," Millie said.

"What?" Richard barked.

"It's just that we all keep thinking of her as a human," Millie said. "But she's a halfblood. And is it really fair to blame her for that? Whatever her parents did, it's not her fault."

Luis looked troubled, but Richard sneered. "She's the living result of Sam's betrayal of his own family. See? I can call it a she too. That doesn't change the facts."

Gabriel felt a wave of exhaustion, a heavy, almost nauseating feeling.

"It's almost sunrise. We've got to sleep," Luis said, his voice thick.

"You're sure the halfblood is secure?" Richard asked Millie.

Millie nodded, but her eyes darted to Gabriel again. Gabriel allowed himself a wry smile. He didn't need the communion to know that his family was confused. Now that he was back, should they look to him for guidance, or to Richard?

Look to Richard, he wanted to say. *I won't be here for long.* He'd come home expecting his family's acceptance, and he still wished he could convince them that Shay had the right to be here. But he couldn't take the time, not with her so close to death. He'd have to escape with her, now, tonight, and never look back.

The thought was painful. He loved Millie. Loved his father, loved them all. They had been his entire world. But that was Shay now.

Luis headed toward the hallway that led to their sleeping chambers. Everyone had their own room, except Richard and Tamara, who shared. It hadn't been that way in Gabriel's first vampire family. Back in Greece, he and Sam and Ernst had slept in one big cave along with the rest of their family. It felt more natural that way. But after the massacre Ernst had insisted on separate rooms. He thought it would be harder for humans to kill them all at once if it meant breaking into several different rooms.

Richard followed, his feet dragging.

Gabriel's limbs felt like lead. Just standing up made his head swim. The sun sapped his strength more than Martin's IV lines ever had. Sleep pulled at him.

"I hope Tamara found a place to hide," he said, forcing the words out as they walked toward their rooms.

"She did," Richard replied. Even though there was no anger in his voice—how could there be, through the exhaustion?—the words stung Gabriel. Of course, the others could *feel* Tamara. They could tell from her emotions that she was safe.

"I wanted to talk to Ernst." Millie's voice, beside him, was weak. "Why is he still in the caves?"

"He's safe there. We would feel it if he was in trouble," Richard murmured before closing his thick metal door. Only Millie and Gabriel were left in the hallway.

"I didn't tie her hands," Millie slurred. "She called someone."

A sharp pang of worry stabbed through the tiredness. "Shay did?" Gabriel asked.

"I took the phone. She said she didn't tell anyone where we were, but I don't trust her. Do you trust her?" Millie was swaying on her feet, clinging to Gabriel's arm. Her eyes held fear, but he could see that she was losing her battle with the death sleep.

"I trust her," he whispered. He caught his sister as she stumbled and helped her into her room. Millie fell like a rock onto the hard cot, dead to the world.

Gabriel pulled her door closed and leaned against the wall, watching the hallway swim around him. Blackness crowded his vision.

I've got to get to Shay.

The sun felt like a fire in Gabriel's mind. He hadn't seen it in almost four hundred years, but he could feel it now as if he were lying on the beach in Greece, baking in the Mediterranean heat. The orange light glowing through the lids of his closed eyes, the strong beams of light pulling the strength from his arms . . . his lungs . . . his heart. It was difficult just to take a breath. Difficult to move. So much easier to lie down, pinned by the heat of the sun.

Gabriel forced his eyes open. The fluorescent lights of the hall danced through the darkness of his vision. He had to sleep.

I've got to get to Shay.

It was their only chance. Now, while his family slumbered. If he got her out, she could handle the rest. Shay wasn't in thrall to the death sleep. She could be awake enough for them both.

Gabriel took a step—and fell.

The sun is too strong. I'm not meant to conquer it. Gabriel's thoughts swam, confusion crossing an eternity of time.

With all his strength, Gabriel got to his hands and knees and crawled forward. He had never fought the death sleep before, but it could be done. Ernst had done it the night of the massacre and had even managed to wake him and Sam. Sam had done it once as well, to be with Gabriel on his final day as a human.

The day on the beach. Sam in the cave above, Gabriel lying in the sun, its warmth wrapping around him like a blanket.

His arms collapsed beneath him, his head slamming onto the rough carpet of the hallway. Gabriel groaned, desperation swirling beneath the exhaustion. How could he fight the death sleep? It meant fighting the sun itself. It burned him now, pulling at him, heating his blood just like it had that day on the beach.

Sam in the cave.

"You should sleep," Gabriel had told Sam. His brother looked so tired.

"I've wakened for this long; I can make it through the day." Sam had smiled weakly. "I will wait."

He knew I would need him, Gabriel thought. *I needed my brother to comfort me as I bid farewell to the sun.*

Love. That's how Sam fought the death sleep. He loved Gabriel, and it gave him strength.

I love Shay, Gabriel thought. *I love her, and she needs me.*

He drew in a long, labored breath. He loved her. But would it be enough?

"Wonky lock," Shay said under her breath. "Yeah, maybe if you're superstrong." She'd been twisting and pulling at the doorknob for what seemed like an hour, and it hadn't budged at all. The lock was a dead bolt. How could there be anything wonky about that?

Shay sighed in frustration and forced herself to back away from the door. She needed a breather. Her body was weakening, and the fact that she hadn't slept all night didn't help. It had to be morning now. She couldn't feel the sun and the moon the way Gabriel could, but she knew it had been a long time since Millie left. And nobody had come to yell at her about the doorknob turning. The vampires must be sleeping. Nothing could wake them up when they were like that.

"It's okay," Shay said, talking out loud just to keep herself from going nuts. "I have all day to find a way out." She refused to think about what she'd do once she escaped from this little room, or about how she'd get far enough away from the remote lab that the vampires couldn't catch up to her in five minutes once they woke up. She knew they could hunt her by her smell. They were practically bloodhounds that way. *Bloodhounds,* Shay thought, a hysterical little laugh bubbling up in her throat.

She looked around the closet. Maybe that letter opener Millie had used could work to force the lock? Shay grabbed it, turned to the door, and had no idea what to do. She tried to pry the faceplate off the lock, but that just bent the flimsy metal letter opener. The rest of the supplies in here were of the paper goods/manila folders/mechanical pencils variety. And some printer cartridges. Nothing that screamed "break the wonky lock."

On TV, they'd just kick the door in, she thought. Kaz had explained it to her once, on one of those nights that Olivia dragged him over to make poor, sick Shay feel normal by watching lame shows together. Kaz only ever wanted to watch things with guns and explosions, and

Olivia wanted reality shows about obnoxious people. They always ended up bickering for most of the night.

"Kick right next to the doorknob," she murmured, remembering Kaz's withering tone as he dissected the stupidity of TV thugs. "Kick next to the lock and you splinter the wood. Don't kick in the middle, moron." Shay smiled. Just thinking about something as basic as Kaz's voice made her feel better. Olivia's boyfriend was solid, dependable, *normal*. Just like Olivia. Shay had never appreciated normal before, because it was something she could never have, not with her blood disease. But right now a little normal would be nice.

She studied the door. The knob—and the lock—were at hip level. Could she even get her leg up that high? Kickboxing was not a thing that sick girls practiced. Walking from one classroom to the next at school took about the limit of Shay's strength on a typical day.

I have to try, she thought. She focused her eyes on a spot about two inches to the right of the metal lock. If she hit the wood hard enough there, it would give. But the metal lock wouldn't, and so the wood would shatter around it. Once it was broken, she could shove the door open. It seemed almost impossible.

Shay took a deep breath and thought about Gabriel, about how she had inhabited his body whenever she drank from him or received a transfusion of his blood. Each time, she had known what it felt like to be Gabriel, to enjoy his effortless strength. Gabriel would kick this door in without so much as a thought.

Be Gabriel. Not the sick girl.

She kicked. High up and as hard as she could. Her boot hit the door exactly where she wanted it to, and a jolt of pain shot up her leg. Shay winced, stumbling, but there was a loud splintering sound. The door had cracked. Shay gazed at it, stunned that it had worked.

Before she could think about it any further, she hurled herself against the door with her entire body. The wood shattered the rest of the way, and the door swung open, sending Shay falling out into the hallway.

The floor was hard and cold, made of cement, and Shay's entire body hurt from the impact. She'd fallen on her shoulder, so now that entire arm hurt along with her leg. She lay there for a moment, feeling stupid. Nobody on Kaz's shows ever broke through a door with this much injury.

That's because they're stunt people, she thought. And because they didn't need vampire blood to give them strength. Shay sat up slowly, running through a self-check. Breaking out of the room had taken its toll. She felt close to Shay-normal, which was ten steps below regular strength for most people. She doubted that she would have the stamina to get outside.

"Maybe there's a phone in the lobby," she whispered, climbing slowly to her feet and starting down the hall. This was officially a laboratory funded by Duke University. They had to have a phone line. And maybe if she called for help during the day, and the vampires were sleeping, she could come up with some kind of story to keep the authorities from discovering the truth about Gabriel and his family. She could say she got lost and they let her use the phone, but they went into the caves to work. Or something. It wouldn't matter. If she got the fire department here, they'd see that she was sick. They'd focus on getting her to a hospital.

And they'll call Mom and Martin. They'll give me a blood transfusion of human blood. I'll put my mother near the vampires who want to kill her, I'll be back in Martin's clutches, and I'll end up dead from lack of vampire blood anyway.

Shay started up the stairs, then paused. It seemed hopeless. Maybe the Escalade was still here and she could drive herself to a hospital without putting anyone in danger. She could stay off the grid, steal some blood and IV supplies. A transfusion would keep her alive for a day or two. Long enough for Gabriel to find her.

She kept climbing, hanging on to the cold metal railing for help. One thing was clear: She couldn't stay here, where they thought she was an abomination.

At the top was the door leading to the research center. Shay waited until her heartbeat had slowed a bit, then pushed it open.

The hand grabbed her immediately.

"No!" Shay cried, instinctively jerking her arm away. It wasn't fair to get caught now. The vampires should be sleeping.

"It's me. Shay, it's me." Gabriel's voice was rough. It was the most wonderful thing Shay had ever heard.

Shay threw her arms around him, pressing her body against his as he hugged her back. It felt incredible. It felt like life. But it wasn't enough. She needed more. She buried her face in the side of his neck, breathing in the scent of him. Not enough. She shoved her hands under his shirt and ran her fingers over his bare back. Yes, this is what she needed. She needed the feel of his flesh. She needed proof that he was really there with her. She tightened her hold on him, her fingernails digging into his skin.

Gabriel groaned, deep in his throat. He wound his fingers through her hair and urged her face up toward his. Then his mouth was on hers, his tongue brushing against hers, and Shay let herself get lost in the sensation.

He pulled away a tiny bit and gazed into her eyes, cupping her face with his hands. "I love you. I saw them pulling you away and it was . . . and I knew. I love you, Shay."

She wouldn't have believed there was anything better than the relief of feeling his arms around her, his mouth on hers. But hearing those words, it was. Completely, totally, *exponentially* better.

"I love you too," Shay breathed. "I didn't want to. It seemed like a stupid, stupid idea. But I couldn't help it."

Gabriel smiled at her. She hadn't been sure she'd ever see his smile again. "It *was* a stupid idea. Stupid and wonderful." He stepped back, his voice becoming urgent. "But, Shay, we need to get out of here."

Shay jerked away from him. "No!" she cried. "I'm not going back down there."

Gabriel's eyes widened . . . and then he got it. She could see it on his face—the shock, the fear, the devastation. Everything she had felt a split second before, when she saw Ernst appear in the doorway of the lab room across the hall.

She cowered away from Gabriel, ignoring Ernst, pretending she hadn't spotted him. "Just let me go. I won't tell anyone anything."

Play along with me, Gabriel, she silently begged. She didn't know what would happen if the other vampires discovered that he'd been about to escape with her. He might end up locked away somewhere too.

"What is going on here?" Ernst demanded. "Gabriel. How are you awake?"

"I thought she might try to get out, so I wanted to keep watch. I thought you'd decided to sleep in the caves," Gabriel said. "I fought the death sleep with all my strength." His eyes were still locked with Shay's, and she could see the torment of his emotions. He *had* conquered the death sleep, and she couldn't imagine what it had cost him. And now it was all for nothing.

They couldn't fight Ernst. He was old and strong. Shay was too weak to do much of anything, and even Gabriel looked drawn and tired. He'd always said that it was nearly impossible for a vampire to stay awake during the day. And she couldn't ask him to battle his own father anyway.

"Well done, my son." Ernst lay his hand on Gabriel's shoulder. "You go back to your chamber now. I'll handle the halfblood."

Shay blinked away tears, gazing at Gabriel's face. He looked as if he'd been punched in the gut. Devastated.

"What will you do with her?" he whispered.

"We can't have her wandering around when we're vulnerable," Ernst replied. "We need her someplace more secure until we spring the trap. I'm moving her to the vault."

He grabbed her arm and jerked her roughly through the lab room and past a thick metal door. Gabriel gasped in horror, but Shay didn't dare turn back to look at him. She didn't want Ernst to think there was anything between them. It was bad enough that she was a prisoner. She couldn't risk Gabriel's freedom as well.

Ernst dragged her down a long corridor and through a door that led to another stairwell. The door slammed shut behind them, cutting her off from Gabriel.

Shay bit back a sob. Would she ever see him again?

THREE

○ ○ ○ ○ ○ ○ ○ ○ ○ ○ ○ ○ ○ ○ ○ ○

IT'S FRIDAY. *I don't know what time, not since Millie took my phone. The weird thing is that Ernst didn't say anything about that. Maybe Millie didn't tell him? I thought they all had a psychic link, but I guess it doesn't mean they have a hive mind or something. Gabriel said it was more that they shared emotions, they could tell when a family member was upset or in danger. So it's not mind reading. Still, I didn't think Millie would cover for me.*

I'm in a different room now. Ernst called it "the vault," which freaked me out because it sounds like something out of a horror movie, but it's really just another storage room. It's in a different part of the compound, under the lodge where they live, I think. I saw a tricked-out living room through an open doorway when I was being dragged down the hall.

This room has paper, so now it's my journal. Why bother? I'm not sure. Maybe Gabriel can get these pages to Mom after I'm dead? Or maybe it's just to keep me sane. Martin always said that habit = comfort. And I am in the habit of writing a journal.

So . . . Friday. Daytime still, I think.

Gabriel looked like hell. I mean, he looked gorgeous. He can't help that. But he's never been able to stay awake during the day before, and I could see the effort on his face and in his eyes. I don't think he'll manage it again tomorrow. But it doesn't matter. Obviously, Ernst will keep defying the death sleep as long as I'm here. He wasn't nearly as wrecked as Gabriel—I wonder how often he stays awake during the day? Gabriel said the older the vampire, the easier it is to resist the sleep. But Gabriel isn't young. He's been a vampire since the seventeenth century, and he could barely stay awake to give Ernst an explanation of what had happened. So how old must Ernst be?

It's strange that I don't know. There's so much about them I don't know. When Gabriel and I were running from Martin, I was so focused on learning about the vampires' strengths and weaknesses, all their rules, I guess you'd call it. I didn't think about their history.

Ernst made this family, that's all I know. He was always the father, even back with the family in Greece before they were all killed. Even Sam—Dad? Sam. Too weird to call him Dad when I never met him. Even Sam considered Ernst to be his father. But when was that? How long ago? And was it in Greece? Did Sam come from Greece like Gabriel did?

You would think I'd know things like this about my own father. His age, his history. What happened to him.

They all call him a traitor, like he did some awful thing just by loving my mom. Even Gabriel thought that, back before he knew me. So what happened? Did they expel him from their family? Or did he leave because they were angry?

Mom always hated my father because he left her. I always hated him for leaving me before I was even born. But now I'm starting to wonder if maybe Sam left us in order to keep Ernst from finding us. Because Ernst wants me dead. I can see it in his eyes.

Shay dropped the pen and shook her hand, trying to ease the muscle cramp in her fingers. That was a new symptom—she'd never had trouble writing in her journal before. But then, she'd never gone for so long without blood *or* food either. And Martin had told her she was getting worse. He'd said she couldn't live without Gabriel's blood for more than a few days. It had been a day and a half since she'd had any blood.

Are they going to let me starve? she thought, hugging herself against the chills that had begun to wrack her body. *Is that what it is, starving?* For a vampire, maybe. To live without blood would be to starve. But for a half vampire? Who knew?

There was no point in thinking about what would happen now. She couldn't escape, and Gabriel wouldn't have another chance to save her.

Had Ernst believed that Gabriel was trying to stop Shay from escaping? She'd been as convincing as she could, but Gabriel's whole family knew he brought her to them because he thought she'd be safe. If Ernst didn't believe the lie, what would happen to Gabriel for going against Ernst's wishes?

She needed something to distract her. She'd go crazy if she kept thinking about what she and Gabriel were facing. Shay glanced around the room. The vault. It was a mess. Cardboard boxes covered with dust, ancient chests made of wood, a huge old filing cabinet that looked as if it came from an office on *Mad Men*. It seemed more like an attic than some kind of dungeon.

She could reach the bottom drawer of the filing cabinet without having to stand up. Shay grabbed the handle and yanked as hard as she could, which wasn't very hard. It took three more tries to get the drawer open enough to look inside.

"Files," she murmured. "Shocker!"

The manila folders were yellowish, and the edges of them were curled and flaked. *Old*, she thought. Like everything else in this place, including the vampires who lived here. She flipped open one folder and skimmed through the documents inside. They were dated from the 1950s, and they seemed to be research reports on bats and sonar for some government project. Shay ran her finger over the names listed at the end: Ernest Frankel, PhD; Rick Scott, PhD; Gabe Kahn, PhD. . . .

"Gabriel," Shay breathed. She'd never asked his last name, and it shocked her to see it. But Ernest and Rick—that was probably Ernst and Richard, using whatever names they hid behind back then. Who knew where the last names came from? The names probably changed every time the vampire family switched identities. Gabriel had told her they needed to do that every twenty years or so, to avoid detection by humans. So his last name wasn't really Kahn, any more than Ernst's was Frankel.

She flipped to the next page, and her heart seemed to freeze. It was a letter to some navy science officer, and it was signed by Samuel Westcliff, PhD.

Sam. Dad. The words swam in front of Shay's eyes until she realized that she was crying. It was her father's signature. Just a scrawl of letters on a yellowed old sheet of paper. But it was the first concrete evidence of her dad's life that she'd ever seen. She had the locket he'd given her mother, the one etched with two birds in a sky that contained both a sun and a moon. But it had come to Shay through her mom. And the visions she'd had of Sam, his life, had come from Gabriel. Shay herself had never met her father, never known a single thing about him, never touched him or hugged him or heard him say her name.

She traced his signature with the tip of her finger, trying to feel the microscopic bumps left behind by the ink. If only she could magically feel what her dad had felt when he wrote this.

He was probably bored to tears, she thought, smiling. The Sam she had seen in her visions of Gabriel's life was a happy, loving person. The kind of guy who wanted to be out among people, not holed up in a lab writing reports. Though that was before the massacre of the family in Greece. Gabriel had told her that everything changed after that. Sam hadn't fully recovered his interest in life until he met her mother, decades after he wrote this letter.

Shay dug through the rest of the papers. More stuff about sonar and something about submarines. The vampires did research for a college now, but back then they were government contractors. She didn't see any mention of Luis or Tamara, but Millie's name popped up here and there as a secretary. Shay couldn't help a smile—the vampires knew how to fit in, right down to making the woman take dictation while all the men were scientists. Pretty typical for the '50s.

She pulled herself up to her knees and managed to get one of the higher drawers open. More files. Shay grabbed a handful at random and dropped quickly back down to the ground, her head swimming and blackness closing in around the edges of her vision. Papers flew out all over the place, but she didn't care. If Ernst wanted to hold her captive, she got to make a mess.

When her head cleared a little, Shay pulled a bunch of papers onto her lap and started reading. These were even older—from the 1910s. The paper was some kind of thin, crinkly stuff, and everything was written by hand. The research seemed to be about bats, but it was much more basic, just identifying different traits in order to distinguish various species. The money came from Hamilton College, and the vampire family had been based in upstate New York. This time Luis was in there—Luis Gonzalez. Gabriel's name then had been Gabriel Makos, and Sam's was Samuel Kazan.

"Greek names," Shay murmured. Were those their real last names? She knew that Gabriel had been raised in an orphanage in Greece—well, at least until Ernst had raided the place and taken him when he was five years old. Sam had been with Ernst, already an adult vampire. But they spoke as if the family had been in Greece for a long time, and Shay had always assumed that Sam was Greek. She had long, thick dark hair that her mother had always envied. Her mom's hair was fine and blond, Irish. There was nothing Irish about Shay but her blue eyes. If Sam had been Greek, that meant Shay was half Greek.

She felt a tiny thrill of excitement, just knowing something like that. All this family history stored here—it was *her* family history.

There had to be something more about Sam. Maybe a picture or a personal letter. *Something.*

Shay pulled herself to her feet and tried to ignore the dizziness the movement caused. There were shelves along all the walls and a collection of chests and boxes stacked on them. Some were ornate and others were just basic pine boxes. A few of them had locks, and a couple had been labeled, though the words were in some other language. German, she thought. Shay had taken two years of German in school, but these labels were so faded that it was hard to tell for sure. The one thing all the stuff in here had in common was that it all looked ancient.

Shay opened a simple wooden box and peered inside. There was a moth-eaten doll wearing a long dress and a yellowed envelope with a lock of hair tied with a ribbon. On the envelope someone had written *Millicent* in beautiful script. Shay's breath caught in her throat. This was Millie's stuff, things from her life before she joined the family. Shay had seen a vision of the house where Millie lived as a child—in a rural place, somewhere in America. Millie had joined the family here in the U.S., just like Richard and Luis and Tamara. They were Ernst's second family, after the massacre killed most of the first family back in Greece.

Shay knew that Millie's parents died of influenza. Maybe Ernst and Gabriel had somehow gotten inside the house, collected some of Millie's things to take with her when they brought her into their vampire family?

She moved to the next box, this one a tiny chest painted black. There were photos inside, the sort of sepia-toned ones you would find in history textbooks. Gingerly, Shay leafed through them, afraid they would fall apart. She gazed at the faces, searching for Gabriel or for her father. But the only person she recognized was Tamara, sitting rigidly on a chair next to a man who looked just like her. The clothes were fancy, but dated. Long skirts, a hat on the man. It was impossible to tell when the picture had been taken, but it definitely looked older than anything else Shay had seen yet. She turned it over. There was a stamp on the back, probably from the photographer. But the letters were from the Russian alphabet.

"Tamara's life," Shay murmured. She had joined the family late, already a vampire. Gabriel hadn't said a lot about Tamara, and Shay wondered if it was because he hadn't helped raise her, the way he had with Millie.

Shay skipped the next few boxes, looking for one that was older or that had Gabriel's stuff in it. There was a box filled with what looked like leather-bound journals, and each was labeled with Ernst's name. But they were just ledgers filled with numbers. Then there was a big chest with iron hinges, and inside was nothing but a bunch of glass vases, each one wrapped in cloth.

"I guess every family has its sentimental attachments," she muttered, thinking about the shoe box full of old Barbies that her mom still had stored up in their attic.

Tucked into the corner of the chest was a smaller box made out of some kind of stone, and inlaid in the top was a design—two birds flying across a sky with a sun and a moon both.

Shay stared at it for a long moment, wondering if she'd gotten so weak that she was seeing things. That design . . . it was the same as the design on her locket.

Fingers trembling, she opened the box. There was a small sheet of fragile, parchmentlike paper inside, covered with spidery writing in thick black ink, complete with smudges and blots.

It was in German.

"This was for my child, but my child went before me," Shay said slowly, translating the old words. "Now it is for you, child of my heart. I cannot bear the pain any longer. I seek the sun. Your love, my Samuel, must be enough for him."

Shay frowned, squinting at the letter. It was written to Sam, that much was clear. Was it a suicide note? For a vampire to seek the sun . . . that was death. The sun burned them; she knew that from her visions of Gabriel's life. Sam had spoken of it on the day that Gabriel became a vampire. Sam had told him of a vampire he'd known, one who had exposed herself to daylight—

"Gret!" Shay cried. The memory rushed back as if it were hers instead of Gabriel's. Sam had told him the story of Gret, Ernst's wife, who had sought the sun. And all they'd found of her was a pile of black ash.

Shay turned the paper over, careful not to jostle it too much. Gret had died before Gabriel was even born, and Gabriel was around four hundred years old. Who knew how old this suicide note was?

There was nothing else. Just the note and the box, with the birds, the sun and moon. Shay reached up and unclasped the chain around her neck, sliding the locket off. She laid it gently in the stone box, where it fit perfectly. Did Gret's note refer to her locket? Had she been walking around with a piece of six-hundred-year-old jewelry around her neck for all this time? She'd had no idea how valuable it was, only that it was meaningful to her because it came from her father.

It was meaningful to him because it came from his mother, Shay thought. *His vampire mother.*

Sam must have kept the locket, with Gret's last letter. Kept it for all those centuries until he fell in love with her mom. She'd seen in her visions that he planned to give it to her mother when they decided to get married. When they knew they were going to have a baby.

She slid the locket back onto her chain and put it around her neck, forcing her weak fingers to work the tiny clasp. Then, exhausted, Shay closed her eyes for a moment, reliving the visions she'd had of Gabriel's long life.

They loved one another, these vampires. Sam and Gabriel considered themselves brothers, and they thought of Ernst as their father. Ernst took orphaned children and raised them like family, and when they grew up, the children became vampires too. There was a ritual, and once they did it, they were joined together. Gabriel always spoke of his family as if it was the most important thing in the world to him. Shay's visions had shown that too.

How do good people do something like this? she thought. *How can they love each other but hate me so much? Not just me—they hate so much of the world, the whole human world.*

She opened her eyes and gazed at the door. Ernst had thrown her in here—literally thrown her. He hadn't even given her a glass of water. And she wasn't sure he would ever come back.

I'm going to die in here, Shay thought. *I won't ever see Gabriel again. And wherever my father went, he won't even know what happened to me. He left us so that this wouldn't happen, and it's happening anyway.*

A tear made its way down her cheek, tickling her skin, but

Shay didn't bother to wipe it away. The effort would take too much strength. She lay down on the cold floor, resting her head because it felt so heavy, like a cinder block. The locket slipped out from under her shirt, and Shay instinctively wrapped her fingers around it. That's what she always did during a transfusion, or when she was stressed, or scared.

"Where did you go, Sam?" she whispered, holding on to the locket. "You could have protected me better if you'd stayed."

He was awake.

Giving in to the death sleep was nothing like falling asleep as a human, not that Gabriel had clear memories of that anymore. But watching Shay sleep during their time together had reminded him of the soft, slow trickle of sleep into a human's body. The death sleep was sudden, overwhelming, complete. The sun came, and your body shut down.

But waking up was the same. Humans woke slowly sometimes, quickly other times. Vampires did too.

Tonight Gabriel was awake immediately. On guard, fear racing through him, just the way he'd finally given in to the death sleep earlier. Ernst must have moved him to his room. He didn't remember anything other than Shay being dragged away and the thick door closing between them. Despair combined with the strength of the sun was too much to fight, and he'd let the death sleep overtake him.

But now the sun was gone and his senses were sharp. He had to get to Shay. She wouldn't survive long without his blood. But how? His brothers and sisters would be awake now too. He couldn't fight them all. He hadn't even been able to fight just Ernst.

"Gabriel, come." Ernst's voice was clipped, but not angry. Gabriel opened his eyes and turned to see his father in the open door. A burst of fury shot through him—the doors locked from the inside, for protection. They all felt safe locked in their rooms, and to violate that privacy was an insult. No one in the family would ever open another's door unless there was some grave emergency.

Ernst never closed my door, he realized. His father had probably sat and watched him sleep all day long, just to be sure that he was safe. Or maybe to be sure that Gabriel didn't wake up again. Maybe Ernst hadn't entirely believed that Gabriel wasn't trying to rescue Shay. It was impossible to tell.

"We're going to restore the communion," Ernst said. "You've been apart from the family for too long."

He walked off into the common room, and Gabriel had no choice but to follow. The others were all there, even Tamara.

"You made it back okay," he said, smiling at her.

"I drove your car off a cliff and hid in the caves. The bats kept me company while I slept," she told him. Her voice was friendly, but he couldn't tell what she was thinking. Even when he'd been in communion with his family, Tamara had been a mystery. She'd been with them for fifty years or so, but she was the only vampire he'd ever met who hadn't grown up in the family. The only vampire besides Ernst, in fact, who he hadn't helped raise from childhood. Richard, Luis, Millie—Gabriel had known them all as tiny children, had taught them the ways of the family, had participated in the blood ritual when they gave up the sun. They were his siblings, but also almost like adopted children to him, the same way he had been to Sam. Sam had been his brother, true, but Sam had also been a second father to him.

"Has anyone checked on the halfblood?" Richard asked.

Gabriel's jaw tightened at the impersonal way he spoke of Shay, but he was afraid to say anything. He had no plan now, no way to get Shay out of the vault. But the longer he could keep the others from knowing that he wanted to save her, the more freedom he would have to figure something out.

"I moved her to the vault," Ernst said. "There's no escape."

True. Even if she somehow made it out of the room itself and then managed to get up the stairs, she'd never make it past the metal door that separated the lodge from the rest of the facility.

Luis glanced at Gabriel. "We're all anxious to begin. It hasn't felt right since you disappeared."

"Not for me either, brother," Gabriel replied truthfully. "I don't think I ever realized how much I rely on our communion. This past month is the first time I've been truly on my own since . . ."

"The Pilgrims landed at Plymouth?" Millie finished for him.

They all laughed, and Gabriel joined in. "Are you saying I'm old? You're no infant yourself, you know."

She grinned at him like she'd done a million times before. But then there was an awkward silence, as if nobody could figure out how to go back to normal. As if they all knew that normal was never going to happen again.

"It feels strange to do a blood ritual in the common room," Richard said finally. "Like we're reality-show vampires hanging out in our fake house. Can we at least turn the overheads off?"

Ernst flicked off the lights, and Gabriel's eyes immediately adjusted to the darkness. "We could go to the caves," he suggested.

"No need," Ernst said. That settled it. Ernst always had the final decision. "I'll begin. You all remember how we brought Tamara into our family?"

Gabriel nodded along with the rest. It was a ritual Ernst had come up with, a sort of miniature version of the blood ritual that created a vampire. When a child raised in the family made the decision to give up the sun, the entire family gathered and together drained the human's blood. Each vampire drank of their new sibling's blood until he or she was emptied. Then, at the moment of death, the candidate drank from the family—one at a time, taking the blood of each family member in, and with it, their very life essences. When it was done, the new vampire shared in the communion of the family. The new vampire could feel the emotions of each one he'd drunk from, and they could feel his.

Tamara had already been a vampire when Richard brought her to them. They couldn't empty her of blood, and she couldn't drink their blood, because vampire blood was poison to another vampire. So Ernst had made up a new ritual: Tamara drank a drop of blood from each of them, just enough to burn the tongue, not enough to cause any damage. And then they all fed from her, just a tiny bit. It had made everyone a little sick, but it had also worked. She became linked to them. And their healing powers had cleared the effects of the poison within an hour.

Tamara's communion has never been that strong, Gabriel thought now. He'd always wondered if it was because they hadn't shared as much blood during her ritual. It used to make him sad, but now it seemed like a blessing. If this ritual allowed Gabriel's family to access only a tiny portion of his emotions, maybe they wouldn't realize how madly, utterly in love with Shay he was. Maybe they wouldn't be horrified enough to storm down to the vault and kill her immediately.

I can't think about that. I can't think about Shay at all, Gabriel told himself as Ernst approached him. He couldn't let his strong emotions for her into his mind as they drank. *I'll think about Martin instead, about how he captured me and tortured me. Maybe the strength of my fury at him will mask the strength of my love.*

Ernst nicked a vein on his wrist and held his arm out to Gabriel. "Drink, my son, and rejoin your family," he said.

Gabriel obediently bent his head to his father's wrist. He took only a taste of Ernst's blood, powerful and old, toxic to Gabriel. It burned like lava in his mouth, but even so, it was *Ernst.* His life in all its joy and sorrow shot through Gabriel: love for Gret, his wife; anger at Sam, his son; horror and fear and fury at the humans who murdered their family in Greece; relief at seeing Gabriel home safe.

Gabriel lifted his eyes to Ernst's, and smiled.

"Richard?" Ernst said.

Richard stepped forward, opening his vein. Gabriel lifted his brother's arm and drank. The essence of Richard filled him—his happy youth with the family, how he'd adored Sam and Gabriel back when he was a child in New York; the shot of pure love he felt when he met Tamara; and then the misery over Sam. And something new, too, a feeling that Gabriel didn't remember ever having gotten from Richard: jealousy. Jealousy toward Gabriel.

He dropped Richard's arm, surprised. But there was nothing unusual in Richard's expression, and he leaned over to put his arm around Gabriel's shoulders, a brief hug.

Now Luis offered his blood. Gabriel was starting to feel a little dizzy from the poison, but he forced the feeling aside. He drank from Luis, taking in the distant sadness of Luis's parents dying on their Texas farm; the impatience to become a vampire as he stood guard over Ernst, Gabriel, and Sam while they slept; the overwhelming boredom of the bat research; the guilt about Sam.

"I thought I'd lost another brother," Luis said when Gabriel stopped drinking. "I'm glad you're safe."

"So am I," Gabriel told him.

"My turn," Millie said. She held out her wrist and grinned at Gabriel. "Feeling sick?"

"I am," he admitted. "But it's worth it."

He fed from Millie, reveling in the familiar emotions of her. She loved wholeheartedly—him, Sam, Ernst, the other vampires, the bats. She yearned for something more, excitement and fun and novelty. Worry and confusion about Shay snaked through her every emotion, mixing with confusion about Sam. And she felt overwhelming relief that Gabriel was back among them.

When he moved his mouth away from her skin, Millie threw her arms around his neck. He hugged her back. "I missed you, Mils."

Gabriel turned to Tamara, the last one of his family. Her gray eyes stared back at him blankly. Did she have the same theory he did—that this mini-ritual didn't create as complete a communion as the full blood ritual? He'd never said anything to Tamara about how he felt less connected to her than to the others. He'd never even thought much about it. But maybe Tamara had known it all along.

"Welcome home, Gabriel," she said, holding out her arm, a thin trickle of blood snaking its way down her wrist.

"Thank you," he murmured, feeling almost sorry for her. She'd been with them for decades. Had she felt like an outsider the whole time?

Gabriel drank from her, and the rush of her feelings was as strong as the others. Tamara's life was unknown to him, but he felt the emotions: love for her twin brother, devastation over his long-ago death, intense loneliness from her years of wandering the world on her own, and finally gratitude and love for Richard.

Tamara pulled her wrist away, and Gabriel stepped back. *She's the only one who didn't feel Sam*, he thought. *The only one whose life wasn't impacted forever by what happened.*

"Gabriel?" Ernst asked.

"I'm all right. The blood burns, but I didn't take too much," Gabriel said. "I . . . I feel you all again." He felt tears rise to his eyes. He'd missed the communion so much. And if there was less intensity to it than before, if it felt like the communion through a layer of gauze, well, it was still an incredible comfort to him. Maybe that's how Tamara felt about it.

If it goes both ways, if the others feel my emotions less intensely, that can only be good, he thought. He didn't want them to feel his constant worry for Shay, his desperate fear that she was getting sicker by the minute, locked away from him and his blood.

"Prepare yourself, my son," Ernst said. "Now we will all drink of you, and our communion will be restored."

Think about Martin. About how I felt lying in the exam room, chained to the table. Martin stealing my blood, Gabriel told himself. He held his arms out, his head thrown back. His family approached. Gabriel closed his eyes and felt mouths on his pulse points—his neck, the hollow inside his elbows, the throbbing veins in his wrists.

Not Shay. Martin, he thought. *The coldness in his voice as he told me he would synthesize what made me a vampire. He would achieve historic greatness by taking my blood, get a Nobel Prize for holding me against my will and studying me like a lab rat. Studying my blood in Shay's body—*

Gabriel's eyes jerked open. He couldn't think about Shay, couldn't let himself feel anything for Shay right now. Only anger. Rage against Martin for tearing him apart from his family, for harvesting his blood, for imprisoning him. From now on, Gabriel had to feel only rage.

His family was drinking of him. The blood slipped from his body, a hot line straight to their mouths. It felt like a release, and a purplish haze stole over his vision. He was giving himself to them just like any other Giver. When a vampire fed from you, you were helpless. Your essence flowed to him even if you were a vampire yourself.

They are my family, one with me, Gabriel thought. *My feelings are theirs. My fury, my need for vengeance . . . my love for Shay.*

"Enough!" Ernst stumbled back from Gabriel, blood on his lips, shock in his eyes.

Richard shoved Gabriel's arm away, and the warmth of his mouth on Gabriel's wrist vanished, along with the feel of Tamara's mouth in the crook of his arm. Tamara retched, turning her back.

"Gabriel . . ." Millie had released his other wrist and stood staring at him in horror. Luis wrapped his arm around her shoulders, not even bothering to wipe Gabriel's blood from his chin.

Gabriel stared at them, his heart pounding from the sudden return to reality. "Did it work?"

"You love that thing, that halfblood," Tamara whispered. "I felt love."

"Love for an abomination," Ernst spat. "For the creature that cost us Sam."

Gabriel's head swam, the emotions of his family pressing into his mind. The communion was back. He could sense their feelings, maybe not as strongly as before, but strong enough: They were horrified. All of them. Sickened by the idea of his love for Shay, disappointed and frightened and most of all angry. The weight of their fury felt like a boulder threatening to crush him.

"She's not an abomination. She's the best person I've known in a life that's spanned centuries. She saved my life, when she had every reason to fear me," Gabriel whispered. How could he have been so self-deluded as to think they wouldn't feel his love?

"He must not be left alone," Ernst said slowly, his rage calming into something more like worry. "He can't be trusted near the half-blood. One of us must stay with Gabriel until it's over."

Until it's over, Gabriel thought, sinking to his knees. *Until Shay is dead.*

FOUR

○ ○ ○ ○ ○ ○ ○ ○ ○ ○ ○ ○ ○ ○ ○ ○ ○

"MAKE THE CALL," ERNST SAID. He held out a cell phone, not the laboratory's phone. "It's the halfblood's phone. It should have Martin's number in it."

"I found it in the storeroom," Millie volunteered, her gaze darting from person to person without staying long on anyone.

"I don't want to hear his voice ever again," Gabriel said. It was the truth. Martin's voice was seared into his memory along with the feeling of being trapped, chained down on a table, drained of blood. He'd refused to speak to the man, but Martin continually talked to him, telling Gabriel all his grandiose plans. Being restrained on that table, listening to him, was almost as dark a memory as the night the family was massacred in Greece, or the night of Sam's blood ritual.

"He'll recognize you. We don't want him to know there are more of us," Ernst said reasonably. "An ambush only works if it's a surprise."

Gabriel actually laughed. He had taken Shay away from Martin—rescued her rather than staying to fight with Martin the way he'd wanted to. Martin wouldn't believe for a second that he was going to kill her. More than that, Martin wouldn't care.

"This man won't come for Shay. He only wants a vampire to study," Gabriel said. There was no point in lying to his family anymore. "I tried to tell you, my original plan had been to use her as bait, but then I learned that it wouldn't work. He's after *us*, and the only reason you know about it is because Shay broke me out of Martin's lab and saved my life. Because of her, I could come home and tell you about this threat. And yet you have her locked in the vault."

"Enough of this talk!" Richard burst out suddenly. "If the halfblood is useless, why don't we just kill it now?"

"The doctor may come to recapture his vampire, but the woman will come for the halfblood," Ernst said, the words sending a chill through Gabriel.

"I told you, I never saw the woman," he protested.

His father didn't even bother answering him. "Either way, it costs us nothing to keep the halfblood alive for another day." He thrust the phone at Gabriel again. "Make the call."

"Why can't you do it? Or Luis or Richard?" Millie asked. "Gabriel told us he never even spoke to his captor. This Martin won't recognize his voice."

"This is a danger that Gabriel brought on us all," Tamara said. "It's his responsibility to remedy it."

"It's needlessly torturing him after he's already been through hell," Millie argued.

Gabriel didn't move his eyes from his father's. Ernst wasn't even listening to the others. He was simply waiting for Gabriel to obey him, assuming that he would, as he had for hundreds of years.

Gabriel took the phone, found Martin in the contacts list, and made the call.

Martin answered on the first ring. "Shay?" he barked.

"No. You know who I am," Gabriel told him, "and you know you're never going to get me back into your exam room."

Martin snorted. "You wouldn't be calling me if that was all you had to say."

Gabriel felt a trickle of loathing creep up his spine. He hated Martin. As much as he wanted to feel fury, simple and righteous, what he actually felt was more complicated. Hatred and, yes, anger. But also fear. This man had kept him captive and made him weak, had *used* him, studied him, treated him as something less than human.

Maybe he was something less than human. Maybe they all were. Why else would they have done what they did to Sam, just for falling in love? Why else would they have Shay locked up like . . . well, like something less than human? An acid mix of guilt and shame swept through Gabriel's body.

"I have Shay. If you want her back, you'll meet me in Asheville, North Carolina. Sunday night. There's an abandoned gas station off Route 70."

"Tell him she's in bad shape," Millie whispered, her voice anxious.

"Be there," Gabriel said. "You know Shay can't live without transfusions. She won't last long."

He hung up before he could hear Martin's reply. He was afraid it would be laughter. Martin didn't care if Shay lived any more than Ernst did. All Gabriel could hope for was that Martin wanted to keep Shay's mother happy. If he did, he might come to save Shay. And maybe, just maybe, there would be a moment of confusion during the ambush when Gabriel could grab Shay and run.

If she was even still alive.

I like Luis better. Richard came in here once and found me looking through a box of old tintype photos, and he grabbed them away from me and spat on the floor. I mean, literally, he spat on the floor like an old lady trying to show her disdain. I didn't care that he took them. I didn't recognize anyone in the tintypes. For all I know, it was just someone's childhood collection of weird pictures. I've gone through half the boxes in the vault, and there is some strange stuff.

Then later Luis came. I was trying to rest. I can't really sleep anymore, or maybe it's that I can't tell when I'm dreaming and when I'm just thinking. Maybe I'm dreaming right now. Although if I'm dreaming, why couldn't I be dreaming that Gabriel and I are together, back in the barn, no humans, no vampires, just Gabriel and me?

I'm pretty sure I'm writing in my so-called journal and not dreaming at all, but I don't trust myself too much. My grasp on reality is basically gone. And let's face it, once there were vampires, reality didn't seem quite as rock-solid as it used to anyway.

So Luis came in, and I was lying there in the middle of all these papers and little china dolls that I'd found in an old pillowcase. His face was an exact replica of Mr. Bonetto's whenever we wouldn't clean the beakers carefully enough in AP bio. I get the feeling Luis is a neat freak. Anyway, I said sorry for the mess, didn't mean to skeeve you out.

And he smiled. It was only for a second. Maybe I imagined it. But I could swear he smiled at me before he remembered he wasn't supposed to. Then he left.

They don't say anything to me; I think they're just checking to see if I'm still alive.

It's never Gabriel. They probably don't trust him to come near me. When I try to think of his face, I can't remember what he looks like.

Did I dream him?

Shay dropped the pen. Or the pen fell. It was probably that the pen fell. She had to concentrate to make her fingers wrap around it now, and it was difficult to press hard enough for the ink to mark the paper. Writing words was hard too—she had to think of each letter, how to write it, and then what the next letter was, and the next. It was as if her brain couldn't comprehend an entire word at once, not when she was looking at it on paper. She could still think, though.

She sighed, rolling onto her back again. She hadn't sat up in a while—she'd been writing in that weird half-reclining position she used in her hospital bed at home. It was easier than trying to stay upright. The small room seemed to swim around her, the shelves spinning slowly past, holding their secrets packed away in the boxes and chests and bags. She couldn't reach the top shelves, but she'd made her way through the bottom ones, searching for any more information on her father.

"Why don't *you* have any collections of crap stored in here?" she whispered, reaching for the locket around her neck.

"These vampires are young," Sam said. "Their childhoods haven't disintegrated yet."

Shay snorted with laughter. "I don't think a single one of them is under a hundred years old."

"Vampire time. A century is nothing," Sam told her. "It was barely even the Renaissance when I was born. You try carting around a collection of doggy statuettes for that long."

"Doggy statuettes?" Shay grinned and rolled onto her side to look at him.

He wasn't there. Of course he wasn't there. Her father was long gone, and she'd never met him. He wouldn't just show up in the basement of a bat laboratory in Tennessee. Gabriel had told her that once Sam left the family, he never contacted them again.

So now she was hallucinating. Well, at least it was new. The fatigue and the cold dizzy feelings, those were familiar from her long illness. She'd never been quite this exhausted and weak before, but the symptoms themselves hadn't changed. Seeing things, though, that was a surprise.

He felt real, Shay thought sadly. *He felt just like he did when I had visions of Gabriel's life. He seemed like the Sam I saw through Gabriel's eyes.*

"This is appalling," a sharp voice said, cutting through the haze in Shay's brain. "How dare you touch our things?"

Shay didn't have the energy to move. She just gazed up at Tamara, confused. "You have me locked up in a room without even giving me water, and you think *I* have a lot of nerve?" she asked, her voice coming out in a croak.

Tamara snatched up the china dolls and shoved them back into their pillowcase.

"I'm looking for my father's things," Shay said. "I have a right to them."

Tamara frowned. "You'll find nothing of his here. This room stores our *family's* belongings. Your father isn't in that category."

"He was with Ernst even before Gabriel. He was part of the original family in Greece," Shay protested. "He's more a part of this family than you are."

"Sam betrayed us," Tamara barked. "If I could wipe his memory from my mind, I would."

She stormed out of the room, or at least Shay assumed she did. It was too much trouble to turn her head enough to watch Tamara leave.

Gabriel didn't tell me much about her, Shay thought idly. *Maybe he doesn't like her much. Millie seems a lot less prickly.*

It was odd, seeing these people with her own eyes. In all her visions of Gabriel's life, she hadn't gotten much sense of his family. Not this family, anyway. She'd seen his early life in Greece, and she'd experienced the horror of the massacre that killed his original vampire family. There had been Sam. And Ernst, always Ernst. Those were the two who showed up again and again. The only member of his American vampire family that Shay had gotten a vision of was Millie.

Maybe there was some kind of guiding principle to the visions I saw, she thought. *I didn't notice a pattern then, but maybe I only saw visions of things that were most important to Gabriel, events and people that he was most attached to.*

"He told you that you didn't have the complete picture of his life," Sam said. "Gabriel told you that you'd glimpsed only tiny pieces, not his whole self."

"I know," Shay murmured, too tired to tell her father that he was imaginary. Besides, it was nice to have someone to talk to. "I guess he was right. I was surprised by how modern he seemed when I finally met him, and he was all 'I *am* modern, crazy girl.'"

Sam laughed, the same warm laugh she'd heard in her visions of Gabriel's life. Sam had been some strange cross between big brother, best friend, and surrogate father to Gabriel. That's what he was now, to Shay.

"You know, it would've been more useful if I had gotten visions of Gabriel's modern life," Shay said. "If I'd seen Richard and Tamara, and the way Ernst really is now...."

"You would have refused to come anywhere near here," Sam said.

"Yeah. If I'd known how much they hate you, I would have realized that they wouldn't welcome me."

Sam sighed. "Even Gabriel didn't realize that. Perhaps because even after everything that happened, he still managed to love me enough to want to keep my daughter safe."

"He was in denial about how Ernst and the others would feel," Shay said. "Believe me, I know denial. My mom has spent my whole life in denial about my disease—she would never admit to herself that I was terminal."

Sam was silent. Shay took a deep breath, or at least as deep a breath as she could. There seemed to be a permanent block in her lungs now, something that kept her from drawing in enough air. Maybe that's why she was hallucinating. She didn't have to look to know that Sam was gone again.

Not that he'd ever really been there.

"I guess I can give up on searching for any more of your stuff," she said aloud. "Tamara told me there wouldn't be any."

The box with the locket was hidden, Sam's thought seemed to say. Or maybe it was Shay's own thought. She couldn't tell anymore. *It was hidden away so none of the other vampires could find it. So Ernst couldn't find it.*

"So it's true. You've plundered our possessions," Ernst said.

Shay opened her eyes, squinting against the light. Ernst hadn't been there a second ago. "Are you another hallucination?" she asked.

"Hardly." His voice was clipped, but not angry.

She wanted to ask him how Gabriel was, but she knew that was ridiculous. If they'd managed to convince Ernst that Gabriel was returning her to her prison the night before, showing any concern for Gabriel now would only make him suspicious again.

Shay tried to move, to sit up. It felt wrong to lie down while her main captor watched. She should show more strength, more defiance. But she couldn't even lift her head.

"I'm worse than I was when Tamara was here," she murmured. "I must've fallen asleep. How long has it been? Is it daytime again—is that why it's you and not one of the others?"

"I'm not here to answer your questions," Ernst said.

Shay closed her eyes again. Maybe she'd drift back to sleep and he would be gone when she woke up again. *If* she woke up again.

A cool, wet sensation wormed its way through her lips, into her mouth. Shay choked, coughing, as the water hit her throat. She sputtered, then swallowed. It had been so long since she'd drunk that her body didn't feel sure what to do.

Ernst frowned, then reached over and grabbed her under the arms, hauling her to an upright position. He leaned her back against one of the shelves so that she was sitting up and held out a water bottle.

Shay reached for it. She could swear she did. But her hands stayed where they were, down at her sides. Not even a single finger twitched.

"Sorry. Guess I'm too far gone," she croaked. It was weird how she didn't care. Caring took energy, and she had none left.

Ernst rolled his eyes. He knelt down and held the bottle up to her lips, tilting it so more water ran into her mouth. This time her throat remembered how to swallow, and she drank eagerly—until he pulled the bottle away.

I'm not saying thank you, she thought.

"Just like your father. Petulant," Ernst said.

Shay felt a stab of surprise. It wasn't what she had expected to hear. "I never saw Sam acting petulant."

Now Ernst looked surprised. "You never saw him, period."

"I did. In my visions. When my stepfather gave me transfusions of Gabriel's blood, I experienced parts of Gabriel's life," Shay said. She decided not to mention the visions she had when she was actually drinking from Gabriel, her mouth on his skin, his blood warm in her throat. Those visions were even more immediate, more intense.

Ernst's lip curled in disgust. "Everything about you is wrong," he muttered.

Shay shrugged, or tried to. "I saw Sam through Gabriel's eyes. If it's all I'll ever get of my father, I'll take it. I don't care if you think it's wrong."

"There are no visions. We don't have visions." Ernst practically spat the words out.

"Well, I do," she replied. "I think it's like the rush of emotions you get from a Giver when you drink from them. Except my Giver was a vampire, and I'm half vampire, so it . . . changed . . . somehow. It became more clear, less a jumble of feelings."

Ernst was staring at her now, as if she were some rare and dangerous—and revolting—animal. A snake or a Komodo dragon. Something fascinating and sickening all at once.

"I drank from a Giver in my very first vision," she explained. "I mean, Gabriel drank, but I experienced his memory as if it were happening for the first time. I was Gabriel, and I was feeding, and I got a rush of sensations from the Giver. And you were there, telling me when to stop."

Ernst drew in a breath, the air hissing through his teeth.

"I loved you. Gabriel did, and I felt it," Shay went on. "I saw you in a lot of visions. You were like a father. Sometimes you scared me, but mostly I loved you. I didn't expect you to be such an ass in real life."

Ernst backed away from her, his forehead furrowed. "I shouldn't have come down here," he said. "I shouldn't have allowed my curiosity to get the better of me."

Shay barely heard him. Her mind had gotten stuck on the thought of Gabriel, of the way it felt to be in his body when she had a vision. Which led to the memory of the way it felt to be in his arms the night before they came here. She missed him. It was like a physical ache.

She began to ask about him, even though she knew she shouldn't. But Ernst was already on his way out, the door slamming behind him.

Shay's gaze went to the water bottle, on the floor near her hand. She stretched out her fingers as far as she could, but the movement threw her off balance. She collapsed to the ground, not even able to catch herself with her arms. Her head hit the hard concrete, and darkness exploded through her brain, warring with jagged edges of light.

The darkness won.

Is this it? Shay's thought asked.

But Sam wasn't there to answer her. And neither was Gabriel, even though it was him she wanted most of all.

"You're seething. Try to calm down," Millie said, taking Gabriel's hand.

"We're no better than Martin. He treated me like a lab rat. We're treating Shay like a worm on a hook." Gabriel looked around the common room, and it didn't seem like home. More like a jail. All night long, they'd kept him here. Talking about the bats and their disease. Watching stupid TV. Sometimes just sitting there in awkward silence. But always, always pretending that Gabriel was still a family member, not a prisoner.

"Would it really be so bad to give her some food or blood? The meeting with Martin isn't until tomorrow night," Millie said softly. "I know we're . . . I know what's planned, but that doesn't mean she should be starved."

Starved. The word made Gabriel want to run to Shay and kick down the door. But if he'd gotten up, made a move toward the stairs, his brothers and sisters would've tackled him. They were going to keep him away from Shay, no matter what. As much as they could feel his anger, he could feel their determination to follow Ernst's order.

"Her stepfather starved Gabriel. Why should we be any different?" Tamara said dismissively.

Gabriel slammed his fist against the hard wood of the coffee table. "So we're no better than *him?*"

No one answered.

"What will we do when the death sleep comes?" Luis murmured to Richard. "We can't guard him then. And with the way he feels for her, he can't be trusted."

"I'll be asleep too," Gabriel said. "And no doubt Ernst will sit there and watch me like he did yesterday."

"I'm sorry," Luis told him. "I didn't mean for you to hear."

"My senses are as strong as ever, brother," Gabriel replied. "Just because I've been through something terrible doesn't make me less of a vampire."

"Gabriel . . ." Millie's voice trailed off. Gabriel squeezed her hand. He knew she wanted to comfort him, but what was there to say?

"This is making me crazy," Richard exploded suddenly. "How can you be so upset about a halfblood? I feel your hatred—and it's aimed at your own family!"

"Because my family is acting like a bunch of strangers," Gabriel shot back, jumping to his feet. "Shay saved my life. Why doesn't that mean anything to you? What kind of people are you?"

"The kind who protect our own," Tamara shot back. "And

you're such a hypocrite! Thinking you're in love with a human. *You're* the one—"

"I've learned that humans aren't all the same," Gabriel cut her off. "Some of them are decent, loving people—"

"Enough!" Luis shouted, shocking them all. He never raised his voice, and he looked just as surprised as everyone else that he'd done it now.

"Please, I don't want us to fight," Millie said in the silence. "The family felt broken when you were gone, Gabriel. We should be happy now, not arguing all the time."

"Do you really expect me to be happy when you're acting like a bunch of thugs?" Gabriel snapped, letting go of her hand.

They all stared at him for a moment, then Millie sighed. "Martin is the one who should be punished. The girl, Shay, she did save our brother's life." She looked from Luis to Richard to Tamara. "Doesn't she deserve to live for that alone? Not here, but somewhere? If she were going to betray us, why would she have—"

"He's poisoned your mind," Richard snapped.

"You've always had a tender heart," Luis told Millie. "But it's naive to—"

"Don't be so condescending, Luis," Millie shot back. "You're ten years older than I am. Ten. That's nothing to us. It's a blink. Just because I'm daring to disagree doesn't mean I'm softheaded."

Gabriel was grateful to Millie for being open-minded enough to see beyond the hatred for humans she'd been taught. He could feel how much it hurt her to go up against the family. She'd always been the peacemaker.

"I thought you just said we should all be happy and not

arguing," Tamara pointed out, raising one eyebrow.

"Isn't it almost day?" Richard ran his hand through his hair. "I can't take his anger anymore."

"How do you think I feel?" Gabriel cried. Their anger, confusion, pain, and feelings of betrayal were constantly bombarding him.

"It won't last much longer." Ernst stood just inside the doorway, his face pale and drawn. "Dawn approaches. When we wake tonight, it will be time to spring our trap."

"Are we all going to Asheville?" Millie asked hopefully.

"No. Gabriel and I will go alone." Ernst's eyes found Gabriel's, and he smiled ever so slightly.

Gabriel felt a wave of shock and anger from Richard. Millie and Luis turned toward him, but Gabriel kept his eyes on Ernst. "Together we'll avenge you, my son," Ernst told him.

"What about the halfblood?" Richard spat. "You can't be in the car alone with Gabriel, not if she's there too. He'll try to save her."

"I just left her. She won't make it through the day," Ernst said.

Gabriel staggered backward as if he'd been punched.

"You said the woman wouldn't come unless the halfblood was there," Tamara said. Her voice sounded distant, lost amid the horror rushing through Gabriel's mind. *Shay . . .*

"If she dies during the day, we'll put her body in the car. That will be enough to lure the woman," Ernst said.

"No." The moan felt as if it came from Gabriel's gut.

"Ernst, that's cruel." Millie wrapped her arms around Gabriel as if she were trying to hold him together, but she didn't repeat her plea for mercy. "You can't expect him to sit in a car with . . ."

With Shay, Gabriel finished silently. *Shay, dead.*

FIVE

○ ○ ○ ○ ○ ○ ○ ○ ○ ○ ○ ○ ○ ○ ○

"GABRIEL! GABRIEL, WAKE UP!"

It was Ernst's voice, sharp with urgency. The cave had been invaded. The smell of blood, his family's blood, filled his nose and mouth and throat, suffocating him.

"Gabriel, I need you!" The sun was still up. Gabriel could feel it filtering into his nightmare of the massacre, that terrible day when Ernst had woken him to the smell of death. His brothers and sisters. Lysander. Philo. Lizette.

"Gabriel, *now!*"

Hands gripped his shoulders, pulling him up from his cot. Gabriel forced his eyelids open. Not a dream. Ernst was here, waking him in the middle of the day, just as he had all those years ago, in the caves in Greece.

Gabriel tried to focus, tried to ignore the feel of the sun sapping his strength. He forced his eyes open. "What is it?" he asked, trying to shake off the remnants of his dream.

"The alarm's been triggered," Ernst replied. "Someone's coming."

Gabriel stared at him stupidly, trying to force the words to make sense. He felt so . . . *heavy.*

"Protect the others," Ernst ordered, yanking Gabriel to his feet. "I'm going up front to see what's happening."

Ernst tugged Gabriel's arm, pulling him roughly out to the common room.

"Gabriel." The word was a question.

"I'm awake," Gabriel said. "Go."

Ernst took off toward the hallway at a speed no human could match, vanishing in less than a second. Gabriel drew in a breath, convincing himself that he was actually standing upright, shaking off the death sleep for the second time in two days. It was disorienting, and his body trembled with the shock of it.

A blaring siren wormed its way into his awareness, loud enough that it hurt his eardrums. *Loud enough to wake the dead,* Gabriel thought ruefully. But it wouldn't have woken him, not on its own.

"The alarm is triggered from two miles away," he said out loud, even though his voice was lost in the blaring Klaxon. The physical act of speaking forced his mind to work through the fog. "From the base of the hill."

Any time a car crossed the mountain road after the last turn-off, the alarm would blare inside the lodge. It was loudest in Ernst's sleeping chamber, since he was the only one who could be reliably awakened. The system only went on during the day. If anyone was insane enough to show up at night, well, they'd have six powerful vampires to deal with.

Gabriel took another deep breath. Still awake. He glanced around the lodge—the doors were closed, all except his and Ernst's. Had Ernst been standing guard at Gabriel's door again? Or had he just awoken Gabriel because he was the next oldest, the second-in-command, the automatic choice? That's how it would have been in previous days, before Martin.

Before Shay.

I've got to get to Shay. Gabriel felt a sudden jolt at the thought, and he was finally fully awake. Shay was locked in the vault. Ernst had gone to check the lobby, in the lab building. Everyone else was in the throes of the death sleep.

This was his chance, maybe his last chance, to save the girl he loved.

Gabriel took three steps toward the vault before the guilt hit him. Someone was coming. It could be nothing, just a family of vacation-ers lost on the mountain roads, people who would turn around in the parking lot when they saw that the road dead-ended in a closed research facility. Or it could be an attack.

The screams of his dying family echoed through Gabriel's mind. His brothers and sisters in Greece, slaughtered while they slept, defenseless, waking only as the blades slit their throats and the fire ignited their bedclothes.

I can't leave my family unprotected, Gabriel thought. The last time he had been younger and weaker. He would've died too, except that

Ernst had woken him up and Sam had shouted for Gabriel to run. Only the three of them had survived to start their new family—Ernst, Sam, and Gabriel.

Ernst woke both Sam and me that day, Gabriel thought. Without giving himself time to consider what he was doing, Gabriel whirled around and ran for Richard's door. The sleeping chambers locked from inside, but there was an override. Gabriel typed the emergency code into the keypad next to Richard's door and pulled it open so fast that the door slammed into the wall behind it, leaving a dent.

"Richard!" he yelled. Richard and Tamara slept together, both of them unmoving. "Richard, wake up. I know you can. Richard!"

Gabriel grabbed his brother's shoulders and shook, using all his vampire strength. Like Ernst had done all those years ago.

Richard lay like a dead man, unresponsive.

"Richard, wake up. Fight the sleep," Gabriel urged him. "The alarm has been triggered. We're under attack. Wake up!" Desperate, he hit Richard across the face.

"Wha . . ." Richard's eyelids fluttered, and Gabriel felt a burst of hope.

"Get up!" He hit his brother again. "Refuse the death sleep. I've done it. You can do it too. I need you to protect the family."

This time Richard's eyes opened all the way, but there was no awareness in them. Gabriel hit him a third time.

"What . . . ," Richard murmured again, voice thick with sleep.

"The alarm. Get up." Gabriel hauled him to his feet. "You have to protect the family. Are you awake?"

Richard bent over double, retching.

"Fight it, fight the sleep. You're old enough now, you're strong enough. It's an emergency," Gabriel told him. "The family needs you."

"Why is the alarm ringing?" Richard asked, baffled.

"Ernst went to check. I'm going to follow him." Gabriel felt a stab of guilt at the lie, but he didn't hesitate. "You stay here. Stay awake, in case you have to protect the others."

Richard frowned. "Ernst?"

"He wants the family protected. That's your job now," Gabriel insisted. "Richard, do you understand?"

"Yes." Richard was swaying on his feet but staying upright. "I'm awake," he told Gabriel. "I am. Go."

Gabriel ran.

But instead of taking the corridor to the lab building as Ernst had done, he raced downstairs to the vault. The door stood open. Papers and boxes lay strewn about, a mess. But no Shay.

Gabriel's heart seemed to roll over in his chest. Where was she?

Shay. . . . He smelled her scent, but that could be because she'd been here earlier. What had happened to her? Ernst said she wouldn't make it through the day. Was she dead?

"No. No no no no." Gabriel turned and sprinted for the stairs. He didn't think, he just ran. She wasn't in the vault. She wasn't in the lodge, or he would've seen her. The only place she could be was the lab building.

Maybe Ernst didn't wake with the alarm. Maybe he stayed awake on his own, like yesterday, Gabriel thought as he raced down the corridor connecting the buildings. *Ernst must have moved her during the day.*

It was the only explanation. But had he moved her in case Gabriel fought the death sleep again? Ernst must have realized by now that

Gabriel had been trying to save Shay when he caught them. Or had he moved her because she'd died?

Gabriel didn't slow as he approached the lab building. The thick metal door that was their first line of defense against intruders was standing open—but that made sense since Ernst had come this way to check on the alarm. It seemed odd that he hadn't closed it behind him to protect the sleeping family, but maybe he'd been panicked.

Can't stop to figure it out. I've got to get to Shay, Gabriel thought.

As soon as he entered the lab building, he veered right. There was a shortcut through the lab room to get to the stairs. And his vampire senses told him there was a heartbeat—a human heartbeat—downstairs.

The smell isn't right, his brain screamed at him as he ran through the room. *Shay's scent isn't entirely human, but there's an overpowering human smell.*

Gabriel ignored the thought and tore open the stairwell door, jumping to the bottom of the stairs in one leap.

The storeroom door was still hanging open, shattered. No Shay.

But he smelled her more strongly now, her own unique half-human scent.

Gabriel grabbed the handle of the door to the broom closet. It was the only other place that could be secured. He yanked, discovering that someone had driven nails through the flimsy wooden door and into the door frame. *Nails to keep the door closed, to prevent escape.* Gabriel felt a burst of hope.

Sure enough, Shay lay slumped inside the tiny closet, her head resting awkwardly on a mop bucket, her arms limp at her sides. *She's no threat to anyone in this condition, but Ernst still had to nail the door shut?* Gabriel thought, infuriated.

"Shay." He knelt beside her. Her eyes were closed, her dark hair wet with sweat. He'd never seen her so pale, and he felt a rush of panic. "Shay, it's me."

She didn't respond. Not even a twitch.

"I know you're alive. I can hear your pulse," he said, slipping his arms underneath her. He lifted her as gently as he could. "I don't have time to give you my blood, not here."

"Gabriel . . ." Shay's voice was barely even a whisper, but it sent a shock of relief through him.

"Yes. I've got to get you out of here, somewhere safe enough to let you feed from me." He crept up the stairs. "We have to get to the caves. We can reach them through the lodge. It's still daylight. We can't go out the front doors."

It meant going back to where Richard was, awake. It was a risk. But Gabriel had no choice. The tunnel to the caves was there, in the basement. And he'd had to rouse his brother to protect the family. He'd assumed that Shay was still in the vault, that he could res-cue her and go straight to the tunnel, all without going back up to the common room. But the only thing he could do now was hope that Richard had stayed in his chamber like Gabriel told him to. Somehow he had to get Shay past his brother without being seen.

He hesitated when he reached the top of the stairs. The overpow-ering human smell was here again. It was a familiar scent.

". . . think you're a dream," Shay murmured, drawing his attention.

"No. I'm real and I'm going to save you." Gabriel tried to sound confident, but he had a hard time hiding his fear. She seemed to weigh nothing in his arms, yet she was scaldingly hot to the touch. Would his blood be enough? She had never been so far gone before. "Stay quiet, okay?" He used one hand to press her head against his chest.

He pushed open the stairwell door and stepped out into the hallway. But before he could cross to the lab room, a voice yelled from the lobby: "Strong enough to blow you all into dust!"

"And yourself with us," Ernst bellowed back.

But it was the first voice that had stopped Gabriel cold. He recognized the human scent now. Shay was rigid in his arms. "Martin," she whispered. Her tone was steady and her eyes clear.

"Yes." Gabriel would know it anywhere. That man's voice haunted his dreams.

"How . . . ," Shay began.

"He must have tracked your cell phone," Gabriel said. "Is that even allowed?"

"He pays the bills," Shay murmured. "And he's famous and rich. If he told the phone company his stepdaughter was missing—"

"They'd help him, whether it's legal or not." Gabriel groaned. "I can't believe we didn't think of that."

The voices in the lobby raised again, Ernst and Martin yelling. Gabriel forced himself to move, heading for the lab room. If he went through there, he could reach the corridor without going into the lobby. Ernst wouldn't see him. Every step was agony, since it meant leaving his father behind with a human—a dangerous human. But he had to save Shay.

"No. Stop," Shay whispered, squirming weakly in his grip.

"I can't." He pressed her head tighter against his chest, willing her to stay quiet. The fight with Martin would keep Ernst distracted so he couldn't track Gabriel. His communion with the family was weaker than it used to be. He had to get as far away as he could before he was forced to stop and let Shay feed. Going now was their only chance.

"Wait," Shay insisted. "Gabriel—what if my mother is with him? Can you see?"

Gabriel froze. It hadn't even occurred to him that her mother might have come too. It was too dangerous to check, it meant risking being caught by Ernst. But Shay would never forgive him if he let her mother be hurt.

Gabriel slowly turned away from the lab room and inched down the hallway toward the lobby. He peered around the corner, trying to see without being seen.

Martin stood with his back to the glass doors that led outside. He held a heavy-looking backpack in front of him like a weapon as Ernst inched toward him. There was a gurney next to Martin, and through the doors, Gabriel spotted a van in the parking lot, its back open. Even through the glass, the sunlight dazzled his eyes and he had to look away.

Ernst was having the same problem, Gabriel could tell. There was a long awning over the glass doors to block any direct sunlight from reaching inside the lobby. But it was still daytime, and any light at all was almost unbearable. They weren't supposed to be awake, and even an overcast day or the most indirect sunlight could hurt them. Where Gabriel stood, far back from the entrance, he felt safe. No sun could touch him. But if Ernst took even one more step toward Martin— toward the natural light coming through the doors—he risked burning.

"You can't imagine the magnitude of your mistake," Ernst said. "One man against a family of vampires. Your research didn't teach you enough about our strength."

Out of the corner of his eye, Gabriel saw the door that led from the conference room to the lobby inch open. *Richard*. Gabriel heard the hiss as Richard sucked in a breath, taking in Ernst standing so close to a human.

"I watched the other one long enough to know that vampires are like blocks of stone during daylight hours." Martin's voice was detached, like always, but Gabriel detected an undercurrent of fear. "You're no vampire."

"Then come closer," Ernst replied. "Find out for yourself."

He knows he can't attack Martin, Gabriel realized. *Not unless Martin leaves the light.*

Gabriel's eyes darted back to Richard. He was poised in the doorway, muscles tensed.

"Or maybe I'll just set off the C4 and destroy the whole place," Martin said. "Fire kills everything, even vampires. My research told me that much."

Shay let out a whimper. Gabriel was the only one who noticed. The room almost crackled with the tension between Martin and Ernst. Richard took a step forward. What was he going to do? He couldn't get any closer to Martin than Ernst could. If Richard got near enough to attack, it would mean stepping into the sunlight.

"You went to all this trouble." Ernst's voice took on a mocking tone. "I thought you were a scientist. Don't tell me you're really a vampire hunter! Out to kill us all?"

Martin pulled a detonator out of his jacket pocket and pushed a button. "Now it's armed. Still doubt me?" He swung the backpack back and forth by one strap, preparing to throw it. "I'll be outside before it goes off. But it's a nice, sunny day out there, so there's nowhere to run for you."

Gabriel felt Shay begin to tremble, her body sending tremors into his own. He couldn't tear his eyes away from the scene in the lobby. Martin was right. If he detonated the C4, none of the family would escape. They'd all burn, just like his family in Greece.

But he couldn't help them. He had Shay to think about.

"So you're willing to leave here without a captive vampire?" Ernst asked, as if he hadn't even noticed the detonator. "Funny, I thought you still needed a laboratory specimen. Someone to torture the way you tortured my son."

Martin's eyes widened. Richard took another step forward.

"That's right. You're dealing with an old one now." Ernst chuckled. "You locked my son in your lab; I've locked your daughter in my cellar. I think she's dead, though."

Gabriel turned away abruptly. "Your mother isn't here," he whispered into Shay's ear. "I don't see her, and I don't smell her." He moved slowly so as not to attract attention from Ernst, Martin, or Richard. If he was going to save Shay, he had to leave now.

"But—," Shay murmured.

"We're leaving." Gabriel's veins felt filled with lava. His father had used Shay's death as a way to taunt Martin. They were the same, both angry old men intent on vengeance. Let them fight. Neither of them could afford for the C4 to go off. Martin wanted a specimen too badly, and Ernst had the family to protect.

Gabriel would get Shay to the caves and he would save her life. As for Richard, all Gabriel could do was pray that he stayed where he was.

Quickly, Gabriel made his way through the lab room. There would be only one brief moment of exposure to the lobby, and then he would be through the metal door and in the corridor. He took a deep breath, gathered Shay closer in his arms, and stepped out of the lab room.

Almost there . . .

A sharp sound came from the lobby—a gasp, or a cry. Gabriel didn't have time to process which. He whirled around. Ernst had spotted him. He stared at Gabriel, and a mix of anger, betrayal, and fear pulsed through the communion from him.

Martin raised his arm, lifting something . . .

"Ernst!" Gabriel yelled. But it was too late.

A dart flew through the air, shot like a bullet from the gun in Martin's hand. Ernst reached up to knock it aside, his vampire reflexes as fast as lightning. The dart pierced his hand.

Ernst dropped like a rock.

Hawthorn, Gabriel thought. The same paralyzing substance that Martin had used to capture him.

"No!" Richard took off across the lobby. Martin ran for Ernst, grabbing his feet to pull him toward the door.

Gabriel stood rooted in place, too torn to even move.

Martin saw Richard coming, and he hurled the backpack of C4 at him. Richard caught it instinctively, and Martin sprinted back toward the entrance, leaving Ernst behind. He fumbled with the detonator as he tried to escape from the attacking vampire.

"Richard, it's a bomb!" Gabriel yelled. "Get rid of it! Throw it!"

But it was too late. Martin pushed the button as he raced through the glass doors.

Richard didn't even hesitate. Clutching the backpack, he put on a burst of speed, vampire speed, and ran outside.

Into the sunlight.

When the bomb went off, Richard was a thousand yards away from the lab. There was a ravine with a river at its bottom, and he hurled the backpack into it, his body turning to ash even as his arm arced through the air. He crumbled into nothingness as Gabriel watched in horror.

Rocks flew and trees exploded into flame, and from the ravine came the sound, loud in Gabriel's vampire ears.

Martin's van sped from the scene, the back doors still open. He wouldn't want to be anywhere in sight when the firefighters arrived.

"Gabriel . . ." Shay's voice was barely a whisper.

Dragging his eyes away from his brother, Gabriel gently put Shay on the floor. "Right back," he promised her. He ran to his father.

Ernst's body was paralyzed. Gabriel remembered the feeling all too well. The hawthorn rendered him unable to move, to speak, to defend himself. But he'd been able to watch, and think, and feel.

Against his will, his eyes went to Ernst's. His father was conscious in there, and his gaze burned with fury and grief. He had seen Richard run outside. He knew that Gabriel had stood by and let his brother sacrifice himself. He knew that Gabriel had woken Richard in the first place so that he could go and get Shay. He'd seen them, and he knew what it meant, and he knew what it had cost: Richard's life.

"I won't let you die," Gabriel told his father. He jerked the hawthorn dart out of Ernst's hand, then scooped him up and put him on Martin's gurney. There was some kind of thick black cloth—or maybe a body bag—on the gurney, presumably to protect Martin's vampire prize from the sun. He'd come prepared.

I'll kill him, Gabriel promised himself. *If I ever see Martin again, I'll kill him.*

But for now he had to help Ernst. Turning his back on the flames outside, he steered the gurney through the lobby, past the metal door, and down the corridor to the lodge. He pounded through the common room and straight to Richard's sleeping quarters. Inside, Tamara still slept like the dead.

Gabriel left Ernst on the gurney beside the bed. When Tamara awoke tonight, she would find him and she would help him.

As he turned toward the door, guilt and fear slammed into him. Martin would be back. He would do anything to get another vampire to study. The family would have no warning, not with Ernst paralyzed.

He won't come back today. Not with the firefighters around, Gabriel told himself. *Or tonight. He knows better than to come at night when we're all awake.*

But the fire. What if it climbed all the way up to the lab? Gabriel was the only one who could move his sleeping family members to safety. He wouldn't be able to wake them.

He let out a groan. It felt as if his heart were being torn in half. Shay or his family. He had to make the choice again. The decision came almost instantly. Shay. His family might be in danger. But Shay would absolutely die if he didn't get to her right away.

Without another word to his father, he left the room, pulling the heavy door closed behind him. He sprinted back to the lobby and flipped the switch behind the reception counter, engaging the electric lock on the main doors. When the firefighters arrived at the blaze, they would think the lab was closed. That nobody was inside. They wouldn't try to force open the interior doors unless the place was on fire.

The forest fire is mostly down in the ravine, he thought. *It should stay there.*

If it didn't, his family would die. If he didn't stay to warn them about Martin, they could die.

Gabriel did the only thing his ravaged heart would allow. He gathered Shay up, unconscious, into his arms and stepped into the corridor, pulling the thick metal door closed behind him. As he ran to the lodge and then down the stairs, rushing toward the caves, it was the only thought in his mind: He had chosen Shay over his family. It had cost Richard his life.

And his father would never forgive him.

CHAPTER

SIX

○ ○ ○ ○ ○ ○ ○ ○ ○ ○ ○ ○ ○ ○ ○ ○

"HOLD ON," GABRIEL SAID, repeating it over and over as he ran through the winding stone tunnel that led from the lodge to the caves. "Hold on, Shay, just a little longer."

They had built the tunnel themselves, blasting it out of the rock like miners. Each member of the family had gone to graduate school several times over, but they'd also managed to pick up other skills in their long lives. They had to stay out of the sun, which meant they had to have access to the underground in case of an attack. That's just how it was. There was an official entrance to the caves from a trail in the woods behind the lab. Gabriel hadn't used it since they completed their own private way in, one that would

let them escape during the daytime without ever having to set foot
outside.

It wasn't too far to the caves, not when you had vampire speed.
But every second was precious now. Shay's heart rate had slowed to
the point that Gabriel could barely sense it. And her scent was . . .
wrong. He had smelled enough death to recognize the smell.

"Please hold on," he begged her aloud. He didn't want to stop in
the tunnel. Ernst couldn't come after him for as long as the effects
of the hawthorn lasted. But Gabriel had no way of knowing how
much hawthorn was in the dart that Martin shot. Ernst was old and
strong. He could fight off the death sleep with much more ease than
Gabriel had ever realized, so maybe Ernst would be able to shake off
the poison much faster than Gabriel had.

"In the caves we can hide better," Gabriel said aloud, even
though Shay was now unconscious in his arms. "The tunnel is just
too close to home. The caverns are endless." It wouldn't matter.
The vampires would be able to smell Shay a mile off, and they
could track Gabriel by his strong emotions. Their communion
let them feel everything the others did, and when the feelings
were heightened, it was like a beacon, powerful enough to follow.
Usually, that was a good thing—it let them find one another in
times of trouble. But right now Gabriel didn't want to be found.
He wished he could calm himself, but his emotions were all over
the place—guilt, grief, fear, love. He couldn't even think straight.
He just knew he needed to be deep underground, away from the
chaos back at home.

Home. Gabriel felt bile rise in his throat. *It will never be my home
again, not after this. None of them will forgive me for choosing the love*

of an outsider over my family. He almost reeled with the realization. *I'm just like Sam.*

The tunnel was more like a series of small caves—they had blasted out the rock in between to connect the open spaces. Gabriel knew each area by heart, and he put on a burst of speed when he reached the final two turns. Soon he'd be in the first cavern, the huge, high space that held the closest bat colony. The colony would be hibernating now, the bats' hearts beating only about once every ten minutes.

He sprinted through the limestone cavern and jumped up about thirty feet onto a rock shelf on the far side of the colony. It was a flat space at least ten feet wide, and it was hidden from the ground by a grouping of stalactites that the bats liked to hang on. It was the closest cover he could find. It would have to do. Shay didn't have enough time for him to locate a better hiding spot from his family.

Gabriel knelt and eased Shay onto the hard ground as gently as possible.

"Shay?" he said. "Can you hear me?"

Her eyelids didn't even flutter. Gabriel pushed her dark hair back from her face and tried again. "Shay?" he said, louder this time. "Wake up. You need to drink."

But she was too far gone. Fighting down his panic, Gabriel nicked a vein in his wrist, then lifted Shay into his lap and held the blood to her mouth. Her lips were hot, but they didn't close around his wound. She just lay passively as his blood trickled onto her chin.

"Please try," he begged. He lifted her to a more upright position and forced his wrist tighter against her mouth.

Shay sputtered and began to cough.

"You're okay," he told her quickly, relieved to see any sign of life. "Just breathe for a minute."

Shay's beautiful blue eyes finally opened, and she gazed up at him uncomprehendingly.

"We're safe for now. You need blood," he told her. "Drink."

He held his wrist up again, and Shay obediently opened her mouth. Gabriel felt the weak suckling, and he prepared himself for the sensation he always felt when she fed from him—the feeling of connection, a line of fire from his blood to hers, painful and pleasurable at the same time.

"No—" Shay turned her head, coughing violently. Whatever blood she'd managed to drink spilled back out, and she retched.

"Okay, it's okay. Try again." Gabriel tried to keep the desperation from his voice, but he'd never felt so terrified in his life. She had to have vampire blood. She would die without it. She *was* dying without it.

"I can't." Shay's voice was rough from the coughing, and he had to lean close to hear her. ". . . too late."

"No. You'll feel better once you've fed." Gabriel pushed his arm toward her again.

Shay tried to turn her head, but instead, it lolled back against him. *She's too weak to even control her movements*, he realized. A tear ran down Shay's cheek, but otherwise, she didn't move.

"Please. Shay, please." Gabriel didn't know what else to say. Didn't know what to think. "I can't lose you. I love you. Please."

"Love you," she whispered, her eyes finding his although her head didn't move. "Sorry."

"No." Gabriel swallowed, hard. "I will not let you die. I never understood why Sam cared so much about your mother, but now I do. He loved her, like I love you. You're the first person who's ever taught me how to truly trust, Shay. I will not live without you."

Shay didn't answer. Her eyes looked glassy. Gabriel didn't know if she could even hear him anymore.

"I'll do a blood ritual. I'll make you a vampire," he said.

Shay's gaze sharpened, her brow furrowing ever so slightly.

"Yes. That's what we'll do." Gabriel hadn't given a single thought to this before, but it suddenly seemed the most obvious thing in the world. "You're half vampire already. That's what's killing you, what's always been killing you. So I'll make you a full vampire. You'll live."

Shay's lips moved, but he couldn't hear what she was saying. He leaned down, so close that he could feel her shallow breath on his skin. "No," she whispered.

"It's not what you want. It's not what I want for you. But you'll still be here. We'll be together," he said. "Please. We haven't had enough time."

Shay was watching him. He knew she understood.

"Shay. It's not easy. You have to . . . die. I have to drain your blood, all of it, before I give you my own blood to transform you." Gabriel took a shaky breath. "I've never—In my family we perform this blood ritual together, as a group. I've never done it alone." Gabriel gently swept her long hair away from her pale, beautiful neck. "But I will. I'll do it for you."

Shay twisted away from him, shocking him with her sudden strength. She managed to get herself into a sitting position, her back against the wall of the cave, before her burst of vitality—or adrenaline—gave out.

"*No.* Just hold me and let me die," she whispered. "If you drink my blood, it will kill you."

"Shay—"

"It's poison to you. Don't you remember?"

He did remember, of course. The very first night he'd seen Shay, she had rescued him from Martin's exam room. She'd unchained him and helped him get out of the building . . . and he had repaid her by taking her captive. At the earliest opportunity, he'd dragged her into a motel room and fed from her to restore his stolen strength. Her blood had almost killed him.

"When I drank from you, your veins were filled with *my* blood," he told her now. "You'd been having transfusions of it. It's vampire blood that is poisonous to me. Not half-vampire blood."

"You don't know that," Shay said. She had already begun to slump down, too weak to hold herself up. "I might be poison."

"You haven't have vampire blood in days now. It's why you're dying—your body is trying to function on your own blood, and it doesn't work," Gabriel said.

"It's too big a risk." Shay's voice was fading, her eyes closing again.

She was right. He didn't know if half-vampire blood would hurt him. Nobody knew the science behind it, if indeed it was science and not magic. They didn't know why vampire blood made them sick, what particular aspect of it was poisonous, or even if it was the fault of the blood rather than of their bodies' ability to process it.

Why didn't we ever study this? Gabriel thought. *Decades spent in doctoral programs, centuries as scientists, and we've never studied ourselves.*

Only Martin had experimented on their blood. Only he might know the secrets it held.

"I don't care about the danger," Gabriel said, even though Shay might be too far gone again to hear him. He gazed at her pale face, still and beautiful like a marble statue. Even after he had kidnapped her and fed from her, she had stayed with him. He had collapsed, sick from the vampire blood, and she could have fled. But instead, she went and got bags of human blood. She fed him and nursed him back to health, and she didn't expect anything in return. She was the most selfless—and fearless—person he'd met in four centuries of life. Even now, she wasn't afraid of the blood ritual because it would kill her. She was only afraid that it might kill *him*.

"Maybe your blood will kill me, Shay," Gabriel said. "But I don't care. I would rather die than live without you."

She didn't reply. Her pulse was slow now, almost imperceptible even with his vampire hearing.

"I love you, Shay," Gabriel murmured. Then he bent his mouth to her neck, and began to drink.

Mommy looks scared. She thinks I don't notice, but I do. This time I've been in the hospital for three weeks. That's a new record. I'm getting sick of the SpongeBob *repeats they always have on here. Olivia sent me a picture from school with Mr. O'Leary and the whole class waving at me. I wish I could go home.*

Shay stopped writing in her journal and looked up at her mother's worried face—just as it changed. Well, the face was the same, and the worry was the same. But everything else around Mom morphed into a different place and time. They were on the beach in Florida, and Shay felt cold even though it was hot out.

"I'm fine," she lied, not wanting to admit that their vacation was over. It was the only vacation she and Mom had ever taken, and it was only three days sandwiched in between the visit to the specialist in Miami and the long Greyhound ride back home to Massachusetts. They couldn't afford any more nights than that at the motel.

"It's a hundred degrees out and you're shivering. You're not fine," her mother said sadly. "I think we'd better get you to bed, don't you?"

Shay wanted to cry or scream, but she was too tired. "Why can't they just find what's wrong with me?" she asked.

"I think it's a unique disease," Martin answered, and Shay felt a jolt of surprise to see him there. Suddenly, she was in a hospital bed, the one in New York, where they'd first met Martin. He was visiting from Texas, and Mom had basically stalked him until he agreed to see Shay.

"How can that be?" Shay mumbled. But she wasn't talking out loud, she suddenly realized. She couldn't; she was too weak to even move her mouth.

Dying, she thought. *I'm dying and my life is flashing before my eyes.* That's what people meant when they said that, apparently—that you saw all kinds of random memories.

Gabriel. Shay tried to say his name, and for one shocking instant, she realized with great clarity just what was happening. She lay in a strange, white-walled cave, locked in Gabriel's embrace, his lips on her neck, his fangs in her flesh, her blood flowing into his mouth. He shouldn't be doing that. Her blood could kill him.

Then reality slipped away again, blending softly into another memory. Olivia on the swing set in her backyard, her mouth opening in a scream as Shay collapsed off the swing next to her, too dizzy to hold on.

Olivia's ten-year-old face blended into her seventeen-year-old one, and she was yelling at Shay for kissing Kaz while half the senior class looked on.

"It didn't mean anything. I'm drunk," Shay protested. She glanced around at her classmates. Chris Briglia was staring at her with a smirk on his face.

And then she was in the water, swimming in the Black River with Chris, both of them pushing hard for the island in the middle of the current. It was freezing.

"Don't be afraid, honey," her mother's voice said, and now Shay was in the hospital again. The tunnel vision had gotten so bad this time that Shay could barely see, and her heart was pounding, *loud*.

The sound drowned out her mother's voice.

Was it a memory? Or was it reality?

Her heart slammed desperately against her chest, fighting for life. She could swear her eyes were open, but they saw nothing but blackness. Shay tried to pull in a breath, but her lungs didn't work. *Dying.*

Gabriel's mouth was still warm against her skin, but Shay felt as if she were moving farther and farther away from the sensation. Farther from the cave, and from Gabriel, and from her own body.

It's okay, Mom, her thought whispered. *I'm not scared.*

For a moment she floated there, in the cave and out of it at the same time. In her body and out of it. Alive and dead.

And then Gabriel's blood filled her mouth.

Instantly, she was back in her body. The salty-sweet taste of his blood returning her to the present, to Gabriel. She became aware that she was swallowing the thick liquid, but only slowly, not really drinking as much as letting it trickle down her throat.

"Drink, Shay, you have to try." Gabriel's voice sounded strange, far away and sort of muffled.

She closed her lips around the wound in his wrist and tried to suck.

More blood. And with it, emotions. *Gabriel's* emotions. Fear and anger and exhilaration and love all jumbled together. She felt a moment of confusion, and she knew it was her own confusion.

And then suddenly, Shay was gone, and she was Gabriel. Like every other time she'd taken his blood into her body, she was in a vision from Gabriel's long life. Shay stood in Gabriel's place, thinking his thoughts, feeling his emotions, watching the world with his eyes.

It had never been this clear before. Each scent wafting by on the warm breeze was almost overwhelming in its intensity. Each star in the black Greek sky seemed blindingly bright. Each grain of sand on Gabriel's bare foot tickled individually. The visions had always been strong, but this was something beyond ordinary strength. It was superhuman.

"They are gone. We need to leave the past to the past," Ernst said.

Shay turned—*Gabriel* turned—and faced his father. "We cannot go on living like animals," he agreed.

"So we leave. Go to Italy or to Germany," Sam said.

Sam! The thought was Shay's, breaking in to the vision. *My father.*

Then Gabriel spoke, and Shay's consciousness retreated again. "Leave our home? Abandon our family?"

Sam put his hand on Gabriel's shoulder, and the weight of it felt comforting. "Our brothers and sisters are dead. We must look to the future now, for what is left of the family. The three of us. We will start again, build a new home. But not here, Gabriel."

"There is too much danger. The island is small, and the humans know some of us escaped their massacre," Ernst said, anger dripping from his voice.

"I've never left the island." Gabriel knew he sounded like a child even though he'd lived several lifetimes. He was afraid.

"Do not fear. We will be together, always," Sam said.

Gabriel moved, pulling his wrist from Shay's mouth for only a split second, but it was enough to startle her into awareness. From the warmth of the darkened beach in Greece to the chilly cave in Tennessee. The change made her feel disoriented, and then Gabriel's blood filled her mouth again. This time Shay didn't need to tell herself to suck—her body did it automatically.

Millie and Luis were fighting, their yelling getting louder and louder as they ran through the halls of the house in New York. Shay—*Gabriel*—winced at the noise. "Quiet! The neighbors will hear."

From beside him on the sofa, Sam laughed. "There are no neighbors for a mile. It's only your vampire hearing magnifying the noise."

"They're supernaturally loud," Gabriel grumbled.

"They're still human children," Sam replied. "They are not as loud as you think."

Gabriel watched as they ran into the room—Millie's red pigtails a mess, her elfin face filled with rage as Luis held the doll out of her reach.

"Luis, give it back. It's nearly time for Millie to go to bed," Gabriel said.

Luis rolled his eyes, but he handed over the doll.

"It's not fair. Why doesn't Luis have to go to sleep?" Millie demanded.

"Because he's ten years older than you. He gets to stay up later," Sam told her. He glanced at Gabriel. "She reminds me of Lysander. Always wanting to be treated like the older kids."

Gabriel didn't answer. He couldn't—the rush of pain he felt at the mention of Lysander was too great. The younger boy had been taken from the orphanage with him, had grown up in the vampire family with him, just as Millie and Luis were growing up together. As siblings. As family. When they were teenagers, they went through the blood ritual and became vampires, just as Millie and Luis would. They lived for more than two hundred years afterward as brothers . . . until Sander was murdered by the humans.

How can Sam talk about him so casually?

"We have a new family," Sam said quietly. It wasn't the communion—Sam had always been able to tell what Gabriel was thinking. "You cannot live a long life if you hold on to the pain of the past. You're going to be here for centuries, Gabriel. Tragedies will happen. You must let them go."

Gabriel turned away, frowning. Sam was his best friend, his brother. But sometimes he seemed like a stranger. How could he "let go" of the pain of losing their family? Gabriel never would, even if he lived for a thousand years.

"Don't be like Ernst," Sam said. "He's grown more bitter with each loss—first Gret, then our family. . . ."

"Why shouldn't he be bitter?" Gabriel cried.

"It's going to twist him eventually. Gret always said that anger hurts more than grief."

Gabriel just shook his head. Sam was being naive. He wanted to see the good in things, but sometimes he went too far.

"Shay—" Gabriel's voice broke into Shay's mind. "Stop."

He pulled his wrist from her mouth, and Shay moaned as reality crashed back in around her. The cold air, the eerie limestone of the cave . . . but she could see more now, details of the whitish rock walls. Was it just her imagination? She was looking through her own eyes, but it felt more like one of the visions when she looked through Gabriel's eyes.

"I need . . ." Gabriel's voice was weak, and she studied his face. His eyes were different—not their typical dark color, but lighter, almost purple. It was beautiful. But other than that, he looked tired. Exhausted, really. She felt a stab of worry—had her blood sickened him? If she kept taking his own blood, she could weaken him too much. It might kill him. But she wanted more. She craved it. She couldn't control herself. Shay pulled his wrist to her lips and drank.

"It's all right," Gabriel murmured, the purplish cast to his eyes growing even more intense. "You need enough to transform. I've never done it by myself." His other hand stroked her hair for just a moment, and Shay felt a sense of warmth steal through her.

Or maybe it was the sun beating down on Gabriel as he swam in the waters off the island in Greece. Shay sank into the vision, but her own thoughts hung on longer than before. Hot sun . . . he wasn't a vampire yet. Next to him swam Lysander, grinning widely.

"How can you be so happy?" Gabriel asked, turning to float on his back.

"I am enjoying the day, brother. Tonight I join the family!" Sander dove like a dolphin and vanished under the waves.

Lysander was in the last vision, too. They talked about him, Shay's thought whispered from somewhere.

It was enough to interrupt the vision, and then suddenly, she was in the sleeping cave in Greece. She recognized it immediately, or rather Gabriel recognized it. They stood in a circle, the entire family, with Lysander on the floor in the middle. Ernst knelt next to the youth, drinking from his neck. He stopped and looked up. "He's dead."

Gabriel felt a momentary pang of fear. He wasn't in the circle with the others, because he hadn't given up the sun yet. He stood behind them, watching. Learning. He'd known what to expect, of course. Ernst had explained it many times. But seeing Lysander dead on the floor . . . it frightened him.

And then Sam stepped forward. He was the eldest of them— other than Ernst—and, therefore, he would take the first turn. Sam knelt at Lysander's side and lifted the young man in his arms. He nicked a vein in his wrist and held it to Sander's mouth. "Drink, brother," Sam said simply.

Immediately, all of Gabriel's fear vanished. Sam would take care of Lysander. He always took care of all the younger ones. If Ernst was their stern father, Sam was their nurturing father. Gabriel smiled. Or else Sam was their mother. He wasn't, of course. But Sam had told him once that he tried to be as much a mother as he could, ever since Gret had sought the sun and turned to ash. Sam had grown up in the vampire family with a mother, Gret. The rest of them hadn't. Sam thought it wasn't fair.

He would've been an amazing dad, Shay thought. And she knew instantly that it was her own thought, not Gabriel's. She was still there, in the vision. Still in Gabriel's body, watching the blood ritual with Gabriel's eyes and thinking Gabriel's thoughts.

But suddenly, her own consciousness was there too. Shay, separate from Gabriel. Shay's thoughts. Shay's emotions.

It's because I'm becoming a vampire, she realized. *The visions have never been like this before because I have never been like this before. I'm changing. I'm drinking Gabriel's blood as I have before, but this time it's turning me into something else.*

Sam held Lysander, letting him drink. Transforming him into a vampire.

Sam. Shay stared at him, her father. He was the one she wanted to watch. She had seen so many parts of Gabriel's life through these visions . . . but she didn't need to live his life to know him. She had the real Gabriel now, in her life, in her arms. He loved her, he was saving her. When they were done, she would be a vampire and they would be together forever. But Sam—she had never met him and she didn't know if she ever would. The only way to know her father was through these visions, through Gabriel's experiences with Sam.

I'll follow him, she thought. *I'll focus on Sam and follow him through the visions. I'll take control of what I see.*

But nothing happened. The vision continued just as before, with Shay watching through Gabriel's eyes as Sam gently eased Lysander's mouth away and another member of the family took his place, guiding Sander to drink from her vein.

The blood ritual, Shay thought. *It's on Gabriel's mind because he's performing it right now, on me. Somehow I'm seeing visions about the blood ritual and the people Gabriel has seen go through it.*

Shay summoned all the strength she had and forced her mind away from the vision and back to reality. She was feeding from

Gabriel. On some level she knew that. She herself was participating in a blood ritual. She had to stop.

"Shay, keep going," Gabriel whispered.

Shay blinked, back in her own body again. The cave surrounded them, and Gabriel slumped against the stone wall, pale and sweating. Shay frowned.

"Can you feed on your own yet? Is it working?" Gabriel asked weakly. "Your eyeteeth—can you release them?"

Shay automatically ran her tongue over her teeth, not sure what he meant.

"You have to keep going," he breathed.

"I'm killing you. If I take more blood, you'll be too weak." Shay's voice sounded strange in her ears. It was the first time she'd spoken since she died.

"I'll recover." Gabriel met her eyes and smiled, a ghost of his usual smile. "Vampire strength."

Shay nodded, the movement causing the cave to spin around her. She was still weak too, maybe even half dead. What was she, exactly? A vampire? A dead girl? Something in between?

"You feed. Do it yourself," he said. "The transformation, it takes . . . a lot."

Shay thought of the ritual she'd seen, the whole family waiting their turn to give their blood to Lysander. Would there even be enough blood in Gabriel's body for them both?

He leaned his head back, exposing his throat. Shay stared at it, focusing on him to stop the cave from whirling. A strange sliding sensation in her mouth caught her attention, and she used her tongue again to explore it. *Fangs.*

Gabriel's smooth tawny skin seemed to draw her forward. Her fangs ached with wanting him.

Shay bent to his neck and inhaled the scent of him. Then her teeth sank into his flesh, blood flowing into her mouth, her consciousness spiraling down into another vision.

Sam, Shay thought. *I want to see Sam.*

"The only choice is a blood ritual," Ernst said, his voice muffled by the still air of the cellar under the old house.

Shay frowned—*Gabriel* frowned. She stood in Gabriel's body, speaking Gabriel's words, just like always in a vision. But there was something different. A wall of tension, an undercurrent of confusion. "But if Sam were willing to give up the woman . . . ," Gabriel began.

"I won't. You know that better than anyone, brother," Sam spat, his voice filled with fury. "You knew it when you told Ernst about my love for Emma."

Gabriel refused to look at Sam, shackled to the dirt floor. But he felt Sam's anger like a physical blow.

What is going on? Shay thought frantically. It was her own thought, not Gabriel's, but the turmoil of Gabriel's feelings made it hard to figure out what was happening in this strange vision. And there was something else—other emotions that came from outside of Gabriel. Anger from Sam, who lay on the ground. A cold hatred from Ernst. Fear from Millie . . . and Millie wasn't even in the room.

"It would take more than giving her up. The human woman is a threat as long as she knows about us. We have to kill her." Ernst sounded annoyed at the prospect, like it was an unpleasant errand he had to run.

"No." Sam's voice was half fury, half fear. But the emotion coming from him was suddenly an all-encompassing terror. Shay felt sick from the intensity of it—or was it Gabriel feeling sick?

I don't understand. Shay's own thought again, or at least she assumed so.

"Did he tell you where she is, who she is?" Ernst asked Gabriel.

"No. Just the name, Emma," Gabriel replied.

My mother, Shay's thought said. *Mymothermymothermymother.*

"During the blood ritual, when he is weakened, he will tell us how to find her," Ernst said.

Now Gabriel felt afraid. He loved Sam, even after this betrayal of the family, he still loved Sam. "Maybe there's a way to avoid a blood ritual," Gabriel said desperately. "If Sam did it, if he killed her. Then we could forgive him, couldn't we?"

Shay felt a wave of astonishment wash over her at the words that had just come out of her own mouth.

Not my mouth, she thought. *Gabriel's mouth.*

She pulled away from him, jerking her fangs from his flesh, the reality of the cave crashing back in on her like a train wreck. Nausea spread through her body when Gabriel's blood stopped sliding down her throat, and she moaned.

"Keep feeding," he whispered. "The transformation's not complete."

"I felt other people's feelings," she said. "In the vision. Not just yours." It was too much. Too overwhelming. Had she even seen a true vision? It had been hard to tell where Gabriel's thoughts ended and the others began.

"It's the communion. We feel one another's emotions," Gabriel said. "It's why the whole family participates in a ritual—so that we're all linked. But I'm the only one this time. You should only be linked to me." His brow furrowed in confusion, but he didn't move otherwise. He looked worn out.

"The visions are changing. Everything seems sharper, like smells and sights. And I can think my own thoughts," Shay said, forcing herself to take a deep breath. "I felt the others' emotions, but I think it was because you felt them. Gabriel"—she looked him in the eyes—"what happened to Sam? You told Ernst about him and my mother."

Gabriel gasped, panic on his face. He pulled away from her, the first burst of strength he'd shown since their private blood ritual began.

"Shay. Don't," he said.

Shay crawled toward him, extended her fangs, and bit his throat. The blood flowed freely. She could almost feel its strength taking over her body, reaching now to each tiny capillary, to every part of her. Transforming her.

Sam, she thought.

And there he was. Her father was shackled to the ground, heavy chains driven into the dirt that made up the cellar floor of the old farmhouse. There were chains around his legs and one around his waist, and he was fighting. Writhing, panting, hysterical.

Shay gaped at him. She'd seen Sam in so many visions now, through so many years of Gabriel's life. He had always been calm, comforting, in control.

Now he looked like a mindless animal crazed with fear.

And then his emotions hit her—hit *Gabriel*. Fury, hatred, terror. Gabriel turned away, unable to face his brother. The one who had been by his side for hundreds of years. The one who he himself had turned in.

Millie stood next to him, with Luis and Richard arranged so that they formed a circle around Sam. Richard's new partner, Tamara, was there too. On Gabriel's other side stood Ernst.

"The youngest will begin," Ernst announced. "Then on to the next youngest, and so on. Drink only what your body can handle. The ritual will last for three nights—none of us need get sick from the poison of his blood."

My turn comes last, except for Ernst, Gabriel thought. Their new family had been made here, in America. They were all younger than Gabriel and Sam, much younger. Even Tamara had been made a vampire little more than a century ago, or so she said.

"How can you? How can you do this?" Sam wailed, pure desperation in his voice.

Millie knelt beside him, hands shaking. Fear and doubt flowing from her in waves, she turned and gazed at Gabriel. So did Sam.

"Gabriel? I held you when you were little more than a baby," Sam said, suddenly quiet. "I trusted you with my secret. I wanted to share my joy with you as I've shared my whole life with you."

"Begin," Ernst commanded Millie.

Her gaze stayed on Gabriel, an unspoken question in her eyes.

"He put the family in danger, Millie," Gabriel whispered. "Begin the ritual."

Millie nodded, eyes brimming with tears. She bent and sank her eyeteeth into Sam's shackled wrist. He screamed, like a horse with a broken leg, like a pig at slaughter, like a madman in an asylum. Gabriel flinched, steeling himself against the onslaught of fury that shot through the communion from Sam.

Sam . . . they're draining him, Shay thought as she watched Millie drink. *One at a time, they're going to drain him.* She wanted out of this vision, she wanted back to the safety of the cave with Gabriel—Gabriel, who loved her; Gabriel, who was saving her.

"Gabriel, how can you do this?" Sam asked, panting and panicked as Millie drank.

"You saw our family slaughtered in Greece. Humans did that," Gabriel said, choking on the words. "Yet you revealed our secret to one."

"To one I love," Sam cried, anguished. "How can you punish me for love? When your turn comes, will you really do this, brother?" His eyes burned into Gabriel as his terror seeped through the communion. "Will you kill me?"

"Yes," Gabriel said. "I will."

Shay tore her fangs from Gabriel's vein, rending his flesh. The cave around them was bright as day, and she could smell each individual bat hibernating above. She could hear their slow heartbeats and the drip of water somewhere far away, and she could see each crag of rock and each grain of dirt between them. She felt the strength in her arms, her legs, her lungs, her heart . . . in every cell of her body.

The sick girl was gone.

Shay was a vampire now.

Gabriel lay on the rock shelf, pale and feeble, his breathing fast, his eyes wide with horror. "Shay . . ."

I've drained him. My blood made him sick, and then I drained him almost dry, she thought. *He's weak. And I'm strong.*

"Shay. What did you see?" Gabriel whispered.

"I saw *you*," she told him. "You murdered my father."

○ ○ ○ ○ ○ ○ ○ ○ ○ ○ ○ ○ ○ ○ ○ ○

Lichen. Stagnant water. *Bat dung.*

Shay doubled over, feeling sick. The caves swam around her, end-less and dank, one after another after another.

A drop of water, moisture from the roof falling to the floor. A single drop.

"It's too much," she moaned, pressing her hands to her ears. That one drip might have been a mile away, but she'd heard it as if it were right next to her head. She heard the breathing of the bats that slept above her, heard each individual heartbeat, heard the barest whisper of wind making its way though the labyrinth of caves.

And the smells. Every scent of this strange, underground world came to her as its own thing. It wasn't just a stuffy, dank, bad scent. It was a bat, a rat, a decomposing fish in a dark stream. It was water, and air that had been inside for too long, and *rock*. Who knew that rocks had a smell?

Gabriel had told her about vampire senses—that every sensation was heightened. She'd known that he could smell things and hear things from far off. She'd known that he could see in the dark.

But not like this.

I should be grateful for the night vision, Shay thought miserably. It was better than being trapped underground in a strange place with no lights at all. If she were still human, the darkness of these caverns would have driven her mad.

But she wasn't human. And the fact that she could see every detail of a place that she knew—she *knew*—was pitch black, well, it freaked her out.

Shay wrapped her arms around herself and sank to the ground. *I thought it would be like in the visions.* When she'd experienced Gabriel's life through her visions, she had also experienced his vampire senses. She'd seen in the dark, and tasted the individual flavors in a Giver's blood, and felt the rush of strength in his muscles. She'd just assumed that that was the way it felt to be a vampire. But the visions hadn't been what she thought. She had been in Gabriel's body and she'd experienced his life, but it was as if there were a layer of gauze over everything. She hadn't known it at the time, but now she did.

What Gabriel had felt and seen and experienced was a hundred times more complex and detailed than anything she'd felt in the visions. Her senses weren't just heightened, they were a whole different thing. This wasn't seeing in the dark, this was nighttime turned to day—and then viewed through a telescope. To use the word "hearing" to describe this ability to detect the tiniest sound . . . it was just wrong. This wasn't hearing. This was something else Something superhuman.

Something *un*human.

"I'm a vampire," Shay murmured, dizzy and terrified by the truth of it. "I'm dead and I'm a vampire."

She wanted to cry, but her body was just too stunned to do it. Or maybe vampires couldn't cry. Had she ever seen Gabriel cry in a vision?

I should have stayed with him, she thought. *He could have explained all this so I wouldn't feel so overwhelmed.*

It didn't matter now. She'd run away from Gabriel hours ago. For all she knew, he'd died up there on that rock shelf. He had been weak as a kitten—whether from her drinking so much of his blood or from his having been poisoned by her blood, she didn't know. And she didn't care. She'd jumped off the shelf and run off at an impossible speed, and Gabriel hadn't followed her. He'd barely lifted his head. He hadn't said a word after she told him what she saw.

He killed my father.

He hadn't even tried to deny it. Sam had told Gabriel about his love for Shay's mother. He'd told Gabriel that she was pregnant and that he was happy about it.

And then Gabriel had turned on him and told Ernst about it. *He said it was verboten,* Shay remembered. *That love between a vampire and a human was an abomination, a horror.* But he had never told her that it was punishable by death. She had never in her darkest dreams imagined that Gabriel and his family had killed Sam. All these years she had no father, all these years her mother thought Sam had abandoned her . . .

And all this time Gabriel had let her fall in love with him, and he'd never told her the truth.

She'd even asked him once what had happened to Sam, and Gabriel said he didn't know. He had chained her father to the floor and participated in a blood ritual to murder him, and then he'd looked Shay straight in the eye and lied about it.

"I can handle this on my own," Shay whispered. "I don't need Gabriel for anything. He's no better than the rest of them."

Shay took a deep breath, strangely comforted by the hatred that seeped through her at the thought of Gabriel. Until now she'd been running, darting through the endless caves like an animal, terrified by the sounds and smells and the unfamiliar surroundings. Terrified by the strength in her own limbs, by the fact that her eyes could see things they shouldn't see. She'd been running from Gabriel—from the truth about Gabriel—but she hadn't been thinking about him.

Now that she had, the hysteria was dying down.

She was hungry.

Shay hugged herself tighter. She was hopelessly lost in the caverns. She had no idea how far they stretched under the mountains in Tennessee. She'd never even known there were mountains in Tennessee.

It didn't matter. She would find her way out. She wasn't some weak little sick girl anymore, she was a supernatural creature with outrageous strength and speed. She'd figure it out. She couldn't spend the rest of eternity being overwhelmed by her own senses. This was reality now. She would handle it.

Tentatively, Shay sniffed the air, turning her head to face different directions.

Stale air. Stale air. Toxic air. Another bat colony.

Focus on the air, she told herself. *Just the air.*

Rocks. Fetid water. Some kind of insect hive.

How do I even know what these scents are? she wondered. She'd never smelled a hive of wasps in her life. Was there some kind of instinctive odor-recognizer in her vampire body? The thought brought the hysteria back, so she shoved it down. *Focus on the air.*

Fungus. Stale air. Maple.

Maple! Shay felt a burst of hope. The scent of maple meant freedom. If the air smelled like maple, that meant it was air coming into the cave from the woods, bringing outside odors in. If she followed that smell, she'd find an opening in the rock. *I'll get outside, and then I'll figure out what to do.*

Shay got to her feet and started moving in the direction that the maple scent had come from. She could do this. She had gone through a thousand awful physical exams over the years—spinal taps and bone marrow tests and lots of other scary and painful things. She had gotten through them all, somehow. She had gotten through Martin's betrayal, when he hit her across the face. She had gotten through being held captive by Gabriel. And later by his family.

She had gotten through dying.

So she could get through this. She just had to find her way out of these caves and get away from Ernst and his murderous vampire family.

The scent of maple grew stronger as she scrambled through another narrow cave. It opened into a larger space, but the outside air was coming through a tiny fissure in the wall of that cave. Shay stuck her leg into the fissure and tried to squeeze through. She was incredibly skinny from being sick all her life, and yet she was too big for that small opening.

Don't panic. Focus, she told herself.

Shay put her face to the fissure and breathed deeply. Maple and now oak.

I will not be trapped in here. Shay thrust her arm through the fissure, dug her fingers into the hard rock, and pulled as hard as she could. There was a snapping and cracking sound, and the opening crumbled like a little avalanche, sending bits of rock tumbling and dust flying into the air.

Shay jumped back in surprise, fast enough to avoid getting hit by the rocks. Then she peered at the fissure. Still small, but bigger than it had been. She had broken through solid rock with her bare hands.

"Well, that's pretty cool," she said aloud. She inched up to the opening again and squeezed herself inside. Maybe it would collapse on top of her now that she'd weakened the rock. But maybe she'd be strong enough to live through it if it did.

She shimmied and twisted her way through the fissure. It was tight, but she managed to make it through. On the other side was a narrow space, more a tunnel than a cave. About ten feet later, it opened out into a cavern. The scent of trees came from somewhere high above.

Shay tilted her head back and squinted into the distance. There, about seventy feet up, was a patch of gray light. She blinked, shocked to see anything other than blackness. Shay reached for a handhold and pulled herself up onto a spire of rock. The air smelled of more than just trees now, it smelled of flowers, and rain, and animals. *Fresh air.*

There was some kind of ledge up there, maybe a rock shelf like the one she'd left Gabriel on. It was impossibly far away.

Shay gathered herself and jumped. Straight up, pushing off of the spire with her feet. In her life she had barely had the stamina to play a game of hopscotch. Back when Olivia would play jump rope at recess, Shay always had to sit reading a book. Now, though, it was effortless. One push and she was flying upward, the damp air of the cave rushing past her face. She reached out and grabbed on to the ledge, her fingers tightening automatically. Without thinking, she pulled herself up and over the edge, landing on her feet on a wide shelf of rock.

"Wow," Shay breathed. Her body had gone from house cat to lion in the space of one day. She felt the dizzy disorientation begin to fade. She was strong. She'd found her way here, and now she would get out of the caverns and away from Gabriel's family.

The gray light came from a cave mouth at one end of the rock shelf, about thirty feet away. It was raining outside—Shay could hear each drop as it hit the stone of the cave, and she could smell the sweet and earthwormy scent of it. The air up here was wet, coating her skin in a fine mist.

"Thank God. I'm finally out," Shay said. She didn't care if she got drenched—no more worrying about catching cold and getting sick. She'd never be sick again. She was a vampire, indestructible.

She stepped toward the cave entrance, eager for the fresh air and the rain. The dreary gray daylight washed over her—and she shrieked in pain.

Shay hurled herself backward, tumbling over the edge of the shelf and falling through the empty air. She landed flat on her back on the rock far below. Stars exploded in front of her eyes.

The sun. The thought reached Shay from somewhere beyond the pain in the back of her skull. *It's still daytime, and I can't go out. Not even in the rain. Not ever again.*

Her incredible vampire vision blurred with tears. She wasn't strong. She was scared. She was a vampire, and she was alone. Forever.

The sun began to go down.

Relief flooded through Gabriel as he felt it. He'd been lying on the cold stone shelf ever since Shay ran off earlier that day. The only other times he'd defeated the death sleep—exactly twice in his long life—the sun had sapped his strength and put him to sleep as soon as the adrenaline rush was over. But not today.

How can I still be awake? he wondered for the hundredth time. He felt the sun like a physical presence even though he was deep underground. It pressed on him, and he imagined he could tell its exact location in the sky as the minutes slowly ticked by. Feeding from Shay had done something to him. It was the only explanation. He'd taken in her half-vampire blood, and then she'd taken almost all of his own strong blood.

He was weak. Maybe even poisoned—if she'd been a full vampire, drinking that much of her toxic blood would surely have killed him. It was anybody's guess what her unique blend of human and vampire blood had done. But to defy the death sleep for the whole day? That was unexpected.

Or possibly he was dying. He felt the pressure of the sun, and yet his body didn't react to it. Not only that, but his body couldn't function at all. He'd lain still for hours, unable to even lift a finger. When Shay ran away, he hadn't been able to go after her. He couldn't get himself back to the lab either, to check on his family. It wasn't like the time he'd been paralyzed by the hawthorn. Then, his body had felt like dead weight, locked in place. He hadn't even been able to talk or blink. Now his body felt feather-light, hollow and weak. And he could still croak out a word or two. Every so often, he'd tried to call for Shay, not that he got an answer.

Where was she? There should be communion between the two of them now, because he had transformed her into a vampire. But he couldn't feel her. There was a swirling confusion, a sort of dizziness and fear that kept overtaking him. That could be Shay, he supposed. She was on her own as a new vampire, with no one to explain things to her. And it was daytime. He'd never heard of a vampire being created while the sun was up. He didn't know how it would work. She hadn't immediately succumbed to the death sleep, which no newborn vampire should be able to resist.

Had the daytime transformation affected the communion? The confusion and fear could be his own. The world had gone crazy in the past few days. Gabriel had been so frantic with worry that he hadn't had time to really think, until today. Lying here, unable to sleep, he could do nothing but think. And it was insane. He was in love with a human. And she was Sam's daughter. His father considered her an abomination, his family had essentially killed her.

Gabriel didn't know how to feel anymore—it was enough to make anyone confused and afraid.

And then Martin, and Ernst, he thought. *And Richard.*

He didn't want to think about that part. He had no idea what he'd left behind in the lab. Had the fire climbed the ravine and reached the building? Were there human firefighters in the family's quarters right now, discovering the sleeping vampires? Was the whole compound ablaze, killing everyone?

Was Ernst all right? He'd been paralyzed by the hawthorn—how long would its effects last?

His family wouldn't know that Gabriel had chosen Shay over them, not unless Ernst recovered from the hawthorn much faster than Gabriel had. But even if they knew, even if they hated him now, he was still driven crazy by the need to keep them safe and to warn them about Martin. If Ernst was still paralyzed, he wouldn't be able to tell them about the attack. They needed to know that Martin wanted a vampire to study—and that he wanted the rest of them dead so that they couldn't come after him.

Richard would have taken over in Ernst's place. He would have told them the lab is compromised, Gabriel thought. *He would have told them they were in danger.* But Richard was dead.

His eyes filled with tears. His brother had died to save the rest of the family. Regardless of the tension between them since Gabriel's return, he still loved Richard. He'd helped to raise him from the time he was a small boy. He'd rejoiced when Richard found love . . . and Richard had reacted with fury when Gabriel found love.

Gabriel blinked away the tears. He was devastated by what had happened. But he couldn't forget what his family had done to Shay.

Just as she'll never forget what I did to Sam.

He closed his eyes. He should have known that Shay would find out eventually. He'd told Sam's plans to Ernst, and he'd stood by accusingly as Ernst sentenced Sam to death. Shay had had visions of so many things in his life, he should have known that she would have a vision of that sooner or later. Of all his experiences, that one—Sam's last blood ritual—was the one that haunted Gabriel the most.

Sam's screams of desperation had lasted through all three nights of the ritual that killed him. When Gabriel closed his eyes every morning, he still heard them. The last image in his mind as he drifted into the death sleep was always Sam's agonized face . . . or at least it had been, until Shay. While Sam was slowly dying, Gabriel had thought there could be nothing worse than the horror of his desperation. But he'd been wrong.

The worst thing was the end. Gabriel was the last to drink from his brother before the entire family drank together, taking the last of Sam's blood. Gabriel felt it as he drank . . . Sam was nearly dead. Gabriel pulled away, removing his eyeteeth from Sam's throat. He'd avoided Sam's gaze since the ritual began, even though he couldn't avoid Sam's emotions blasting through the communion.

But this last time he couldn't help himself—he met his brother's eyes.

Sam was looking back. "You act out of love for your family," Sam whispered. "Someday you'll regret your part in this, and when you do, remember . . . I forgive you."

That was the worst part. The worst moment of Gabriel's life.

He'd still drunk with the rest of his family, taking the very last drops of Sam's blood. The final emotions they'd felt in the communion were love for Emma and for Shay in her mother's womb, followed by forgiveness for all of them who had slowly killed him. That sensation of sweet and piercing forgiveness was what Gabriel had never been able to forget, much as he wanted to. Every time he thought of it, he was struck again by Sam's innate goodness and his deep love of all living things. Every time he thought of it, he was crushed by the knowledge that he had snuffed out that goodness, that love. For so long he'd clung to the belief that what he'd done was right. He'd needed to believe it was necessary for his family's survival.

But now, after meeting Shay and coming to know her, that belief had slipped away and he was forced to face the truth: Sam had trusted Gabriel with his deepest secret, and Gabriel had betrayed him. Gabriel had caused the death of the person he loved as a brother and a best friend.

"If transforming Shay has killed me, I deserve it," he said weakly into the emptiness of the cave. "Maybe it will make me worthy of your forgiveness, Sam." He didn't believe that, though. After what he had done, he would never be worthy.

"Gabriel!" The voice echoed through the cavern, piercing his dark thoughts. "Where are you?"

Millie. He felt her now, fear and agitation and confusion. She must be feeling him, too, using the communion to locate him. It wasn't something they did often, but when necessary, in times of great distress, the link could tell the family where to find one another.

"Here," he croaked. His voice was pathetically quiet. Even with her vampire senses, it was doubtful that his sister would hear it. Gabriel closed his eyes.

It was another five minutes before Millie appeared on the rock shelf next to him. She took one look at him and dropped to her knees at his side. "What happened?"

"Martin," he said. "He must have traced the signal from Shay's cell—" At least he'd been able to get out that warning.

"We found Ernst in Richard and Tamara's room. He can't move," Millie said.

"Hawthorn," Gabriel told her. "Martin shot him with it."

"Is that what's wrong with you? What are you doing in the caves?"

"Mils . . . I need blood." He could feel his consciousness blurring.

"Sorry. I'm sorry. We're all confused." She scooped him up in her arms. "I'll run."

Millie jumped down from the rock shelf, landing without jostling Gabriel. She took off at high speed, cradling him like a baby as she sped through the series of caves. Before long, they were back to the tunnel he'd come through with Shay that morning.

"Gabriel!" Luis cried when they reached the lodge. He glanced at Millie. "Where did you find him?"

"In the caves. He's weak, nearly spent," Millie said.

"I'll get blood." Luis took off toward the refrigerated room where they kept their store of blood bags.

"Was Richard there too?" Tamara asked frantically. She bent over Gabriel. "Where is he? I can't feel him."

Gabriel couldn't answer her. Richard was gone from the communion. He was gone.

"Gabriel was alone. He's not strong enough to talk," Millie said. "Try to stay calm, Tamara."

But Tamara's emotions were in turmoil. It was almost more than Gabriel could bear.

When Luis returned with a bag of blood, Millie opened it and held it to his lips just as Shay had once done. Gabriel tried to shove down the feelings that the memory raised. He didn't know how to explain to his family what had happened. Instead, he focused on the blood. His strength slowly returned, spreading through his limbs as he finished the first bag and reached for another. He felt his brother and sisters watching him as he drank, but he didn't meet their eyes. Only when he'd finished a third bag of blood did he finally turn to them.

"I've never seen anyone take so much at once," Luis commented. "What happened to you?"

Gabriel didn't answer. "Where is Ernst?" he asked instead. The question distracted Luis, and Gabriel was grateful.

"Still in my room. I found him when I awoke, but Richard was gone," Tamara said. "Tell me where he is."

Her voice was steady, but she was brimming with fear. Gabriel knew they all felt it. "Can Ernst talk?"

"No. He isn't moving, isn't talking, and we can't feel him in the communion," Luis said quietly. "But his eyes are open, and he's . . . he's *there*. He's alive. I don't understand it."

"Martin—the doctor—he came to the lab while we slept. The alarm woke Ernst, and Ernst woke me," Gabriel explained. "Martin had a gun with hawthorn darts. And he had a bag filled with explosives. He wanted to knock out a vampire and take him captive. He had a gurney and a windowless van. He was prepared."

"And the explosives?" Millie asked.

Gabriel shrugged. "He's smart. He didn't want to leave any loose ends. I don't think he has any idea how many of us there are, so he brought enough C4 to torch the whole place. He knows fire is one of the only ways to kill us."

"So he shot Ernst?" Tamara said. "What about Richard?"

"He shot Ernst, and the hawthorn severed his communion with us. It's what happened to me when I was Martin's captive," Gabriel said. "I don't know how long it will be before Ernst recovers."

"Did he shoot Richard? Did he *take* Richard?"

Gabriel met Tamara's gaze. He couldn't keep avoiding her questions. "No. I woke Richard from the death sleep."

They all gasped. None of them had ever conquered the sleep before.

"I told him to stay in the lodge, to protect you three. I went to the front to help Ernst," Gabriel said. "But Richard . . . he must have followed me. I didn't know he was there."

It was close enough to the truth that they wouldn't be able to tell. He forced himself to focus on his family, not to think of Shay at all. Their communion had shrunk now to just himself and them, no Ernst. And his connection, like Tamara's, wasn't as strong as it once had been.

"It all went wrong. Martin shot Ernst and tried to drag him outside. Richard ran to stop him, and Martin activated the bomb. It would have blown the whole lab up. It would have killed us all."

Tamara let out a moan.

"Richard grabbed it and ran out into the woods. He threw it in the ravine before it went off," Gabriel said.

"He went *outside*?" Millie whispered. "During the day?" Tamara rocked back and forth, hugging herself, her expression blank.

"He had no choice. He saved us all," Gabriel said. Eventually, they would think to ask what Gabriel had been doing during that time and how he had ended up in the caves, but there were more important things to think about first.

There was a stunned, devastated silence for a moment.

"I'm sorry, Tamara," Gabriel said quietly. "It should have been me."

Tamara looked up at him then. "Yes," she said. "It should have. Ernst woke *you* up to help, not Richard." She dissolved into tears. "Not Richard."

Gabriel closed his eyes, but he couldn't close out the emotions roiling through their communion. Tamara and Richard had been together for years. She was grieving, and it was his fault. All of this was his fault—Ernst's paralysis, Richard's death, Shay's anger . . . and Sam's murder. Because that's what it was, murder. At the time it had seemed like the only choice, like justice for the fact that Sam had chosen love over his family.

I wish I'd been as clear-sighted as Sam, Gabriel thought. *Sam knew that if he wanted to be with Emma, he had to leave the family. If only I'd run away with Shay, if only I'd never brought her here . . .*

It didn't matter. Shay would still have found out the truth about what happened to her father. She'd never forgive Gabriel, and it was right that she shouldn't. He didn't deserve her forgiveness. But while he couldn't save his relationship with Shay, maybe he could still save his family.

"What about the fire? Did the humans come here?" he asked aloud.

Millie and Luis shook their heads. "We didn't even know about a fire," Luis said. "We haven't left the lodge, except when Millie followed you to the cave."

"And Ernst is unresponsive?"

"Yes." Millie sounded scared.

"Luis, check the front. The forest outside was on fire, but it started down in the ravine. It's a fifty-foot drop. It's possible that the fire stayed mostly down there or went up the other side. Richard threw the explosives there on purpose."

Tamara moaned.

Luis frowned. "The fire alarms aren't going off."

"But the firefighters may have tried to get in anyway, to use the lab as a base of operations or to evacuate anyone inside," Gabriel said. "It's okay if they see you now—make up a story about being in the caves with the bats. We're all awake. I just couldn't risk them finding out we were here during our death sleep."

Luis nodded and headed off toward the lobby.

"It will be better if we can say the fire damaged our facility," Gabriel said. "In fact, I'll turn the sprinkler system on and let the water destroy the place. It gives us an excuse to drop the bat research and close down the lab."

"Close it down? You mean leave?" Tamara asked. Her voice was dull, but her emotions were still out of control.

"We have to, as soon as possible. Tonight," Gabriel said. It meant leaving Shay alone as a new vampire. Now that he was stronger, and the sun was gone, he could feel his communion with her. He felt hunger, fear, and desperation. She needed him, and her emotions were strong enough that he could follow them to her. But she'd never accept help from him—not after what she'd found out. She had run from him, and he still felt anger boiling beneath her other feelings. He had lost her forever.

At least he could be here for his family. Get them to safety. After that . . . what did it matter? He'd lost her. "Our location is compromised—Martin knows where we are, and he won't come alone next time," Gabriel told his brother and sisters. "And besides, we can't risk staying here. Even if the firefighters didn't come today, they'll come soon. The university will send people to check on the lab. The authorities will notice if we're not around during business hours. This is only a safe place for us if we're left alone."

"But the people at Duke . . ." Millie's voice trailed off.

"If necessary, we simply disappear. I'd prefer to use the fire as an excuse so we don't raise too many questions." Gabriel took a deep breath. "Tamara, get all the research off the computers— just send everything we have to the university. Millie, take care of Ernst. We'll have to go to the house in Indiana, which means leaving within the hour."

"What about our things? The vault?" Millie asked.

She was asking about Shay. But Gabriel wasn't about to discuss that, not yet. "We don't have time," he said. "We'll have to leave everything."

"But—"

"Go! We have to move fast," Gabriel barked. "We can deal with loose ends once we're safe."

Millie nodded, wide-eyed. They had emergency plans in place for times like this, but it was usually Ernst giving the orders. Gabriel felt like a fraud taking charge. He was the next oldest, Ernst's second-in-command—his family would do what he said.

But he knew that the instant the hawthorn wore off and Ernst could talk, he would tell them all what Gabriel had done. And once they knew Gabriel had chosen to save Shay instead of Richard, they would turn on him.

I'll get them to safety first, Gabriel told himself. *They're still my family, and I'm the one who has put them in danger.*

It wouldn't be enough. But it was all he could do.

Shay took a deep breath, and for the first time all day, her shoulders relaxed. Suddenly, her head felt clear. Well, more clear than it had, anyway.

The sun went down.

She knew it as certainly as if she were outside watching the sunset over the horizon. It was gone from the sky, and the pressure of it was gone from her body.

Shay didn't move from her spot in the dark cave. She hadn't moved since she fell down here, at first because it hurt too much, and then because the feeling of her cracked skull healing itself had freaked her out too much. She hadn't been aware of the sun—even when she was up there near the cave entrance, it had been overcast and gray. But apparently, her vampire senses had been tracking the sun all day.

Fighting with the sun all day, she corrected herself. *I wasn't even supposed to be awake during daytime. No wonder I felt like I was losing my mind.*

She sat up slowly, waiting for her head to spin the way it had earlier. But it didn't. Everything in the cave looked as sharp and clear as before, and she could still hear water dripping from a mile away. But her brain didn't seem stuffed with cotton anymore.

Maybe if you become a vampire during the day, it messes up the system, she thought. Well, why should this be any different? Her body had never done what it was supposed to when she was human either.

"Okay. Let's try this again," she said aloud, hoping the sound of her own voice would stave off the loneliness she felt. By herself, at the bottom of a cave somewhere in the mountains in Tennessee, far from her mother or her friends . . . or Gabriel. If she thought about it, the terror of her situation might crush her. So instead, she focused on the one thing she felt more than anything else.

Hunger.

She was ravenous.

Her body had fully recovered from that fall onto solid rock, and she felt incredibly strong. She peered up at the ledge she'd tumbled off of. In her visions Gabriel had jumped distances like that. Shay bent her knees and gave it a try, springing upward with almost no effort. This time she landed on the cliff. The cave entrance smelled different—less plant and more animal. Or maybe that was her hunger?

It was dark outside, and she didn't hesitate. She ran right through the cave, ducking down to fit under the three-foot-high overhang of rock. The rain had stopped, but the ground was still wet.

Shay stood still and looked around, enjoying the cold air on her skin. She was on a mountainside, but at a low elevation. There were trees everywhere and thick underbrush. She couldn't see a path or a road or even an electric light. *I am really in the middle of nowhere,* she thought.

Something moved in the bushes, and Shay's head snapped toward it. Her hunger was growing by the second. It wasn't like anything she'd ever felt before. No rumbling stomach or head rush from low blood sugar. This was a full-body ache, like there was some vital part of herself that was missing. She thought that she might die if she didn't eat soon.

Eat what? she thought. *What does that even mean?*

She was a vampire. She had to drink blood. Gabriel had told her that his body couldn't even digest regular food.

The thought made Shay queasy. She'd drunk blood from Gabriel on several occasions. It hadn't bothered her—she'd needed his blood to live. It gave her strength. So this was no different. She needed blood to live.

But it won't be Gabriel's blood, she thought. And that's where the queasiness came in. Gabriel had wanted her to drink, and she'd been almost in a trance every time she did. She'd been so immersed in the visions of his life that she was barely even aware of the actual blood in her mouth and throat.

But it wouldn't be Gabriel's blood this time—or ever again. And there wouldn't be visions. He'd said that vampires didn't get visions, and none of his family had seemed to believe her that she had them. Gabriel had figured it must be some strange side effect of her half-vampire nature. *I'm a full vampire now, so no more blood visions,* she thought a little sadly.

It made her long for Gabriel, just for a second. She didn't want to see him, not now that she knew what he'd done to her father. But she desperately wished she could go back to the Gabriel she had thought he was, the one who loved her and who saved her. The one who was her father's best friend.

That was never true, she told herself. *Gabriel was lying to me about*

Sam the entire time. He knew that he'd murdered my father, and he didn't tell me. I can't ever forgive him for that.

The bushes moved again, and a fox suddenly darted out and sped off down the hill. Shay stared after it for a moment, wondering what on earth had happened to her. Sick girls weren't allowed to go wandering around deserted mountainsides after dark, hanging with wild nocturnal animals. Her mother didn't even like it when Shay stayed at Olivia's house after dinnertime.

Slowly, she began walking down the steep hill, following the direction the fox had taken. She felt worried. She didn't know what she was doing, and becoming a vampire was disorienting even with the whole family there for support.

Shay stopped short. That hadn't been her thought.

It hadn't really been a thought at all, she realized. Just a feeling. Worry. Concern over the strangeness of her situation.

But it wasn't her own worry. Her worry had more to do with the fact that she was so, so hungry. Shay frowned. She began to jog. The sooner she found some kind of food, the sooner she'd feel better.

The sound of running water caught her attention, and she automatically turned toward it, breaking into a run. She was heading straight downhill, and at a pretty steep angle, but she wasn't scared. Her feet hit the ground with total confidence, and she sped around trees and jumped small bushes without even thinking. She wasn't the least bit tired.

Before long, she found the water—a medium-size stream flowing from somewhere higher up.

Shay stopped and looked around. Now what?

A burst of guilt hit her, so strong and bitter that she gasped.

Guilt, depression, misery . . . it brought tears to her eyes.

But why? She shook her head, trying to shove the feeling away. It made no sense. She had nothing to feel guilty about. She'd been thinking about how to find blood, and suddenly this overwhelming emotion. *It's not my feeling,* she thought. *Just like the worry from before. It's not me.*

Shay drew in a breath, forcing herself to concentrate. The guilt melted away. But before she could relax, it was replaced by something else. *Love.* Deep and strong. And then guilt again.

"Oh my God, it's Gabriel," she muttered. "It's his psychic link thing."

He'd told her about it a few times, and she had felt it—sort of—during the blood ritual to transform her. The communion, he'd called it. He'd said that she would be linked to him because he transformed her.

Shay groaned. Gabriel was the only guy she'd ever loved, and he had taken away her family before she was even born. Because of him, her mother had been angry and miserable for years. She herself had felt abandoned since the day she was born. Because of Gabriel, she would never know her father.

And now she had to have him in her head, forever? Of all people in the world, she had to feel Gabriel's emotions? The one person she never wanted to think about, and there he was, shoving his feelings at her.

"Screw that," she said, jumping the stream. There was some kind of animal on the other side, a beaver or a muskrat or something. It was busily chewing on a log along the banks. Shay didn't let herself think, and she definitely didn't let herself *feel*, because who knew whether it would be her own emotion or Gabriel's? She just snatched up the animal with the lightning-fast speed she now had, and she brought it to her mouth.

Her fangs extended instantly, and she bit.

Blood. Finally, blood to satisfy her hunger.

The animal twitched in her hands, but she ignored that and drank.

Disgust. Danger. Horror.

They weren't her feelings. It was Gabriel, but it was stronger than before. His feelings overwhelmed her, as if they were pushing at her, trying to . . .

Trying to stop me, Shay thought. The emotions were stronger because Gabriel was reacting to Shay.

The realization hit her a split second before the sickness did.

Shay retched violently, dropping the half-dead animal. She turned and vomited onto the stream bank again and again. Her entire body seemed to fold in on itself, and waves of nausea and dizziness washed over her. Shay gazed at the bright red blood all over her hands, and she puked again.

When it finally stopped, she collapsed onto the ground, her legs in the water, the trees and the stars and the mountainside going in and out of focus.

Not animal blood. I can only drink human, she thought in some detached part of her mind. *The animal's blood made me sick.*

Shay didn't know how long she stayed there, waiting for the reaction to end. Whenever she tried to move, she retched again, so eventually, she gave up and closed her eyes. The world felt as if it were slowly spinning beneath her, but at least she didn't have to watch the focus changing.

Urgency. The feeling prodded her back to reality.

Shay blinked, not sure how long she'd been lying on the bank of the stream. The sky was still dark, but the sounds had changed—fewer insects, she decided. And somewhere far off, a lone bird was cooing.

Slowly, she became aware of a pressure building inside of her. But it wasn't a physical sensation. It was more like a pressure in her mind. Something heavy and irresistible.

Sleep, Shay thought. *That's what it is. I need to sleep.*

But that didn't make any sense. She'd been lying on the ground for who knew how long, and even though she wasn't sure it could be called sleep, it had to at least count as rest. There was no reason to be tired now.

Still, the pressure mounted. Shay pulled herself up to a sitting position, trying not to squirm from the feeling of weight. And heat.

"The sun," she gasped.

As soon as the thought occurred to her, she knew she was right. Sunrise was coming, and she felt it somehow, just as she'd felt it when the sun went down.

She was so tired. Not just sleepy, but bone tired. Exhausted. She didn't even know a word for this kind of fatigue. Hunger was wrenching at her stomach, but Shay leaned back on her elbows, wanting only to sink onto the ground and go to sleep.

Panic.

Shay jumped to her feet, staring around the forest. The sudden feeling of terror had been so strong that her pulse now pounded wildly. But was it her panic? Or Gabriel's? The waves of fear seemed too intense to come from herself alone.

Run. Hide. Find shelter.

Shay shook off her doubts. It didn't matter whether it was the communion with Gabriel or her own instincts, she had to listen. The sun would come up soon, and she would die if it touched her.

Her first thought was to get back to the cave. But she'd run pretty far from the entrance, and when she retraced her steps back along the stream, she couldn't see anything that looked familiar. Just trees and bushes and mountainside. *Why didn't I pay more attention when I came out of the cavern?* she thought.

"Because I was busy being a freakin' vampire for the first time," she muttered. "And nearly killing myself with a muskrat."

Shay stopped running and glanced around, forcing herself to think. She had to find somewhere dark. When she and Gabriel had been on the run, they'd stayed in hotels. As long as the door was closed and the curtains tightly shut, Gabriel had been okay during the day. So she didn't have to find a cave. She just needed shelter, enough to block the light.

Can I run to a hotel? Or a ranger station or something? Shay wondered. She looked in every direction, using her incredible new vision . . . and she saw nothing. No shelter of any kind.

The panic was rising along with the pressure of the sun. She had to get inside, now.

Shay ran, searching for anything that could offer some protection. Hiding under a bush wouldn't cut it. Could she dig a deep enough hole to hide in? But it wasn't as if she could bury herself alive . . . or undead . . . or whatever she was. She still needed to breathe, didn't she? Did she?

Get inside.

She spotted a tree up ahead, a tall, black twisted one that looked dead. Shay slowed down and stared at the trunk.

"Hollow," she said, and made a beeline for it. The trunk had a hole at the base barely big enough for an animal to fit through, but Shay managed to squeeze herself inside somehow, saying a silent thanks for being so skinny from her long illness.

She was bent almost double, her knees up to her face and her arms squished against her chest. There was tall grass around the trunk, and the forest was dense here—but her hip was right up against the hole. Sunlight would touch her there, if it managed to find its way through the tree cover.

So tired. Shay felt heaviness infecting her limbs, pressing on her skull and her lungs, slowing her heart. With every ounce of will-power she had, she forced herself to untangle her right arm and reach outside the tree trunk. She grabbed hold of the first thing her fingers hit—a large branch that must've fallen from her dead tree.

The weight of the sun was too much to bear now. The pressure got more intense with every second. Shay could barely tell if she was awake or asleep, alive or dead.

This is the death sleep. This is how Gabriel's family members were when the humans massacred them in Greece, she thought. She knew with bone-chilling certainty that if someone attacked her right now, there was no way she could defend herself. She couldn't even move. She was completely vulnerable.

If I don't move my hand back in, I'll die, she thought. It should've been enough to fill her with adrenaline. But she lay still, her arm outside, hand clutching the branch.

A rush of fear and urgency hit her like a hurricane wind, and she knew it wasn't her emotion. But she was so dead tired that she couldn't even come up with Gabriel's name. The urgency spurred her to move, and she jerked her arm back, dragging the branch over the opening of the tree trunk. She pulled her arm inside.

Maybe the branch would cover her from the day. Probably not.

I'll turn to ash. I'll never wake up, she thought.

But the death sleep draped over her like a dark black cloud. It was dawn. And she was helpless.

She slept.

EIGHT

○ ○ ○ ○ ○ ○ ○ ○ ○ ○ ○ ○ ○ ○ ○ ○

IT TOOK SHAY A FEW SECONDS to remember where she was and why her muscles were tight and cramping. She'd spent the day crunched up inside the base of a tree. She flexed her fingers and toes, tilted her head back and forth. That was about the extent of the motion she could make inside her fortress. "I didn't turn to ash." She said the words aloud just so she could really take in the fact that she'd survived her first day as a vampire.

Carefully, she wriggled back out of the hole in the tree trunk, then shoved herself to her feet. She pushed way too hard with her hands, so hard that she almost landed on the ground again. This vampire strength was tricky. Okay, first things first. That meant getting away from here. She couldn't risk another sunrise out in the wild; she needed shelter.

She started to trot, her gait long, even, and steady. Effortless. Even with everything that had happened, there was a wild joy in that, which nothing could stop from bubbling up inside her. And this strength and this energy were *hers*. They weren't borrowed by a drink of Gabriel's blood.

She leaped over a bush and for a second imagined herself as a track star. Then a stomach cramp hit her, so strong that she had to wrap her arms around herself until it passed.

She was hungry. So hungry, it hurt. The animal blood had made her sick enough that it had blocked out her hunger, but now it was back, just as strong—stronger—than it had been when she'd left the caves.

What had she been thinking? All this strength and energy had a price—she had to feed to keep it. And soon. She needed to find more than just shelter tonight. She needed to find a place where there were humans. Givers. That's what Gabriel and his family called the people they drank from. Maybe she should call them that too. Givers. It was a nice word. But not an accurate one. The humans weren't giving anything. Something was being stolen from them.

I don't have to kill, she reminded herself. But she would have to grab and bite. She'd have to terrify someone.

Shay began to move again, but almost instantly, another cramp ripped through her stomach. She had to bend over with her hands on her knees until it passed. Victim. Giver. Sacrifice. Blood cow. No matter what term she decided to use, she wouldn't survive without feeding on one of them. She had to get out of the woods. She straightened up, tilted her head back, and sniffed.

There was a town close by, at least close enough to smell with her heightened vampire senses. She picked up car exhaust, fast-food fumes, asphalt, rubber, plastic, and blood. Plenty of blood. That was enough to get her moving. Shay ran toward the smell, her mouth flooding with saliva and her fangs aching to be released.

Within ten minutes, she hit a narrow dirt road; well, more of a path. But it quickly widened and soon intersected a two-lane road, paved and everything. There were town scents coming from both directions. Shay went left, where the odors seemed a bit stronger. With her sharpened vision, she could see a string of traffic lights stretching out into the night, headlights and taillights, too, the closest maybe five miles away. She wasn't good at judging distances yet.

It felt good to be heading toward civilization. She'd never exactly been a nature girl. It hadn't been an option with her sickness.

A lime green Volkswagen pulled past her. All three people—and the dog—inside stared at her. Shay ran her tongue over her teeth, doing a fang check, even though her mouth hadn't been hanging open. No fangs. So why were they gaping at her like that? A girl out jogging not so late at night. She was dressed in cords, not sweats, but really, there was no reason to stare.

I'm running too fast, she realized. *Running freakishly fast.* She took it down several notches, then several more. The next time a car went by, she got a glance, but no stares.

She reached the first traffic light and stopped. A gas station sat on one side of the street, and about a block down was a high school. She could hear laughter from the school, and the scents from that direction told her that there were a few kids hanging around, but she wasn't going to go over there. It might be the best place to . . . to feed, but a school felt too close to the life she'd just left.

How was she supposed to choose who to take? Was she supposed to do it like Dexter—and just drink from bad people? Or was she supposed to treat the world as a buffet, grabbing whatever smelled like it would taste the best?

A hospital, she thought. She'd steal herself some blood the way she'd stolen blood for Gabriel. She began jogging again, scenting the air, searching for the familiar odors of antiseptic, bleach, industrial cleaner, pungent chemicals, all with an underlayer of urine, feces, blood, sweat, and illness.

There was definitely one somewhere, close enough that she could smell it. But she couldn't be sure that it was even in this town. Other scents were stronger. And there were so many of them. She was getting an encyclopedia of information with every sniff.

The odor of warm blood grew stronger with every stride. It was overpowering, launching another stomach cramp that forced her to stop and focus on breathing, just breathing, until it passed. It felt as if claws were raking across her belly.

I'm not going to make it to the hospital. Not in time, anyway, Shay thought. She would definitely start stocking up at every hospital she found, but right now she had to drink. She was afraid if she didn't, she might pass out on the side of the road.

At the next light there was a strip mall—Pizza Hut, liquor store, Subway, insurance company, six cars in the lot. She'd do it there. It was too risky to keep going when her body was demanding fuel.

It'll be okay, she thought. *I won't hurt . . . whoever. Other than biting them with my razor-sharp fangs.* She felt repulsed and excited at the same time. Her human brain recoiled, but her vampire body craved the blood. *I'll just take enough to make it to that hospital,* she promised herself.

Shay slowed to a walk and veered into the parking lot. She paused for a moment and ran her fingers through her hair to check for leaves. She knew she didn't look threatening. She was just a tiny girl on the outside. But she wanted to look more than safe. She wanted to look normal. Nice and normal. She smoothed down her shirt and put a smile on her face.

Okay, here I am. A nice, normal girl on my way to Pizza Hut. Kinda hungry.

"Hey, girl. Looking for someone to buy you beer?"

Shay turned toward the voice. A twenty-something guy sat in the front of a pickup parked on the other side of the lot. She'd smelled him, but she'd thought he was inside one of the stores. Sooner or later, she would learn how to gauge things like that.

"Come on over here," he called. "I can hook you up."

This is fate, or luck, or something, Shay thought. She strolled over to the truck, and the guy rolled his window all the way down. "You're looking for someone legal, am I right?"

Shay could smell that he'd already had several beers of his own. "You got me," she said, holding up both hands in mock surrender.

"I just bought a six-pack, and I'm happy to share. Come on and sit with me," the guy said.

He was making this too easy. Shay circled around the truck and got into the passenger side. It was perfect. The parking lot was dimly lit, and no one would be peering into the truck anyway. As long as there was no screaming.

What now? she wondered. *Just grab him and bite? But how do I keep him from yelling?*

She needed to cover his mouth. But she needed to do it gently. She didn't want to end up breaking his neck or anything. All she wanted was a little blood, only enough to make sure she could get to the hospital without collapsing.

"What's your name?" the guy asked. He popped the top of a can of Bud and handed it to her.

"Veronica," she said. She didn't know why she was bothering with an alias. It wasn't as if anyone was going to believe drunk dude here if he started talking about some chick sucking his blood. But she'd always liked that name. And maybe it would make this easier. *I'm not me. I'm Veronica the Vampire. Feeding.*

She pretended to take a sip of the beer. She wasn't sure what would happen if she actually drank it and she didn't want to have some horrible reaction in front of him.

"I'm Billy," he told her.

She wished he hadn't. A name made things personal. She wanted him to stay "drunk dude." It would also help if he was being more obnoxious.

But she wasn't going to stop. The scent of his blood was overwhelming. Her world narrowed down to that one scent. It was everything she wanted. Nothing else mattered. Shay's fangs erupted.

Fast as she had gone after that muskrat back in the woods, Shay jerked toward him, pressed her hand over his mouth—careful, careful, careful—and drove her fangs into his throat. His blood warmed her own throat as she began to feed. In one of her visions she'd been with Gabriel the first time he fed. The sensations had felt so strong that she wouldn't have believed she was receiving them in muted form.

But this was mind-bending. It was like drinking music, so many flavors. And so many emotions—everything her Giver had ever felt was rushing through her, so fast that she didn't have time to individually identify each one. It wasn't like the blood ritual, when the emotions coming from Gabriel were so specific. It was more like sensory overload.

Maybe that's how the communion is formed, she thought. *A vampire's blood gives you access to their emotions slowly. A Giver's blood gives you everything at once.*

And everything at once was incredible. Shay moaned with pleasure.

The guy twisted his body slightly, trying to escape her hand, her teeth. A part of Shay wanted to pull away for a moment and whisper that she wouldn't take much more. But pulling away was impossible. It would be like pulling her veins out of her body.

How did vampires not want to feed all the time? What in life could be more potent, more real, more sweet and satisfying?

Shay let herself sink even deeper into the sensation. Her whole body felt as if it were vibrating, as fast as hummingbird wings. *No, that's his heart,* Shay thought. Her Giver's heart was trembling instead of beating, and she felt it through every inch of herself. It was awesome. Truly awesome in the way that the word should be used.

Still, a part of her was repulsed. Maybe part of her always would be. She hadn't been raised by vampires the way Gabriel and his family had. Maybe that made a difference. At least the pleasure was so intense. Shay could just bury herself in it and leave that little piece of human emotion behind.

The vibrations in the Giver's heart ceased. And the feeling of revulsion grew stronger. Not just revulsion. Horror, too. And terror.

With a hard thunk, the Giver's heart began to beat again. But erratically, in fluttering stops and starts.

He's dying!

The thought was so shocking that Shay jerked her teeth out of the Giver's neck. She released the hand she'd been holding over his mouth, and he slumped forward against the steering wheel.

She shivered, coldness rushing through her where there had been warmth. Had she killed him? She realized that the horror and revulsion and fear hadn't been coming from the remains of her humanity. Those had been Gabriel's feelings. He'd been trying to stop her.

Had he been in time to keep her from becoming a murderer? Shay reached out to put her fingers on the side of the guy's neck, but it was smeared with blood, and even though she'd been drinking it moments before, she didn't want to touch it. Instead, she pressed her fingers to his wrist. He had a pulse, but it was so faint. What was his name? He'd told her his name—what was it?

"Billy!" Shay exclaimed. "Billy, can you hear me?"

He gave a low moan in reply. Shay had to get out of there. She couldn't be found with him. There'd be way too many questions. "I'm getting you help. I promise, Billy." She jumped out of the truck and ran for the liquor store. She stopped for a moment outside to wipe the blood off her mouth, then went in.

"There's a guy passed out in his truck over there." She gestured toward the parking lot. "I don't know if he drank too much or what, but I think he needs an ambulance."

"Crap!" the man behind the counter exclaimed, then he grabbed the phone and began to dial.

Shay ducked out of the store and started to run. *It's okay. He's alive. I stopped in time*, she told herself. But without Gabriel, she wouldn't have. She would have sucked her Giver—*Billy*—dry.

I never wanted to see this place again, Gabriel thought as he sat down in the living room of the Indiana farmhouse that was the family's closest safe house. It was the only place they'd been able to reach in one night. They'd left Tennessee only two hours after sunset, but it had still been a race to get here before the sun. They'd all run straight to their old rooms, barely making it before their death sleep. Gabriel had woken tonight with a sinking feeling in his gut. He hated this house. And he hated to think about the mess they'd left behind—sensitive scientific equipment ruined by the sprinklers, their reputations as scientists permanently destroyed by their sudden disappearance. They would all need new identities now.

But they'd needed to get away. They couldn't risk the forest fire investigators coming to the lab during the day, and they definitely couldn't risk the chance of Martin coming back. The family was small now, vulnerable. Ernst needed time to recuperate from the hawthorn paralysis. They all needed a place to process what had happened to them. Tamara had been in shock when they'd arrived just before sunrise, and she still was, even though she refused to admit it.

Gabriel glanced over at Ernst, who lay motionless on the sofa. He immediately wished he'd kept his eyes on the football game Luis had on TV. Ernst's gaze was sharp and unforgiving. *As soon as he's able to talk again, he'll tell them everything,* Gabriel thought for what had to be the hundredth time.

He couldn't worry about that right now. Tamara, Luis, and Millie had looked to him as a leader, despite everything that had happened. It was second nature to them, or at least to Luis and Millie. He was the oldest. To the two of them, he was part big brother and part father. He'd been in their lives as long as they could remember.

Tamara was so devastated by Richard's death that she hadn't questioned Gabriel taking charge, his decision to bring them to Indiana, or anything else. For the moment at least, she'd retreated deep inside herself. He reminded himself to make sure she drank some of the blood they'd brought with them from the lab. In her grief, she might forget to give her body what it needed to function.

"I wonder if Ernst would be more comfortable back in his bedroom," Gabriel said, shifting in his chair so he wouldn't have to see his father's eyes.

Millie shook her head. "We have so much to figure out. I think Ernst would want to hear our discussions about what to do next, even if he can't talk yet," she said.

"Yeah, he's paralyzed, not dead," Luis added. Realizing what he'd said, he shot an apologetic glance at Tamara. She didn't seem to notice. She was curled up in one of the armchairs, in exactly the same position she'd taken when she first came out of her room a little after sunset. It was almost as if they had two hawthorn victims in the room instead of one.

Gabriel had expected this whole house to feel almost haunted, but it didn't. If he went down into the cellar, though . . . He shuddered, images of Sam chained to the cellar floor filling his mind. Sam had died down there. That was where the family had killed him.

I won't go down there. There's no reason to. The entire farmhouse had blinds that were perfectly fitted and able to keep out all sunlight. The dirt cellar had been deepened and widened to give the family a place to go if the house itself became unsafe. There were two stairways leading to it, one from the kitchen and one from a hatch hidden outside.

"Before anything else, we need to e-mail the people at Duke. They must have already heard about the fire," Millie said, pacing. "They're going to think it's really strange that we've evacuated without contacting them, even if we did send the research."

Gabriel shoved his fingers through his hair. "Anything we say to them will only raise more questions. They'll want to know where we are, when we're coming back. They'll expect us to come in for meetings and to be available during the day. When they get into the facility, they're bound to find the tunnel we blasted without their permission."

"And the security system we installed," Luis put in.

"No contact with Duke. It's time for a complete identity shift," Gabriel said. "We have plenty of money. We can choose a new location and go into hiding for a while." A long while. Long enough for Martin to grow old and give up looking for them. The man had the money and power to mount an intensive search.

"Hiding. Like we weren't in hiding back at the lab," Millie muttered.

"Maybe Ernst will okay you going back to school now," Gabriel said, his eyes automatically sliding over to Ernst, lying there so still. "You always like being in college, Mils. And I should go back too. I need to get a more current degree."

"How can you talk about school and money?" Tamara asked, her voice flat. "Richard is dead."

"We know, Tam," Luis said gently. "We just don't know what to say. It helps to talk about ordinary stuff."

"We should have a service for him, once Ernst is better," Millie suggested. Tamara rested her face in her hands, as if she couldn't stand to even consider it.

Millie turned to Gabriel. "Do we—Should we do something about Shay? You didn't tell us what happened to her, but . . . well . . . are they going to find her body in the lab? Won't that cause too many complications?"

"She's not there," Gabriel said quietly.

"What *did* happen?" Luis asked. "Did Martin take her back?"

They'd find out soon enough that he had chosen to save Shay rather than Richard, but Gabriel wasn't going to volunteer the information. They'd been so busy traveling last night that no one had even asked about Shay. They didn't have a communion with her like he did. The link came from drinking blood, and Shay hadn't shared blood with anyone else in the family. They would only know whatever he told them.

"No, she's not with Martin," Gabriel said. "But she's gone. On her own now." He felt their eyes on him, knew they had questions. But he couldn't face their anger, not yet. He knew how they'd react when they learned the truth. He would have to deal with it eventually. But he wanted a little more time first. Besides, he couldn't be an effective leader to them once they knew what he'd done.

"On her own? Did you just put her out there for the firefighters to find?" Luis's brow furrowed in confusion.

On her own. Gabriel cringed at the words. He hated that Shay was alone. She needed him with her, even if she despised him. No new vampire should have to deal with her overpowering thirst alone. At least he'd been able to reach Shay through her communion and stop her from killing the Giver. He knew she would never be able to forgive herself if she took a life.

"I don't understand. You let her go?" Millie asked. "To die? She won't survive without vampire blood."

"No. I . . . I did a blood ritual. I transformed her," Gabriel admitted.

"What?" Tamara's head snapped up, and her eyes were alert in a way they hadn't been since she learned of Richard's death.

"She would have died if I didn't. She couldn't survive as half vampire and half human, not for even another day," Gabriel said, an edge of defiance creeping into his voice.

A wheezing cough grabbed everyone's attention. They all turned to Ernst. He moved his lips soundlessly for a moment, then looked at Gabriel and spoke. "You will face judgment for what you've done."

○ ○ ○ ○ ○ ○ ○ ○ ○ ○ ○ ○ ○ ○ ○ ○

Slow down, Shay ordered herself. *Slow waaaay down.* She reduced her speed until it felt like she was running through Jell-O, although intellectually, she knew she was still sprinting by human standards.

How far had she run from that guy she'd left lying in his pickup, that guy she'd almost drained?

Almost killed.

Shay swallowed hard. She could still taste his blood in her throat. The blood held traces of the beer he'd been drinking, salty peanuts, and something sharp, almost electric. Not a taste she was familiar with.

Fear. I'm tasting his fear. The thought hit Shay with the power of a punch to the stomach. He'd been terrified when Shay's fangs came down. She'd felt that emotion as if it were her own when they connected, her teeth deep in his neck, his essence flooding her. His blood had to have been charged with adrenaline in that moment, and that's what she was tasting now.

Shay swallowed again, the taste of the blood both thrilling and repulsive. She forced herself to slow down even more and take a careful look at her surroundings. There was another strip mall on her right—Laundromat, Celebrity's Hot Dogs, mini-mart, one car in the parking lot. A sad-looking office complex across the street, with an empty parking lot. And an SUV passing her now, the middle-aged woman driver shooting Shay a concerned look. Concern for the teenage girl out by herself so late at night, not concern at seeing a vampire.

I'm passing for human. Good, Shay thought.

Her knees went weak, her legs suddenly wobbly. Carefully, she lowered herself to the curb. She had to *pretend* to be a human being. She wasn't human anymore. From the moment Gabriel had transformed her, she'd been going on instinct, running, hiding, feeding, surviving. She hadn't considered what she'd become, or at least only in the ways that being a vampire was new and different. She hadn't actually thought about what she had lost.

Her humanity.

A harsh bark of laughter escaped from her throat. *I really am "speh-shul,"* she thought, remembering the journal entry where she'd used that word to describe herself, the way she'd heard everyone else use it to describe her for her entire life. They didn't want to say "sick" or "disabled" or "dying." So they said "special" and they all pretended that it meant something different.

She recalled the definition she'd copied from the dictionary:

"distinguished by some unusual quality; being in some way superior." They'd thought she was special when she was the sick girl. Now, forget about it. There wasn't a special enough word to describe her.

Shay pressed her hands over her ears and squeezed her eyes shut tight, trying to block out the overwhelming rush of sensations. Trying to *think*. What was she supposed to do? She knew she couldn't allow the sun to touch her. She knew she'd have to drink blood to survive. But what was she actually supposed to *do*? With her life?

Her life. Shay had been so used to thinking of her life in terms of years and, lately, in terms of months and days. Now she had decades, centuries, maybe all eternity. For a moment, only a moment, she felt time stretch out in front of her, out, and out, and out. People dying all around her. Shay living on. Alone.

She shuddered, and then she wanted Gabriel more than she'd ever wanted anything. She wanted his arms around her, his mouth on hers. She wanted him with her for every second of that forever.

No. That wasn't true. What she wanted was the old Gabriel, the Gabriel she'd believed she loved. *That* Gabriel hadn't betrayed and murdered her father.

That Gabriel didn't exist.

A car slowed down and came to a stop beside her. She opened her eyes, feeling the vibration of the engine. The passenger window glided down. Shay caught a whiff of tobacco, Wint O Green Life Savers, detergent, shampoo—Suave 2 in 1, she thought—pencil shavings, and underneath all that, the wonderful scent of blood. "You okay?" the driver, a man Shay figured to be in his late seventies, asked.

"Yes." Shay stood up. "I'm fine. I just had a fight with my—my boyfriend. I called someone to pick me up." The old man hesitated, then nodded. The window slid back up as he drove away.

There were hours of night left, but Shay couldn't stand to be out on the streets any longer. She could see the glow of a neon sign about half a mile away. When she focused, she could pick out the sound of the neon's hum from the barrage of other noise. It seemed like the right kind of neighborhood for a cheap motel, the kind that's never full. The kind of motel Gabriel would choose.

Was he still influencing her somehow? Shay knew she wouldn't have been able to stop feeding if Gabriel hadn't somehow reached out and stopped her. Did the impulse to go to that motel and break into a room come from him or from her?

It doesn't matter, she decided. She needed a place to rest. Well, not rest exactly—her body was still revved and ready to run for a few more days without stopping. As horrifying as it had been to nearly kill that Giver, she couldn't deny the effect of his blood. Her vampire body was at full strength again, just like that. It was as if she'd been dead and was now arisen, full of health and strength. But her mind was still her own mind, and she was still her old self. She might not need physical rest, but she needed a place where she could feel safe, so she could begin to figure out what to do with the rest of . . . the rest of forever. Or at least the next couple of days of it.

Shay headed toward the neon light, making sure not to move faster than your regular, ordinary human person. It was a motel. Sleepy Time Motel, specifically. *Original on the naming,* Shay thought as she trotted into the parking lot. It wasn't hard to figure out which of the sixteen rooms was empty. She could hear the beating hearts of the people inside seven of them.

She chose a room that had empty rooms on either side. The door frame splintered as she forced the lock. *Damn!* How long was it going to take her to get used to the power of her vampire body? Shay glanced around, checking to see if the sound of cracking wood had drawn any attention. No. No, she was safe. She ducked into the room. She hadn't screwed up the door to the point that it wouldn't shut. That was something.

Now what? Her eyes darted around the room and stopped on the phone. *Mom.* That's what she wanted. She wanted to talk to her mother. It was completely irrational, but there was a little part of Shay that still believed her mother could fix anything. Without thinking about what she'd say when Mom answered, Shay dropped down on the way-too-soft bed, grabbed up the phone, and dialed. Olivia had said that Shay's mother was coming back from Miami. She should be home by now.

But it was Martin who answered. The sound of his voice was like an ice cube slithering down her spine. She slammed the phone back into the cradle and held it there, hand trembling. A memory screeched through her brain. Martin in the research facility. Shooting Ernst with a dart. Ernst collapsing.

Martin hadn't even looked around to see if she was there. Not that it was a news flash that he didn't give a crap about her. He'd proved that the night he'd hit her in the parking lot, to get her out of the way so he could recapture Gabriel. All her stepfather cared about was securing a vampire for his research. And now she was one. He'd probably love to strap her to a table in his lab, just the way he'd done to Gabriel.

Shay pulled in a deep breath, picked up the phone again, and dialed a phone number that was almost as familiar as her own. "Be there, be there," she muttered as the phone began to ring.

"Talk to me."

Tears sprang to Shay's eyes the moment she heard her best friend's voice. "Olivia. Olivia, it's—"

"Shay!" Olivia interrupted. "What the hell? Do you know how worried I've been? You can't start a call like that and then—"

"I'm sorry. I know. Someone took my phone," Shay told her.

"Who? That guy you're with?"

"No. Anyway, I'm not with him anymore," Shay answered.

"Okay, I'm coming to get you. No argument. Where are you?"

A bubble of hysterical laughter broke out of Shay's throat. That was her second bout of crazed laughter today. Definitely on the mentally unhealthy checklist. "I don't know. I don't even know."

"This gets better and better," Olivia muttered. "How can you not know where you are? Did you faint or something? Martin said you wouldn't make it without your transfusions."

"It's nothing like that," Shay assured her. She spotted a creased sheet of paper with the motel's address and number at the top and the phone rates below that. "I'm in Vinton. It's in Virginia, not that far from the Tennessee border." She hadn't even known which direction she'd run in when she left the caves. Or how far she'd come.

"I'm Googling it," Olivia said.

Shay pressed the phone tighter against her ear. Olivia's voice was like a Valium or something. She felt calmer just listening to it.

"Okay, found it. It looks like it'll take about a day to get there. Can you hold on till then?" Olivia asked.

"Yeah." Shay let out a shuddering breath. "Yeah. Now that I know you're coming."

"I'll leave first thing in the morning. So Kaz and I should hit town Wednesday morning, okay?"

"Yeah. Good. I'll call you on your cell when you're on the road and tell you where to pick me up," Shay replied. She tilted her head from side to side, easing the tension out of her neck.

"And on the way back home, you can—and will—explain every-thing." Olivia had slipped into that mom voice she frequently used with Shay. The did-you-take-your-medicine, have-you-been-getting-enough-rest voice of the best friend of a sick girl.

Shay had always hated that tone of voice. Now it just sounded like home.

"Yes, ma'am," Shay said. "I'll explain—" Her words caught in her throat. What had she been thinking?

She hadn't been thinking. At all. For starters, she couldn't meet Olivia, or do anything else, while the sun was up. She'd be busy death-sleeping.

I should just hang up, Shay thought, panicked. *I should stay away from her. Only badness is going to come from Olivia getting anywhere near me.*

"Shay?"

"I'm here," Shay said. "You know what, I was just freaking out. I'm okay to get home by myself."

"Sure you are," Olivia said. "Shay, you didn't even know where you were when I asked you. You're not okay to do anything. Google just found me a Starbucks on Euclid Ave. Find it. And be there Wednesday morning."

"Can you leave tonight instead?" Shay asked.

"First you don't want me to come, now you want me to leave in the middle of the night? Shay, what is going on?" Olivia demanded. "I think you need to tell me everything right now."

"Let me wait until you get here. Please leave tonight. You're right. I'm not okay to get home. I'm scared, Liv. Completely losing it," Shay admitted. And she wanted her friend with her. She couldn't handle this on her own. None of it. She'd figure out something to tell Olivia.

"All right. I'm calling Kaz. We'll get there as fast as we can. Be at that Starbucks," Olivia instructed.

"I will. I promise. Thanks, Olivia. This is—You don't even know how much this means to me," Shay said. "Go call Kaz."

"Right now. See you soon," Olivia replied.

I need a plan, Shay thought as she hung up. *I can't let them know I'm a vampire.*

She sat for a moment, lost in thought. So far, the major things she'd discovered about her new self were that she was strong, she was fast, and she was hungry. Strong and fast she was already working on, trying to remember to take them down a notch. Hungry was a bigger problem.

The most important thing is to feed before I see Olivia and Kaz. I have to be so full that I have no desire for their blood, she decided.

The hospital. As soon as she woke from her death sleep on Tuesday night, she'd find that hospital she smelled. She'd steal enough blood that feeding wouldn't be an issue. Then she'd come up with some kind of story to tell Olivia and Kaz.

Shay pulled the spread off the bed and dragged it into the bathroom. Perfect—no windows. She locked the door behind her. Not that someone couldn't bust it down while she was in the death sleep, but it made her feel a little safer.

She lay down and rolled herself up in the bedspread. It wasn't time to sleep, but all she wanted to do was lie there, keeping still, keeping safe.

"It'll be okay," she whispered. "It'll be okay. Really."

Gabriel stared up at the ceiling, giving himself over to the feelings the communion brought him from his family. And from Shay. It was easy to tell them apart, as easy as telling one voice from another, one face from another. Besides, Shay's emotions were stronger. The communion between them hadn't been broken and re-formed the way it had with his family.

Shay was calming down, at least a little. Gabriel didn't know why or how, but the knowledge that she didn't feel as if she were in immediate danger soothed him. He tried to lose himself in her emotions, to become one with her in the only way he still could. But other emotions battered him, especially those from Tamara. Tamara was furious, and more than that, Gabriel could feel her lust for vengeance. She was glad that Gabriel was now being held prisoner by his own family, locked away in one of the farmhouse's small bedrooms while the family discussed what should be done with him.

Was Tamara angry enough to want Gabriel dead? Perhaps not. Perhaps she'd be satisfied with the fact that Gabriel had lost everyone he loved. He was grateful that he couldn't feel Ernst's emotions. The hawthorn had severed Ernst's communion with the family.

However bad it was for me to lose my connection, it must be a thousand times more traumatic for Ernst, he thought. His father was unimaginably old, older even than Gabriel knew. Ernst was always vague about his birth. But certainly he had been in communion with at least one other vampire since Gret, who had been born well before Sam. *Ernst is alone now for the first time in more than six hundred years. The shock could be enough to drive him mad.*

But sympathy for his father came tinged with anger. It was because of Ernst's hatred for humans that any of this had happened. If they'd never killed Sam, if he'd been allowed to marry Emma and be a father to Shay . . .

It was no good thinking of things that would never be.

Gabriel allowed himself to focus on Shay's emotions again. Her fear and panic had definitely subsided, leaving anxiety behind, and the heavy pull of sadness. He wouldn't have been surprised to still feel anger in her, after everything that had happened. But there was only the slightest twinge left. The sadness overwhelmed everything else.

She feels my emotions too, Gabriel reminded himself. He thought about focusing on his love for her, trying to make the sensation that reached her as strong as possible, to prove to her that no matter what, his love for her was true. He knew all the members of his family would get the blast of emotion as well, but he didn't care. He wanted them to know how he felt about the person they considered to be an abomination.

Instead, Gabriel clamped down on his love for Shay. She wouldn't want to feel it and it would be wrong to force it on her. She hated him. He deserved her hatred. If she needed his help—the way she had during her first feeding—he would try to give it to her. Otherwise, he'd shield her as much as he could from the emotions he knew she'd be repulsed by.

The sound of the door swinging open pulled Gabriel away from his thoughts. "Come on," Luis said from the doorway. "Ernst is ready for you."

Gabriel pushed himself off the bed, ignoring the way his stomach clenched. He was hundreds of years old, yet he felt like a little boy being called to his father for punishment. As a distraction, Gabriel attempted to pick out Luis's emotions from the powerful mix. His weren't as strong as Tamara's. Millie's either. Millie was pumping out fear, and Gabriel was sure it was fear over what was going to happen to him.

Luis's emotions were muted, held in check. Gabriel decided that it meant Luis was trying to keep an open mind. *That's at least something,* he thought as he followed Luis to the dining room, where his entire family had gathered around the heavy oak table, Ernst at the head. Gabriel slid into the chair opposite the man who was his father in every way that mattered. Millie was to his right. She gave him the barest of nods, and he returned it.

"Millie thinks that we should hear your side of the events," Ernst told Gabriel, without meeting his eyes. "I believe that your actions told us everything we need to know, but you may attempt to defend them if you wish."

Gabriel clasped his hands in front of him, considering how to answer. "My actions led to Richard's death," he said simply, his voice steady as he gazed around the table at his family. "There is no way to defend that." He hesitated for a moment, then added, "If I hadn't done what I did, Shay would be dead. That's the truth of it. I had to choose between them, and I chose her."

"Over your family," Ernst thundered. He sounded like one of the ancient gods, filled with wrath, and this time he looked Gabriel full in the eyes.

"When I joined the family, it was made clear to me that we protect each other at all costs," Tamara said. "Gabriel is right. There is no defense for what he did."

Gabriel stood. He noticed Luis tense, but he didn't rise. "We do always say that we protect each other, always. That the family stands together," Gabriel agreed. "That's what we say. But that's not how we behave."

"You know that is—," Ernst began.

Gabriel held out one hand, silencing him. "You told me you would hear what I had to say."

"Go on." Ernst's voice was tight with held-back emotion.

"We didn't stand with Sam. And we didn't stand with Shay, who, as Sam's daughter, is as much a part of this family as he was," Gabriel said.

"Sam intended to leave the family," Tamara snapped. "You're turning the truth around. He rejected all of us."

"Sam didn't want to leave, he *had* to! He knew we wouldn't support his love for a human. Our hatred for their kind forced him to choose between us and the woman he loved," Gabriel retorted. "By my definition, that wasn't us standing with him."

"You didn't feel that way at the time," Ernst reminded him. "It was you who informed me of Sam's betrayal. And you took part in the blood ritual that killed him."

"I was wrong." Gabriel felt the oily mix of guilt and grief he always did when he thought of Sam. Of what he had done to Sam. "We were wrong." He hadn't believed that until he'd fallen in love with a human himself. He'd hated that Sam had to be killed, but he'd been positive it was necessary for the family's safety. Now he knew better, because of Shay. "Something wonderful happened to Sam. He fell in love. And instead of celebrating his happiness, the way a family should, we murdered him for it."

"He fell in love with a human!" Ernst roared. Now he was on his feet, glaring at Gabriel. "After he'd seen what they do. After he'd seen them kill almost his entire family!"

"In another place. Another century!" Gabriel yelled back. "The humans who massacred our family in Greece are long dead. Sam didn't fall in love with any of them, but with a different kind of person—"

"They are all the same when they find out about vampires," Ernst cut in. "Violent and murderous. Tell a human the truth and that human turns against us. And we were supposed to approve of Sam putting us all at risk like that?"

He strode around the table toward Gabriel. "And you did the same thing. You did the same thing, and now Richard is dead."

"Shay had nothing to do with that. You decided to use her as bait, and the plan went awry. I'm to blame, but so are you. Not Shay," Gabriel burst out, his hands curving into fists as he faced his father. "And Emma wouldn't have done anything to harm us. She knew the truth about our existence, but all she cared about was her love for Sam. She didn't see him as a creature to be feared and hated. There was no reason to believe she would have brought any harm to us."

"But she did," Luis said evenly. "She's the one who told Martin about us."

"Only after we killed the one she loved. We made her believe Sam had abandoned her and left her to raise their baby alone," Gabriel countered.

"Humans can't be trusted," Ernst insisted. It was something he'd said again and again and again over the years.

"*Some* humans," Gabriel corrected, lowering his voice and forcing his hands to unclench. "Not all. Shay taught me that. She risked her life for mine more than once."

"Are you listening, Ernst?" Millie asked. "Please listen."

"You are saying that Richard's death is my fault," Ernst said.

Gabriel sighed. He didn't want to force such a heavy responsibility onto his father's shoulders, not when he himself bore a lot of the blame too. "I'm saying that our beliefs have led us to this place," he said slowly. "We have reasons to fear and hate the humans who massacred us. And Martin, who treated me like less than an animal. But we can't continue to fear and hate all humans. I shouldn't have had to choose between loving Shay and loving my family. Everything would have been so different . . ."

"Different how?" Luis asked, voice neutral.

"I wouldn't have had to decide between saving Shay's life and fighting by Richard's side," Gabriel explained. "Shay wouldn't have been near death. She would have been given the blood she needed. She wouldn't have been locked away by herself. She would have been part of our family."

He rushed on. "I can't be the only one who has come to regret what we did to Sam. To our brother." Tears stung his eyes as he looked at Ernst. "To our son. His death was the result of our prejudice, mine as much as the rest of yours. Yet he still was able to forgive us. We all felt it, even though we've never spoken of it."

Millie let out a sob.

"We could have begun to make things right by treating Sam's daughter as if she belonged with us," Gabriel went on. "But instead—"

"Enough!" Ernst's voice was edged with steel. "Sam was put to death because his actions risked all of our lives. As have yours. And you will meet the same fate."

"No!" Millie cried. "Ernst, no! Please!"

Ernst didn't even glance in her direction. "Gabriel, I hereby sentence you to death."

○ ○ ○ ○ ○ ○ ○ ○ ○ ○ ○ ○ ○ ○ ○ ○

SHAY STARED THROUGH THE WINDOW of Starbucks at her best friend. It had only been a little over a week since she last saw Olivia, but it felt like a lifetime.

It was about an hour after sunset, and Shay had already gorged herself on blood—cold, from a bag, and entirely revolting. But it worked. She was calm and not hungry. Yet here she was lurking in the darkness while Olivia and Kaz sat cheerfully inside. They looked so ... young, Kaz stealing a sip of Olivia's smoothie and Olivia giving him a smack on the arm.

Shay had never really felt like she was the same age they were. In some ways, her school friends had seemed so much older—having love lives, taking road trips to see colleges, even drinking. All things Shay couldn't do because she was so weak. But in most ways, she'd felt light-years more mature than people like Kaz and Olivia. They simply didn't have to think about serious things the way she did. Plus, it had always felt as if hospital time counted like dog years, and Shay had put in a lot of hospital time.

But now, watching them, she felt even older than before, even more separate from her friends. *Why wouldn't I? I'm not even the same species,* she reminded herself.

Olivia suddenly narrowed her eyes, peering through the window. She spotted Shay and shook her head, but her lips curled into a smile, and Shay felt herself smile in response. The feelings of being different and alien and old vanished. Shay rushed inside and over to her friends.

Olivia jumped up and wrapped Shay in a hard hug.

Shay's vampire senses exploded. Olivia's blood thrumming against the walls of her veins. The smell of it, caffeinated and salty-sweet. The feel of her heart pulsing with life. Saliva flooded Shay's mouth, and she felt her fangs start to release.

No, no, no! Shay stumbled away and wrapped her arms around herself. She dug her nails into her skin and concentrated on the small pain, using it to pull her focus away from Olivia's blood.

Olivia studied her. "Well, you look okay. You look great, actually."

"Not about to faint, right?" Shay asked, her fangs safely retracted. It must have been some kind of an instinctive response. Because how could she possibly crave more blood when she'd fed less than an hour ago? She could still feel the new blood cells moving through her, bouncing off one another. She'd never felt more alive.

Not true, a small voice whispered in her mind. *I felt more alive that night Gabriel and I were together.*

That night in the barn, Shay had still been half human. Death had been hovering over her, waiting for the moment when she didn't have vampire blood to keep her body functioning. But when she and Gabriel lay there, bodies tangled together, she'd felt more alive than she ever had or ever would. Sure, right now, her body was pulsing with vitality. But that night with Gabriel, her mind, and body, and heart had been alive with joy and, yes, love.

"Shay Stadium!" Kaz cried. It was an old joke from her old life. It felt good to hear those words, words from before—before she'd had transfusions from a vampire, before that vampire had taken her hostage, before she'd fallen in love with him. . . .

There was no point in thinking about Gabriel. He wasn't who she'd thought he was. But Kaz and Olivia were still themselves. Shay had managed to piss them both off in the last month or so, acting all kinds of crazy with the strength of Gabriel's blood in her veins. And yet here they were, hundreds of miles from home, ready to help her.

"Thanks for coming, you guys," Shay said. "You have no idea how happy I am to see you."

"Like we had a choice, after that phone call," Olivia scolded, her hazel eyes dark with concern. "You're sure you're okay?" she asked, dropping back down at the table.

Shay slid a chair back, getting it a little farther away from Olivia and Kaz before she sat down. It didn't help much. Their scent was in her nose and in her mouth and throat—and so were the scents of the other customers and the baristas. She could pick out each individual person just by their smell.

Gabriel had told her that young vampires needed more blood. But this was ridiculous.

"Shay? Did you hear me?" Olivia asked, tone sharp.

"What? Sorry. I guess not," Shay admitted.

"She just asked if you were okay," Kaz put in. "Even though she already said you looked more than okay. So I don't get it."

"She looks good, actually very good, but she's all twitchy," Olivia told Kaz, her eyes locked on Shay. "So are you okay or not?"

Was Shay all right? She was in almost the same situation as she'd been in when she had her breakdown and called Olivia. She was a vampire. The guy she thought she loved had betrayed her. Martin was off-the-reservation crazy. But being with her friends made her feel so much better. Safer—even though, technically, she was better prepared to defend herself than they were.

"I'm good," she said. "Now that you're here, anyway."

Kaz raised his arms over his head and then grabbed his elbows with the opposite hands, stretching. "So I'm thinking room service. I'm thinking pay-per-view," he announced.

"We aren't watching porn with Shay," Olivia told him firmly.

"Who said porn?" Kaz protested.

"To you, pay-per-view and porn are the same thing," Olivia replied.

"Unjust," Kaz replied, grinning.

It took Shay's brain a few seconds to catch up. "Wait. You want to stay over tonight?" she gasped. Because that would be bad, what with the sun coming up tomorrow and everything. She could picture it perfectly: She would fall into her death sleep, and Olivia would go into panic mode and try to haul Shay to the emergency room, and Shay would turn into a pile of ash.

"Uh, yeah. It was almost a twelve-hour drive, and that was with only one bathroom stop and one pass by a Mickey D's drive-through," Olivia said. "No way are we turning right back around. Besides, you and I need to talk, missy."

"We will," Shay promised, not that she'd figured out exactly what to say. "But I need to get home—fast. Let's just go. I'll drive, and you two can nap. And when you wake up, you can ask me all the questions you want to. I'd rather not go into it all here. It's kind of hard to talk about. I don't want to be the crying-at-Starbucks chick on YouTube." She realized too late that she'd been talking so fast that her words were crashing into each other. She had to try to control the twitchiness.

Olivia and Kaz shared a look, a she-says-she's-okay-but-clearly-not look. Kaz shrugged. "Okay. Whatever. This is all-about-Shay day," Olivia said. "You know, I could have just wired you money for the train or something, if all you really needed was a way back home."

"I needed more than that," Shay reassured her. "I needed not to be alone."

"Just tell me this for now. Do we need to worry about some psycho guy coming after us?" Olivia asked, flicking her long strawberry blond hair off her shoulders.

"No. Gabriel and I are done," Shay said. Although she'd always be able to feel his emotions, so how done could they really be? Right now he was feeling something close to despair. About what had happened to Ernst and Richard? Had his family found out the truth about Gabriel choosing to save her over them?

That was not her problem. She shoved his emotions out of her mind, the one thing she'd gotten pretty good at since becoming a vampire.

"And he knows this?" Olivia asked.

"I made it absolutely clear." Wait. Was that why Gabriel was feeling so horrible? Could that despair be about *her* and not whatever was going on in his family? Losing her?

He killed my father. He deserves whatever despair he feels, she thought.

Olivia got up. "All right. Let's go, then."

Shay stood up so fast that she knocked her chair over.

"You'll probably need a couple of venti coffees if you're going to be driving all night." Kaz took a step toward the counter.

"No, I'm awake. I juiced up on Diet Pepsi Max," Shay lied. Gabriel had managed to eat a little bite of cotton candy that she'd fed him one time, but Shay wasn't sure what coffee—or anything else—would do to her vampire system. After her experience with the muskrat, she'd decided to stick to nothing but human blood from now on.

"Maybe that's why you're so—" Kaz made violent circles with his hands as he led the way to the door and held it open for Shay and Olivia.

"Yeah, I way overdid it," Shay replied, grabbing on to the excuse. "Keys, please," she said when they reached Kaz's SUV.

Olivia started to get in the front seat. "Go in back," Shay urged. "It's better for napping." And it would put her beating heart a tiny bit farther away from Shay. *I'm full*, she reminded herself. *Satisfied. I don't need to feed.* Still, the smell of her friends' blood was impossible to ignore.

Shay powered down the window closest to her as she started the car. "Shay, it's only forty degrees out," Olivia complained.

"Sorry." Shay put the window back up. When they were asleep, she'd at least crack it. As she began to drive, she searched the stations until she found some music that seemed sleep-inducing. Kaz and Olivia were out within ten minutes.

Shay tried to relax. She focused on her technique—this was only the fourth or fifth time she'd ever actually been behind the wheel. Driving with superhuman vision was a little disorienting. She could see so far ahead that it distracted her from what was right in front of her. She concentrated on keeping exactly to the speed limit and sig-naling every time she wanted to change lanes. She needed something besides the smell of blood to concentrate on.

But nothing on the road was enough to distract her. With every mile, her thirst grew more overpowering. She felt as if she were withering inside. Once when she was in the hospital, she hadn't been allowed water for a couple of days. She was being hydrated intrave-nously, but it hadn't felt that way. Her world had narrowed down to pure thirst.

That's how she felt now. But it was the desire for blood that con-sumed her this time. Blood. She needed blood. It was all she could think about.

"Coming over." Olivia wriggled into the front seat. "Time to talk."

"You've hardly slept at all," Shay protested, her fangs nudging at her gums, wanting out. "Only a few hours."

Olivia pressed the scan button on the radio and stopped on a Lady Gaga song. "Riding in a car all day is tiring, but not the kind of tiring where you want to sleep," she said.

"Tell that to Kaz," Shay replied, impressing herself by how normal she sounded. She could do this. Yes, she wanted to drink. Badly. But she could control herself. Could and would.

"Kaz is a world-champion sleeper," Olivia said, giving him an affectionate look over her shoulder, a move that presented her neck to Shay.

Shay tightened her grip on the wheel—kneading it with her fingers just like her mom always did—and ground her teeth together. "So what's the deal on the guy?" Olivia asked.

"He's history," Shay said. Her scalp felt prickly, and her hands shook despite her grasp on the wheel. She'd been insane to call Olivia. Completely out of her mind. It didn't matter what she told herself, she couldn't sit in this car for the hours and hours it would take to get home to Massachusetts, not without blood.

"Shay, you dragged me all the way out here to get you—after you took off, you made me lie to your mom, you slept with some guy I don't even know, and then suddenly you're calling for help and freaking out because you're stranded in Virginia. This is all bizarre."

"You have no idea how bizarre," Shay muttered.

"Well, tell me, then. I will not let you shut me out anymore. Start with the guy or don't, but talk. Now."

"I couldn't stay with him," Shay said after a moment. The devastation of what she'd found out about Gabriel blotted out even her thirst, at least for a few moments. "He just . . . he wasn't a good guy."

"So he had sex with you and then he was done with you?" Olivia asked. Her words were harsh, but her tone was soft.

"No. No, it wasn't like that." Shay shook her head, trying to dispel the dizziness swirling through her body. "God, what ever made me think he was so great in the first place?"

"Did he take you to his friends' place? You said he thought the two of you would be safe there," Olivia said.

"Yeah, we went there. But safe? Not so much. They were *not* happy to see me. I guess maybe he didn't know his friends as well as he thought he did." Even after what he'd done, Shay still felt sure Gabriel had believed that his family would take her in as one of them. He'd been deluding himself—but he hadn't been trying to delude her. Not about that.

"Did his friends blame *you* for what Martin did to Gabriel, holding him captive?"

Shay gave a snort of laughter. "You could say that." She used her tongue to push at her fangs. They'd started to release again.

"Did you tell your mom about Martin?" Olivia asked. "Because she's home now. With him."

"She knows some of it, yeah," Shay replied. "But he's so much worse than she thinks. That's something I've got to deal with when I get there."

I'm getting Mom away from him, Shay promised herself. *I'll drink him dry if he tries to stop me.*

The thought of Martin terrified her. She had distorted, garish memories of him trying to blow up the lab. She'd been clinging to the last shreds of life at that moment. But everything was different now. Now she was the one with the power. Now Martin would fear her. She'd make him fear her.

"Are you going to call the cops on him?" Olivia asked, leaning a little closer, sending a fresh burst of blood-scent over to Shay.

"I haven't figured it out yet," Shay said. "I don't really have any evidence, and cops tend to believe rich doctors over sick teenagers." The truth was, though, that she knew whatever she did to Martin, it wouldn't involve the police. She couldn't afford to attract the attention of the authorities.

She swallowed hard, trying to fight the hunger that increased with every pump of Olivia's warm blood. "Hey, Liv, do you have any perfume? The shower at the hotel was über-grungy, so I didn't use it, and I think I kind of smell."

Olivia twisted around again as she reached for her purse in the backseat. Her scent hit Shay even harder.

"Uh, they like you to drive in one lane or the other," Olivia commented, handing Shay a spritzer of Wakely.

Shay realized that she'd gotten so distracted by the scent of blood that she'd let the car drift. She corrected the wheel with one hand, dousing herself with perfume with the other.

"Forty dollars an ounce," Olivia reminded her.

"I'll buy you more as soon as we're home. I just don't want you and Kaz to have to breathe in my reek." Actually, Shay was hoping the perfume would dull the scent of the blood. And it did, some, burning the inside of her nostrils and making her eyes water. *I'm going to make it. It's going to be okay*, she decided.

"How pissed off at you is Martin going to be—for letting Gabriel go?" Olivia asked. "I still can't believe he had someone chained up in his office. That's complete psycho horror movie behavior."

"I don't know. I hadn't thought about that part," Shay said. Because she didn't care how pissed he was. He couldn't possibly be as mad as her. "I haven't thought about way too many things. I just wanted to see you and get home." She shot a quick glance at Olivia, not quick enough that her eyes didn't have time to seek out the thin blue vein running up the side of her neck.

"Shay, one lane," Olivia cried. "One!"

She'd drifted again. Shay jerked the wheel too hard to the right and almost took them over the edge of the shoulder.

"Stop," Olivia ordered. "I'm driving. I'd like to make it home alive."

"Sorry," Shay said.

"Are we there?" Kaz asked, voice thick with sleep, as Shay pulled over.

"Hardly. We're not even over the state line. This is northern Virginia," Olivia told him. "I'm going to drive. Shay's still got the twitchies."

Shay jumped out of the car and sucked in as many deep breaths of the night air as she could before she had to get back inside, where the air was saturated with the scent of blood. The smell of the perfume was still strong, but Shay's body had changed in so many ways. She was a hunter now, a tracker, and blood drew her, pulling her to the source.

Kaz watched her, one eyebrow lifted. "Do you need medication or something?" he asked after Olivia had pulled back onto the road. "Do you have it with you?"

"No. I'm okay," Shay replied. She noticed Olivia shooting Kaz a worried look in the rearview. "Really," she added.

"Do you think maybe you should go to my house first, instead of going straight home?" Olivia asked. "Your mom could come over and see you, let you know how much trouble you're in with Martin. I don't want him going off on you."

This was so familiar: Olivia worrying about Shay, wanting to manage things for her, protect her. And meanwhile, Shay was using every bit of strength she had to fight the instinct to sink her fangs into Olivia's neck and drink. She shuddered, remembering how she'd almost killed that guy in the pickup.

"Shay, what? Are you cold?" Olivia asked, misunderstanding the way Shay's body was shaking.

"No. But I think I'm going to be sick. Pull over," Shay cried. She had to get out of the car, before she did something unspeakable.

"You just told Kaz you weren't—," Olivia began.

Shay's fangs released fully. There was no time. She reached over and grabbed the wheel, jerking the car over to an exit ramp as Olivia slammed on the brakes. They skidded to a stop, half on and half off the ramp. Shay shoved open the door and ran.

"Shay!" Olivia screamed.

Shay didn't turn back. There was a gas station just off the exit. One car at the pumps. A woman next to it, pumping gas. Giving herself over to her instincts, Shay hurled herself at the woman, knocking the nozzle out of her hand. Before it had the chance to clatter to the ground, Shay's mouth was filled with blood. She had one arm locked around the woman's waist, one hand pressed over her lips to keep her from screaming, as Shay took what she needed.

The dizziness left her body. She felt clear and strong as the blood flowed from the Giver to her, bringing with it a collage of emotion, almost too many feelings to absorb. *Don't take too much,* she told herself. *Not too much.* But she had to have a little more.

"Shay!"

The familiar voice was so full of horror and disgust that Shay instantly released the woman, who slumped to the ground. Not drained, though. A part of Shay was still aware of the blood coursing through the woman even as she turned to face Olivia.

Olivia let out a long, shrill shriek. In her friend's eyes Shay could see her own reflection. Blood dripped from her mouth down her chin. Involuntarily, she licked it away, and Olivia let out a low retching sound.

"It's not—" Shay didn't have time to finish, not that she knew what to say anyway. Olivia turned and tore back toward the car.

"Sorry," Shay said to the lady on the ground. "Sorry, sorry, sorry." Then she chased after Olivia. Too late. Olivia slammed herself into the car. Kaz gaped at Shay, eyes wild, as the automatic door locks went down.

Olivia floored it, and the car sped off, tires squealing.

Shay stared after it, mouth open, still trying to come up with the words that would make Olivia understand.

Like that was even possible.

○ ○ ○ ○ ○ ○ ○ ○ ○ ○ ○ ○ ○ ○ ○ ○ ○

ELEVEN

SOON THEY WOULD COME FOR HIM. The death ritual would begin at three a.m., the soul's midnight, the time of night when more humans let go of life than any other, when the barrier between this world and what lay beyond was the thinnest. It was one of the first things Ernst had taught Gabriel, back when he was still a young human boy. He'd called it superstition back then, but when it had been time to take Sam's life, Ernst had wanted to do it at three o'clock. Gabriel suspected that his father still bought into the "superstitions" he'd learned in his own youth more than even he realized. He was absolutely sure that Ernst would follow the same rules for his own ritual that they'd followed for Sam's.

Let them come, Gabriel thought. He lay in one of the farmhouse bedrooms, waiting. *Let my life end. What is there to live for now?* There was no joy without Shay, who now despised him. Without his family, whom he had betrayed to save her.

And maybe Shay would be happier once she was released from the burden of communion with him.

At least she wasn't in any immediate danger. Several hours before, he'd felt devastation and grief slicing through him. Shay's devastation; Shay's grief. But those feelings had subsided a little. Whatever had happened, she had survived it.

His mind drifted to Sam, and he wondered what had filled his brother's thoughts as Sam waited for the family to begin his final blood ritual. Unlike Gabriel, Sam had had so much to live for—a woman who loved him passionately, a child soon to be born. He had been going wild inside, that much Gabriel knew from their communion.

He usually kept the memories of that night locked in a deep, dark place inside of him. But tonight the memories crashed down on him relentlessly. Sam had fought with all his strength to free himself from the family as they dragged him into the circle where the ritual would take place, screaming at them to release him. Screaming, then begging, with his eyes locked on Gabriel's face. He'd continued to struggle until the last moment of the third night of the ritual, when the last of his life was drained away. When he'd forgiven them.

Why couldn't he have died cursing Gabriel, damning him for what he'd done? After Gabriel had taken everything from Sam, betrayed him in the most awful way, how could his brother still have had the generosity of spirit to think of Gabriel's suffering instead of his own?

Sam's forgiveness has been the hardest burden to bear, he thought. *At least I'll be free of my guilt once I'm dead.*

The smell of smoke permeated Gabriel's room, pulling him from his thoughts, and for a moment memory and reality blurred and blended. That smell . . . it could have come from the night Sam was killed. The night Gabriel helped murder him. It took him a moment to realize that the smell of smoke was from the present, not the past. The circle for his ritual was being prepared down in the cellar. Not much time left. A blink, a sigh, compared to the years he'd already lived.

And what had he done in all those years? What had he accomplished?

I gave Shay life.

That was something. It was enough. And maybe, in its way, saving Sam's daughter had partially made up for what he'd done to Sam. Not that anything could truly absolve him, not even Sam's words.

Gabriel heard the lock click, and a second later the door swung open. Ernst stood there, face expressionless except for the look of steely determination in his eyes. Gabriel got up and went toward him, though neither of them spoke. When Gabriel reached him, Ernst turned and walked down the hall. Gabriel followed, Luis and Tamara falling into place, flanking him on either side.

Tamara was blazing with hatred. And anticipation. She wanted Gabriel dead and she was eager to see him suffer. Her fury ran through the entire communion. Luis's grief over Richard's death hadn't turned to anger the way hers had. From Luis, Gabriel felt a deep sadness along with resignation.

The smell of smoke grew stronger as they moved through the old house. Silent as a funeral procession, as if Gabriel were already dead, they took the stairs from the kitchen to the cellar.

Gabriel wished that the blood ritual could take place outside. The moon was full, and it would illuminate the night. He would rather die in light than darkness, but it was not to be.

Ernst led the way across the empty space to a large perfect circle burned into the dirt floor, smooth gray stones rimming it.

Millie waited for them there inside the scorched ring. She bent and removed one of the stones, allowing them passage into the center of the circle. Her eyes were filled with grief as Gabriel passed her, and he could feel the same grief from her in the communion, but she placed the stone back in place without a word.

He had helped Ernst prepare the circle for Sam's death, trying to harden his heart the entire time. Millie's grief was simple and pure, but Gabriel's had been twisted by his anger—at Sam for falling in love with a human, at all humans for taking yet another brother from him.

He'd asked Ernst how he knew what to do, where the ritual had come from. Ernst hadn't known the answer. He'd learned the runes that had to be painted on the stones in red—red from the blood of the family—from his creator, although they weren't Germanic in origin. Gabriel hadn't seen anything like them before or after Sam's execution. Until tonight. He could smell the blood of his family around him, not quite dry yet on the stones.

Ernst nodded at him. Gabriel knew he was expected to shed his clothes and lie down in the circle. He'd prepared himself for this moment and had been convinced he was ready. But when he looked at Ernst, he knew he didn't want to die without reconciling with the man who was the only father Gabriel had ever known.

"Could we have a private moment?" he asked Ernst. "I'd like to say good-bye to you, Father."

"I didn't have that chance with Richard," Tamara spat.

"Ernst?" Gabriel said.

"You've forgotten how this family works," Ernst replied in a cold voice. "We are bound together. We are one. We share our lives, our emotions, our fate. There is no need for privacy among the family."

It was clear nothing Gabriel said would penetrate the stone wall that Ernst had raised between them. He felt so distant from his father. He could only guess what Ernst was feeling now that the hawthorn had broken the communion between them again. *So let it end. Just let it end*, he told himself.

Gabriel stripped off his clothes and lay in the ash in the middle of the circle. It was still faintly warm, and the cellar air was damp and cold. The heightened awareness of the physical world was the thing Gabriel marveled at the most when he was first transformed. Shay had given him back that sense of wonder. He'd thought it had been lost forever after Sam died, but somehow she had found an ember of it still burning in him and brought it blazing back.

Gabriel sought out the emotions that were Shay's. She was still all right. Getting calmer, pushing down whatever it was that had filled her with devastation and self-loathing. She was strong, stronger than she knew. She would find a way to make her new life matter.

He let that thought comfort him as Luis and Tamara drove four stakes into the ground. They chained each of Gabriel's hands and each of his feet to one of them. It wasn't necessary. It had been for Sam, but Gabriel had no intention of trying to escape the will of his family. He deserved this, for what he'd done to them, to Shay, and to Sam.

When they finished, Ernst began to speak. "As I said, we are a family, with one life that belongs to us all. If one of us is in danger, we all are. If one of us is in danger, we all fight until that danger is gone." He paused. "What has happened to our family is the ultimate betrayal. One who should have been protecting us, fighting by our sides, brought danger into our home, our place of safety and security."

There was no protest. No one spoke out to defend him, to say that what Gabriel had truly brought into their home was another member of their family.

"Because we are all one, we must all take responsibility for what is to be done tonight and the next two nights. We must all share in the ritual. We must all share in the blood, not only because it would be fatal for any one of us to drink so much of the blood of our own kind, but because we must share everything. We must share the grief that it is impossible not to feel. And the guilt."

"I won't ever feel guilty for this," Tamara muttered. "He doesn't feel guilty for what he did."

She was wrong. Gabriel's guilt over Richard's death was heavy within him. He said nothing. No words would convince her.

But Ernst. Did Ernst actually feel guilt and grief over condemning Gabriel to death? Did Ernst still love Gabriel? Did he still see Gabriel as his son? He'd never said so, but Gabriel knew something had broken inside Ernst when the family took Sam's life. Would the ritual leave him shattered this time?

I wish I could tell him I understand, Gabriel thought. *That I know he believes he's doing the right thing, doing what he has to do to prevent another massacre. I felt the same way when we performed Sam's ritual. It was only after falling in love with Shay that I truly understood what we had done, how wrong we were.*

"The youngest will begin," Ernst announced. "Do not take more than your body can safely process. Stop when you feel the nausea and dizziness overtake you. The purpose of the ritual lasting three nights is so that this may be done safely. Tonight I will not drink. I will watch over all of you. My turn will come later." Whatever Ernst was feeling didn't come out in his voice, which was steady, his tone cool.

Gabriel kept his gaze locked on the ceiling, waiting for the fangs of his sister to pierce his flesh. Millie was the youngest. She would go first, followed by Luis, who was older, and Tamara, who was older still.

"Millie," Ernst finally said, the one word an order. Revulsion and sadness and a little anger—he thought at Ernst—pulsed through the communion from Millie as she approached Gabriel. She knelt beside him. He could hear her shifting slightly, hesitating.

He turned his head and looked at her elfin face. "It's okay, Mils."

"No, it's not," she whispered.

"It is. Ernst was right. I didn't mean them to, but my actions got Richard killed. In our family that is punishable by death," Gabriel told her. He willed her to realize that if she refused to take part in the ritual, she would be the next to die. Ernst would never allow the discipline of the family to break down.

He looked back at the ceiling, thinking it would be easier for both of them if there were no eye contact. He tried to imagine the sky, the moon, the stars. He heard Millie sigh, then her hair brushed against his cheek as she brought her mouth to his neck and began to drink.

Sensations bombarded him as a purplish haze stole over his vision. The feeling of his blood being siphoned through his veins. The nausea Millie was already beginning to experience. Tamara's bloodthirsty satisfaction. Luis's revulsion—and his surprise at his own reaction. From Ernst, nothing. They hadn't restored the communion, and Gabriel knew he'd never feel his father's emotions again.

Fragments of memory from his long life competed with his family's emotions for his attention. Watching Elena make flower chains at the orphanage. Playing poker with Sam. Sitting in a lecture hall, uneasy with the number of humans around him. Lying with Shay, her arms and legs wrapped around him.

Dizziness washed through him. Gabriel wasn't sure if it was his or Millie's or both. The memories continued to explode in his mind, some of moments in his life he'd long forgotten. Then, like a sucker punch, he was hit with the picture of him drinking from Sam, helping to kill him. Involuntarily, Gabriel gave a moan. Millie misinterpreted it and pulled away. "I can't . . . Ernst, please."

"Come away, Millie," Ernst answered. "Luis?"

Luis nodded. He strode over and stretched out on the ground next to Gabriel, then slid his teeth into the largest vein in Gabriel's wrist. As Luis drank, Gabriel wished for more of the sweet agony the memories of Shay gave him. Instead, he was blasted with a series of memories of Sam. All so good at the time. And so horrible to recall now that he believed with all his heart that the family shouldn't have killed his brother. Why had Gabriel gone to Ernst with the information about Sam and Emma?

Because I thought it was my only choice. I believed that there was no way for the rest of my family to be safe if Sam involved himself with a human.

The memories dimmed, and Gabriel's body suddenly felt light. He felt as if he were floating up, up, up. Up past the wooden beams of the cellar ceiling, up through the old farmhouse, up into the night, into the brightness of the moon. The feeling shattered as the poison of his blood began to burn through Luis's body, Gabriel experiencing the agony along with Luis.

"That's enough for tonight, Luis," Ernst finally said. "It's Tamara's turn now."

Only seconds after Luis pulled away, Tamara dropped down on top of Gabriel and jabbed her teeth into his neck without hesitation. She sucked so viciously that Gabriel felt as if his blood were being scraped from his veins.

She uttered a growl as another memory of Shay from their one night together in the barn flashed through Gabriel's mind. Gabriel wondered if Tamara realized where the rush of joy and rapture she was getting as she drank came from. Shay straddling him, kissing him. Gabriel gasped with the pain of that memory, its sweetness tempered by having lost Shay. But no matter how much pain it caused, he was grateful to experience that moment again before he died.

Gabriel's stomach cramped as he absorbed Tamara's feelings of nausea and, less powerfully, the nausea that still filled Millie and Luis. Pain exploded behind his eyes, and again he wasn't sure if the sensation was directly from his own body or something that Tamara was experiencing as she sickened from his blood.

If the sensation was from Tamara, it wasn't inhibiting her. She continued swallowing down Gabriel's blood, as if she was planning to take it all right then. That's how badly she wanted him dead. The night of Sam's ritual, she'd done what she needed to do, without pleasure or regret. But with him . . . He'd probably feel the same if the situation were reversed and Tamara's actions had led to Shay's death.

Gabriel realized his muscles had tensed and consciously relaxed them. This was what he wanted. "Forgive me, Tamara," he said. Her only reply was to knot her fingers in his hair and drain his blood more desperately.

Then Tamara's eyeteeth jerked out of his throat. He felt her body being lifted off of his. "Enough!" Ernst cried. "Are you trying to kill yourself? That's not what Richard would want for you." She began to sob. "Enough for tonight." Ernst's voice was gentle now, the voice of a concerned father. "You all did well, and you all need rest. It's time to go back upstairs."

Two more nights, Gabriel told himself as they left him chained there, naked on the cellar floor. *Only two more nights.*

He heard a shuffling sound from the top of the staircase. Ernst.

"You don't have to stay there all night," Gabriel called softly. "I'm too weak to break the chains, but if I could, I wouldn't. Don't you understand? This is what I want." To go through what Sam had, for almost the same reason, for love, felt right, deserved, earned.

There was no reply from Ernst, but Gabriel knew he was still there.

"Shay despises me. I murdered Sam. I betrayed my family. And you hate me," Gabriel burst out. "What is there to stay alive for?"

Again, there was no reply from Ernst.

TWELVE

○ ○ ○ ○ ○ ○ ○ ○ ○ ○ ○ ○ ○ ○ ○ ○

SHAY FINALLY SLOWED DOWN as she entered Black River. No reason to risk a ticket when she was only a couple of miles from home. As if speeding was the worst of it. She'd stolen a car. Somehow she'd become the kind of girl who'd steal a car. Girl. She had to stop thinking of herself as a girl. She was a vampire. She did what she had to do to stay alive. Steal a car. Break into a motel. Drink human blood.

As she pulled to a stop at a red light, the nausea and dizziness she'd been feeling all night intensified. Because she was anxious about facing her mother and Martin? Because she couldn't get Olivia's expression of absolute revulsion out of her head?

Shay sighed. Maybe both those things were part of it, but she knew that mostly the sensations were coming to her through her communion with Gabriel. There was something wrong with him, seriously wrong. He'd drained her of blood, and her blood was poison to him. Was he going to be able to survive it? Or was Gabriel dying?

I told him that transforming me might kill him, Shay told herself, pushing down the emotions from him. *And, anyway, there's nothing I can do. It's not like I can save him. I have my own situation here, my own life. Or afterlife.*

A horn blared behind her, and Shay realized that the light had turned green. *Okay, okay,* she thought as she stepped on the gas. *I can see you have someplace very important to be. So do I. I have to go tell my mother I'm a vampire.*

That was the only plan she'd been able to come up with. She was going to ask her mother for help. And if Mom refused, if she turned on Shay immediately the way Olivia had, then Shay would go outside and let herself burn down to ash when the sun came up. She couldn't handle this by herself, she just couldn't. Olivia thought she was a monster, and Olivia was probably right. Mom had spoken of Gabriel as something less than human, so she'd probably think of Shay that way too. And what was the point of living if everyone she loved hated her? Hated her or was dead.

Two lefts, a right, and she was on her street, the perfectly manicured lawns and lovely McMansions gliding by. Shay felt like she'd drifted into a dream she used to have. When she pulled into the driveway, it didn't feel like coming home.

Maybe because this house, this street were much more Martin's than Shay's or her mother's. When he'd married Mom, he'd swept them away into a bubble with every comfort money could buy. They hadn't known that it was as much of an investment as anything else. Did he have any real feelings for her mom? Had he ever?

Shay turned off the engine and stared at the house. More questions she hadn't allowed herself to think about flooded her. Would Martin be there? He'd answered the phone before. Did her mother know what Martin had done in Tennessee? Had she helped him plan his attack on the vampire family's lab? She had helped him take Gabriel hostage, but that was to save Shay. Would her mother—

Shay shook her head, trying to stop the chatter in her brain. She should use her vampire senses—that would tell her all she needed to know. There was only one heartbeat inside the house. Shay pulled in a deep breath. The strongest scent was her mother's, that mix of honeysuckle perfume and the chemicals of hair coloring, Tide detergent, aloe vera hand lotion, and, more faintly, under the powdery odor of deodorant, the pungent scent of fear sweat.

Mom's alone. Just go in, Shay ordered herself. It was almost six in the morning. There was only about an hour before sunrise. There wasn't enough time for doubt. She stepped out of the car and shut the door softly. When she'd climbed the steps to the front porch, she took the spare key from the hanging pot filled with what her mother called hummingbird fodder—just a bunch of plants that hummingbirds liked.

She felt like a thief as she slid the key into the lock and silently opened the door. *I still live here*, she told herself. Mom would want her to come in. She'd be so excited to see Shay, and so relieved. At least at first. At least until she knew what Shay had become. *She loved Sam once*, Shay reminded herself. *Even though she knew what he was.*

Shay started for the stairs, then hesitated as she heard a clicking sound from the kitchen. The sound was familiar, but she couldn't quite pinpoint it.

Oh. Of course, she thought when she reached the kitchen doorway. The clicks were created when her mom shut one of the little plastic doors on Shay's pill holder. Holders. She had two—one for morning, one for night. Wednesday—click. Thursday—click. Friday—

"Mom."

The bottle of pills her mother had been holding flew out of her fingers. It landed with another click—a louder one—followed by the *ping, ping, ping* of some loose pills, pills Shay no longer had any use for.

"Shay!" Mom scrambled up from her chair. They met in the middle of the room. Shay had to remind herself not to hold her mother as tightly as she wanted to. She was still learning to control her strength, and she could crack one of her mother's ribs if she wasn't careful.

Again, Shay was struck by the realization that she was stronger than the people she kept turning to for protection. Kaz, Olivia, Mom. Maybe she shouldn't have come here. But she hadn't had anywhere else to go. And this way, no matter what, she'd at least be able to say good-bye to her mother.

"Are you okay?" her mom exclaimed as she released Shay, her eyes frantically searching Shay's face. "You look—you look well. But we should get you checked out."

"No," Shay said quickly. "I'm fine."

"I've been frantic. After I talked to you, I came straight home from Miami," Mom said. "I figured this was where you'd come if you wanted me. How did you get here? Where were you? Is the—Is *he* with you?" Fear flickered in her eyes, and the smell of her fright intensified.

"No. *Gabriel* isn't with me." Her mother flinched at the way Shay had emphasized his name. "I meant what I said before, Mom. What you did to Gabriel . . . I know you did it for me."

"I did! It was the only thing I could think of to save you. I—"

"But that doesn't change the fact that you took a person hostage for his blood." Shay felt some of her old anger rising up. What Gabriel had done to her father was unforgivable. But it didn't change the fact that he himself had been treated like a lab rat.

"We both know he isn't a *person*," her mother replied, then she pressed her fingers against her lips. "Let's not do this, Shay. Let's not fight. I was afraid I was never going to see you again."

"Me too," Shay admitted. "Mom, I have so much to tell you. But where's Martin?" His scent was still strong in the house. He'd been there recently.

"He was gone when I got up," her mother said with a shrug. "He's been heading to his office insanely early and staying late. He's going crazy trying to figure out where you are. He feels so responsible for what happened to you."

"That's because he is," Shay snapped.

"We both are. I should have demanded that Martin stop the transfusions. I could see they were making you act recklessly. You never would've gone to Martin's office . . . you never would've found that vampire if I'd just made Martin stop," her mother said.

"If you'd made him stop, I'd be dead," Shay argued. "It wasn't the transfusions that—"

Mom put her hand on Shay's arm, interrupting her. "I can't

believe how good you look. Martin didn't think you'd be able to live more than a few days."

The fear flashed through her eyes again. *Does she know the truth?* Shay wondered. *She has to at least suspect. She knows I was with a vampire. And here I am looking completely healthy, when I shouldn't even be able to keep myself on my feet.*

"Well, you can't believe anything Martin says," Shay replied.

"Oh, sweetie, no. We were both so worried about you."

"Martin doesn't give a crap about me," Shay said flatly. "He never has. He—"

"How can you say that?" her mother exclaimed. "Martin gave up his entire career to find a cure for you!"

God, she's good at denial, Shay thought. *I guess she had to be to survive having a terminally ill kid.*

"Mom, come on. Martin saw me as a way to make one of those historic medical contributions he's always talking about. I was going to be his artificial heart or polio vaccine or whatever. As soon as he figured out a way to use what I was—half human and half vampire." Shay shook her head. "He was hoping he could come up with a cure for death, not for me."

Her mother paled, and she stumbled over to the closest kitchen chair and sat down. She opened her mouth, but no words came out.

"I know the truth, Mom," Shay told her. She sat down across the table. "I know that my father was a vampire."

There was a long pause.

"Martin . . . of course Martin is ambitious," her mother finally said. "And as a doctor, what you are, well, it fascinated him. And he thought the possibilities for using . . . that part of you to help humankind were endless. But he really cares about you, Shay. About both of us. Not just about the glory."

Shay couldn't believe it. Her mother was acting like as long as she didn't acknowledge what Shay had said, it wouldn't be true.

"That's why he—*we*—did what we did," Mom continued. "That's why we tracked down that vampire. We wanted—"

"Mom," Shay interrupted, "are we actually going to sit here and pretend I didn't just say that I know about my dad?"

"It's not something I ever wanted you to find out," her mother whispered. "And it doesn't matter. You're you. You're Shay. That part of you, it has nothing to do with what you actually are."

"It's everything I am!" Shay protested. "It's why I've been sick all my life."

"Okay, that may be true. It is true, at least that's what Martin and I believe," her mother said. "But there's nothing else of your father in you. He never even saw you. Not once. He was never in your life. That's one thing I'll always be grateful for."

"You didn't always feel that way," Shay said. "You loved him once. And he loved you."

"I'm sure you want to think that, but this isn't a fairy tale," Mom said.

"Sam loved you, and I know it," Shay insisted.

Her words shocked her mother into wide-eyed silence. "I know all about him, Mom. Gabriel told me some of it, but some I just *saw*. When Martin gave me transfusions of Gabriel's blood, I had visions of his life, and my father was in his life."

Mom frowned. "You have no reason to believe those visions were true."

"I saw him with the locket." Shay pulled it free from her shirt, running her fingers over the sun and moon etched in the front. "He was so excited about giving it to you." Tears stung Shay's eyes. "He was excited about me, too. He couldn't wait to change diapers. He was happy about me coming, Mom. And he was in love with you."

"No," her mother said, shaking her head. "He abandoned us, honey. He said he would marry me, but he never showed up. He wasn't there when you were born. He did give me the locket, but after that, he just took off. I never heard from him again. Not a letter, not anything."

Shay reached out and took one of her mother's hands in both of hers. "Because he was dead."

For a split second Shay saw shock—and sadness—in her mother's eyes. But that was quickly replaced by doubt.

"You know what he was," Mom said. "Dying isn't . . . It's not something that happens very easily to them, Shay. I understand why you'd want to believe that he didn't willingly desert us, but—"

"His family killed him, because they found out about the two of you, that he loved you, that you were pregnant with his baby." Shay didn't explain how they found out. It was too painful. The words would have felt like shards of glass against her throat and tongue.

And her mom didn't care anyway. Her eyes looked glazed. Shay had the feeling that Mom wasn't seeing her or anything in the kitchen. She seemed to have slipped deep into shock. Shay stood up. "Let me get you a glass of water or something."

She went to the fridge and poured two glasses of pomegranate juice. That's what her mother had usually given her whenever she felt especially weak and shaky. She set the glasses down on the table, but her mom didn't pick hers up. "Mom, drink," Shay urged.

Her mother blinked a few times, gave one of her fake "everything's fine" mother smiles, and took a sip of the juice. "You really believe that?" she asked. "About your . . . about Sam. What his family did?"

"I saw that, too. I saw them kill him," Shay replied quietly. She didn't want to remember this part, but it would be important to Mom. "In the visions it's as if I'm right there. It's not like watching a movie. I can feel things, get smells, tastes, emotions. And I saw Sam . . . he wanted to come back to you. He fought hard—"

A sob escaped her mother's throat. "I should have had more faith in him. I gave up on him so easily. My friends told me that he'd bolted because of the baby—not that they knew what he really was. They convinced me. I didn't even look for him."

"I wouldn't have looked for him either," Shay said. "I'd have thought the same thing. He wouldn't have been the first guy to bolt when he found out his girlfriend was pregnant." Her mother had had to deal with so much sorrow in her life. Shay didn't want her taking on any extra guilt. It wasn't as if she could have saved Sam anyway. If she'd gone looking for Sam, Ernst would have killed her.

Shay glanced at the clock. She had little more than half an hour before her death sleep. She had to tell her mother what she was—and soon. But Mom needed at least a few minutes before she got hit with anything else.

Maybe she'd even be happy, now that she wasn't consumed by hatred for Sam. Maybe she'd be relieved that she would never have to worry about Shay's health again. Shay was going to outlive her mother, something neither of them had ever really believed would happen.

"Was it—Was he in a lot of pain?" her mom asked.

"I only saw a little bit," Shay said. There was no reason for her mother to know the details. It wouldn't change anything, and it would make her feel even worse. "Mom, this is actually a happy thing, in a way. The truth is that he loved us. He never would have wanted you to spend all these years believing he didn't care about us. He seemed like a pretty amazing person, actually."

"You really saw him?"

Shay nodded.

"I'm glad. I know you've always had questions . . ." Her mother hesitated. "I couldn't talk about him. For so many reasons."

"I get it," Shay told her. "He broke your heart."

"But he didn't mean to." Her mother blinked rapidly, fighting tears. "He didn't mean to."

"He didn't mean to," Shay agreed, sneaking another look at the clock. She could wait a few more minutes, but then she'd have to tell her mom the truth.

"Do you want to know how I met him?" Mom asked. This time her smile, though small, wasn't at all fake.

"Definitely," Shay said.

"I was about your age, or a little older. I was supposed to meet my friend Vivian at the movies, but she was late. She was always late—so annoying. I constantly missed the beginnings of movies because of her."

Shay smiled. Her mom suddenly sounded younger.

"Sam was out front too. Looking at the posters, trying to decide what to see. We started talking—I don't remember how exactly—and by the time Viv finally showed, we—"

"Emma, move away from her."

Shay jerked her head toward the kitchen door. Martin stood there, dressed in jogging clothes, face flushed. One of his big hands gripped the door frame so tightly that Shay thought it might splinter.

"Do it, Emma. Now, please," Martin said when her mother didn't move. His voice was flat and calm, but Shay could hear his heart thundering, pounding much too hard and fast to be the result of a jog around the neighborhood. "Can't you see what she is?"

"Gabriel transformed me. I'm like him now. Like my dad," Shay blurted out, not wanting Martin to be the one to tell her mother. "Mom, I'm a vampire."

Her mother gasped, but Shay rushed on. "That's why I look so good. I'm not sick anymore. I won't ever be sick again. Gabriel saved my life."

It was true. Whatever else Gabriel had done, he had given Shay a new life. And he'd risked his own to do it. She could still feel his pain and nausea, his weakness. His helplessness. He'd known he might not survive the blood ritual to transform her, but he'd done it because he loved her. Shay wasn't sure what to feel about him, but she couldn't escape that truth. Gabriel loved her.

She raised her eyes to her mother's. "Even after what you two did to him, Gabriel saved my life," she repeated, trying to gauge her mother's reaction. It was hard. Mom seemed to be feeling a thousand things at once.

"Emma!" Martin's voice was like a whip. "That's not your daughter. Get away from her. I'll take her to the office until we can figure out what to do with her."

"You already know what you're going to do with me!" Shay snarled, leaping to her feet. "You're going to chain me up, exactly the way you did Gabriel. I'll be your test subject—since you didn't manage to kidnap one when you attacked Gabriel's family."

"What?" her mother cried.

"Don't listen to her, she's not even human," Martin said.

"Martin used my cell to track me, and when he found out where I was, he showed up with a bag full of explosives and a dart full of hawthorn," Shay told her mother, never taking her eyes off Martin. "I was practically dead, but Martin didn't bother looking for me. He just wanted to get himself another vampire to experiment on."

"You knew where Shay was?" Her mom's forehead wrinkled as she tried to take in this new information. Shay could almost see Mom's denial falling away, leaving her vulnerable. Shay didn't believe her mother had married Martin for love, at least not the hearts-and-flowers kind of romantic love. But she had respected him. And she'd truly believed that his top priority was curing Shay, and that made her love him in a way.

Martin's mouth curled into a sneer as he stared back at Shay.

"Martin, answer me! You knew where she was?" Her mother's voice rose into a shriek.

Martin didn't bother to reply. Instead, he pulled a syringe out of his jacket pocket.

Hawthorn. Shay knew what it was the instant she smelled it.

Shay's fangs sprang free. Her hands clenched into fists. "I'm not your sick little patient anymore," she warned him. She crouched down, preparing to fight.

"No!" Mom grabbed Shay by the shirt and yanked her backward. Martin took advantage of her split-second loss of balance, charging at Shay with the needle. A drop of hawthorn shone on the tip, glittering like a jewel.

Shay gasped as the drop fell from the needle onto her skin. Instantly, her communion to Gabriel began to fade, his pain and weakness, his dizziness, his sorrow, his shame, and his love for her slipping away.

The expected sensation of the needle piercing her flesh didn't come. Her mother had grabbed Martin's arms with both hands, knocking the syringe to the floor.

Shay dropped to her knees, focusing all her will on keeping the communion with Gabriel. She should be glad to lose it, but as it faded, she instinctively fought to keep it. She wasn't ready to let go. Even after what he'd done, she couldn't bear the idea of being completely severed from him.

More than that, something was very wrong with him. She'd been pushing that knowledge away, but now it flooded her, strengthening her resolve to hold on to him. Vaguely, she was aware of the crunching sound as her mother ground the syringe under her foot.

"She's not Shay," Martin said again, reverting to his reasonable doctor voice. "Did you see those fangs? She was going to kill me!"

"I'd call it self-defense. She was right. You were about to take her to your lab and experiment on her blood until there was nothing left of her," Shay's mother yelled.

"You have to stop thinking of her as human. She's an animal now, with animal instincts," Martin shot back.

"No. She's my Shay, same as she always was, same as she always will be. And you know what? She's more compassionate than either of us. She saw how wrong what we had done was. She looked at . . .

at *Gabriel* chained to that table, and even though she knew he was a vampire, she couldn't leave him there." Shay's mother sucked in a shaky breath. "Oh my God, she's just like her father. He would have done the same thing if he was in that situation."

Shay tried to open herself completely to the communion. What was happening to Gabriel? No matter what he'd done to Sam, he was the man who had saved Shay's life.

"You're being dangerously sentimental," Martin argued. "If she was hungry, and you were the only one around, she'd drain you dry."

"And I'd want her to," Mom snapped. "We've been married for more than three years—how can you not know that I'd do anything to keep my daughter alive? Why do you think I married you in the first place? Because I fell madly in love with you?"

Shay tried to shut out their voices and focus. A faraway sense of anguish . . . that must be Gabriel. Her own emotions were more in the disgust/pity/anger mode right now. Shay took a deep breath and did her best to stem her emotions. Gabriel was in too much pain already. She didn't want him to pick up anything negative from her.

God, why did she still feel responsible for him? After everything? She'd gotten him out of Martin's lab room. She'd saved his life. She'd done enough. Whatever he was going through now was his problem to deal with.

But she could feel the frailty in his body through the communion, and she found it impossible to ignore. Maybe he felt the same way about the numbness taking over her senses. He'd be able to feel it. Shay was sure of that. Experimentally, she tried to flex her fingers. They responded slowly, trembling with the tiny effort.

". . . you thought my research would save Shay, and my money would mean she'd never want for anything," Martin's voice filtered slowly into Shay's mind. "It was a fair trade. She needed my research. You both stood to gain as much as I did."

"Well, she doesn't need you anymore," Shay's mother told him. "And neither do I."

Martin laughed. "I can freeze your bank account with one phone call," he said.

"And with one phone call, I can tell the world what you've done," Mom replied, her voice as cold and steady as Martin's. "You're not going to win a Nobel Prize for experimenting on humans."

Shay realized that outside the window, the sky had changed from deep black to charcoal. The pressure of the sun was building in her mind; sunrise would come soon. She had to get out of this room and into someplace safe. Still, she let herself savor her mother's words for a moment, to let Gabriel—and herself—feel the warmth and happiness again. Her mother loved her, no matter what. Mom was on her side.

She struggled to open her mouth. "Mom," she tried to say. But her tongue was thick with the hawthorn poisoning. The word came out like a grunt.

But that was enough for her mother. She looked at Shay, then looked at the window. Immediately she turned back to Martin. "I want you out of here. Now! Or I'll call the *New York Times*. Or, even better, your good friend Oprah."

"This isn't over," Martin growled. But he obeyed, the door slamming shut behind him. Shay's mother grabbed a kitchen chair and wedged it under the knob.

"At least you didn't get much hawthorn," she murmured as she knelt by Shay. "Only skin exposure. The paralysis shouldn't last too long." She wrapped her arm around Shay's waist and hauled her to her feet. Shay tried to speak again, to explain what she needed.

The words wouldn't come out clearly, but as she almost always did, Mom understood. "Your death sleep is coming. Don't worry. I'll get you into bed and close the shades and curtains."

Relief flooded through Shay. She tried to send it on to Gabriel, even though she could barely feel him anymore. She wanted to keep their communion. She didn't know how she felt about him. He'd killed her father. He'd saved her life. All Shay knew for sure was that she wasn't willing to let him go, not yet.

The sun pressed so heavily on her that Shay stumbled on the way upstairs. But Mom held her up, and Shay didn't feel any sense of panic about the death sleep approaching. Her mother would take care of her. It was incredibly comforting and familiar to have her mom helping her into bed. She'd done it so often when Shay's body had failed her. Shay wished she could at least say thank you, but she was still having trouble forming intelligible words, and now the sun was draining all her energy.

Shay lay still and watched through heavy eyelids as Mom lowered the shades, then closed the curtains over them, checking to make sure that no light could leak around the edges. Had she done this for Sam when it was time for his death sleep?

"You're safe, baby," her mother said as she sat down on the edge of Shay's bed. She brushed Shay's hair out of her face. "Are you hungry?"

Shay was too weak to nod, but her gaze automatically went to her mom's throat. She couldn't help it. Her body demanded blood.

Mom just nodded. She stretched out next to Shay and wrapped

one arm around Shay's shoulder. She coaxed Shay's head down to her throat. "Drink."

Shay didn't try to resist. She was hungry, always hungry. As gently as she could, she began to drink, feeling strength flow into her with her mother's blood.

Mom continued to run her fingers through Shay's hair as Shay fed. "You're home," she said again and again, soft and sweet as a lullaby.

Shay closed her eyes, allowing herself to feel safe and relaxed for the first time in days. The sun's warmth stole into her mind, but it wasn't a threat this time. More like a warm blanket cuddling her as she drifted off to sleep. Everything was all right. Finally.

Agony.

Shay's eyes snapped open, and she jerked away from her mother. Pure pain—physical, emotional—shot through her, filling her with anguish beyond anything she'd ever known.

Gabriel. It's Gabriel's pain. Our communion is still there, she thought.

Shay moaned, almost sick with the intensity of the feeling. Gabriel was awash with hopelessness and despair. It felt as if he'd just lost everything in the world he cared about.

I've got to help him, Shay thought.

But then the sun came up, and she was helpless.

THIRTEEN

○ ○ ○ ○ ○ ○ ○ ○ ○ ○ ○ ○ ○ ○ ○ ○

GABRIEL FLOATED BACK into consciousness. The sun had gone down. He wished he could see it one last time. It would be a better way to die than this, lying here chained in the cellar. He stretched as much as he could with wrists and ankles shackled to the stakes planted deep in the ground.

Immediately, he searched the communion for Shay. He felt his family's communion—Millie's sorrow and panic, and Tamara's fury and hot anticipation of the ritual that would continue later that night. He felt Luis's numbness and resignation. But Shay ... Where was she? Last night, close to dawn, their bond had almost been severed.

The sensation of Shay slipping away from him had sliced through the pain of his blood being stolen from his body. In that last hour before dawn, he'd fought to keep their communion tight and he'd thought . . . it had felt as if she was trying to keep the communion too.

That had to be a delusion, something his brain had conjured up to give him comfort. Shay wouldn't want to be connected with Gabriel. Not now that she knew he was responsible for Sam's death. She hated him.

And last night he'd confirmed for himself that his father did too. If it wasn't hatred, then Ernst would have protested when Gabriel said those words, when he forced himself to say aloud that Ernst hated him. Ernst hadn't protested. He hadn't replied at all. It had been like a bomb going off in Gabriel's chest. His guardian, his mentor, his friend, his *father* hated him. Gabriel had succumbed to the death sleep with that truth filling every cell of his body.

They had lived together for four hundred years. Even after everything Ernst had done to him, to Sam, to Shay, Gabriel still wished for his father's love.

He continued reaching for Shay through the communion. If what he'd felt from her last night was a delusion—and how could it be anything else?—he wanted it again, a sweet drug to ease him through this night and the next. Then he'd be free, free of guilt and shame, free of having betrayed and being betrayed by others, free of the world. Dead. That was still what he wanted. There was nothing left for him in this life.

Shay.

Gabriel drew in a deep breath, relieved. He could feel her, faintly but definitely. Was it his imagination? Could his brain really create this feeling of Shay with such accuracy? Or was it truly her? Gabriel decided to let himself believe he had found her. He focused his entire being on what he could feel from her through their communion.

She was safe. He savored that emotion. She had found a secure place to undergo the death sleep, and she'd fed recently. Shay was hungry, all new vampires were hungry, but the craving for blood wasn't tearing at her. She was in control.

What happened to our communion last night? he wondered. *Why did it almost break?*

Gabriel promised himself he'd be vigilant. He had no reason to think that concentrating on her would strengthen their connection. But it certainly couldn't hurt. His communion with Shay would end forever tomorrow night. While he still had it, though, he wouldn't let his attention wander even for an instant. He played memories of Shay over and over again in his mind, the way a simple touch of her lips had set his entire body on fire when they first kissed, and that moment when he realized he loved her, just as she was being dragged away from him.

When he died, his love for Shay would live on. He was sure of it.

He lived in those memories and in the communion with Shay until the soft sound of footsteps pulled him back to the cellar and the second night of the blood ritual. Gabriel raised his head as much as he could, so he could watch his family return to the circle. Tamara glared back at him, running the tip of her tongue over her lips as if tasting his blood already. Luis kept his eyes straight ahead as he walked over to his position, and Millie didn't look up from the ground as she took hers. Ernst didn't avoid Gabriel's gaze, but his steely eyes told Gabriel nothing of how he felt.

It doesn't matter. I know how he feels—he detests me and blames me for Richard's death. Maybe it was a kindness that Ernst showed so little emotion, a kindness that their communion had been shattered by the hawthorn dart.

"Tonight we act as one," Ernst announced. "That is because in all the ways that matter, we are one. Our lives are so tightly bound together that what is good for one is good for the entire family, and that which threatens one, threatens the entire family. Tonight we continue to take the blood, and the life, of Gabriel, who was once family but is now a stranger who brings danger to us all."

Gabriel let his head fall back onto the ground. A stranger. He might be many things, including a threat to his family, but he could never be a stranger to those gathered around him, much as they might wish he were.

"We will again drink in the order of youngest to oldest," Ernst continued. "You may not be able to withstand as much of the poison blood as you did last night. Take only as much as you are able. This will be the last night you drink deep. Tomorrow night I will finish this, while the rest of you stand witness, until the end. Then together we will take the last drops, sharing the responsibility among us."

This time Millie did not wait for Ernst to call her name, although her footsteps were slow and reluctant as she approached Gabriel. His eyes sought hers, but he didn't try to pick her emotions from the communion. He was concentrating on Shay, only Shay.

Then, suddenly, he heard Millie moving away, rushing toward Ernst.

"I can't do this again," she cried, her voice quavering. "I can't!"

Luis put an arm around her shoulders. "It's okay. It'll all be over soon."

"We're all here with you, Millie," Ernst told her. "I know it's hard, and that's why it's something we do as a family."

"Family?" Millie exclaimed bitterly. "Gabriel was right when he said if we were truly a family, we would have accepted Shay."

"I don't want to hear that name," Ernst warned her.

Tamara jumped in. "If Gabriel cared about his family the way he should have, he would have fought by Richard's side, as a brother should."

"Richard should have stood by his side, too!" Millie insisted. "That's what we're supposed to do. When Gabriel fell in love, we should have shared his joy. Instead, Richard mocked him and hated him for it. We all did."

"Millie—," Ernst began.

"No! If being a part of this family means vengeance and hatred and anger, then I don't want to be in this family."

Gabriel was shocked by her words, by her empathy and bravery. Millie had done what no one had done for Sam. No one had seen Sam's side. Every member of the family, none more than Gabriel, had believed Sam's death was just and necessary.

There was a clatter as Millie ran up the cellar steps. Out of the corner of his eye, Gabriel saw Luis start after her. "No," Ernst told him. "I'll do it."

But first he stepped up to Gabriel's side and stared down at him. "I thought you'd damaged our family as much as was possible. But you continue to destroy us."

"Not me. You." Gabriel wondered why he'd never realized it

before. "I brought a new member to our family. Someone who would have made us stronger and better. You turned her away. It's you who are destroying us, Ernst."

Ernst didn't reply. He signaled for Luis to come and drink, and Luis obeyed.

He loves me. Gabriel loves me. That's true. I can feel it in every bone, every inch of skin. I can feel it deep in my heart, and even deeper in his soul. I can't feel much from him through the communion; Martin's dose of hawthorn almost ripped it apart. But I can feel Gabriel's love.

What do I do with that? He betrayed my father—his own best friend. How many visions did I have of Gabriel with Sam, loving Sam? He thought of Sam as his brother, and still he told Ernst that Sam was going to marry my mom. What did he think Ernst would do? Did he know the punishment for loving a human was death? Because in my vision, Gabriel didn't seem too surprised. And he helped carry it out—he drank Sam's blood. He killed him.

That's all I need to know, right? Gabriel killed my dad. End of story.

But I can't unknow him. He said that to me once. That he had tried to keep from thinking of me as Shay, and to only think of me as "the human girl"—so that he wouldn't feel anything for me. Because I'm human and he's supposed to hate humans, all of them. But he had spent time with me, he knew who I really was. And he couldn't go backward. He couldn't unknow me.

And I can't unknow him. The Gabriel I loved was sensitive and loyal and funny and brave. He suffered a terrible trauma at the hands of human beings, and that's why he hated them—us. I understand that. And he loves his family more than anything. I get that, too. I can't help it, I can't go backward. I fell in love with him. How can I turn off that kind of feeling? No matter what he did in the past, he's still the guy I knew.

But still, to kill a person you love? Your own brother?

It seems unforgivable. Monstrous.

I guess that is all I need to know. My father would still be alive if it wasn't for Gabriel. I'd have a father. I'd always have had a father.

Shay lifted her pen. It felt good to have her actual journal back again. But it wasn't really helping her figure out her emotions. He loved her. But he killed her father. He loved her. But he killed her father. On and on and on, the same argument marched through her brain.

She glanced over at her bed. Her mother lay there, sleeping. She'd stayed up with Shay until about three, then finally dropped off. If she was dreaming, the dream had to be nice. Her forehead was smooth, her lips curved into the beginning of a smile. *Is she dreaming about Sam?* Shay wondered. She hoped so. With all the badness that had happened, at least there was that—Mom had gotten her love back.

How could Gabriel have thought the love between my mother and father was dangerous to his family?

I know the answer. I don't like it, but I know. He thought we were all the same, humans. He thought we were all like those people who slaughtered his family. Ernst thought that too, and so did all the other vampires I saw in Tennessee.

Well, except maybe Millie.

But if you think that, then you think any human who knows of the existence of vampires will automatically want to kill you. Gabriel thought my mother would want to kill him. Kill his family. So in a way, he was acting in self-defense.

He'd never had the chance to know a human, not until me. And then he saw, he really saw, that we aren't all the same. He changed. He let go of his fear and prejudice. He couldn't have fallen in love with me if he didn't.

A sudden blast of vertigo hit her, and the pen slid out of Shay's hand. The room spun and dizziness churned through her—dizziness from Gabriel.

Shay grabbed on to the edge of her desk and dug her fingers into the wood. She forced herself to look at her bedroom and realize that the walls weren't moving. It wasn't her feeling. She wasn't sick and woozy. It was Gabriel.

"I thought he was getting better," she murmured. Ever since she woke from the death sleep tonight, she'd felt love coming through their tenuous communion, but not pain or dizziness.

A jolt of hot agony ripped through her, so strong that it made her gasp. Shay groaned and put her forehead down on the desk, just trying to breathe through the pain. What was happening to him?

My communion with Gabriel is weak, and this is still almost unbearable, she thought. *How must it feel to him, experiencing it firsthand?*

"Shay? Are you okay, sweetie?"

Shay gripped the desk with both hands as another bolt of searing anguish attacked her. "Yeah," she mumbled.

"No, you're not." Her mother jumped off the bed and rushed to Shay's side. "Do you need to feed? What's wrong?"

"Not me. It's Gabriel," Shay managed to say. "Something horrible is happening to him. I thought he was getting better, but he's worse."

"The communion," Mom breathed. "Sam told me everyone in his family was connected through the communion, but I didn't imagine it was so powerful."

"It's weaker than usual," Shay answered. "The hawthorn almost destroyed it. For me to feel so much pain, Gabriel has to be in agony." She wrapped her arms around herself, as if that would help control the waves of dizziness.

"Maybe we could put just another drop on your skin," her mom suggested. "I don't want you suffering like this. We need to break the tie between the two of you."

"No!" Shay cried. She knew she should want the communion broken, but the thought made her feel cold and empty.

"But you said Sam's family killed him. That means Gabriel . . ." Her mother let her words trail off.

"He was there. He . . . he helped," Shay admitted, but she couldn't bring herself to say that Gabriel had been the one who had exposed Sam's relationship with a human. "I don't even know how I'm supposed to feel now. Gabriel saved my life. But he helped kill my father. But then he saved me by transforming me."

Her mom gazed at her for a long moment. "I can see why you're confused," she finally said. "Right now what you need to do is take care of yourself. You've been through so much, Shay. You need time to recover and to learn how to deal with . . . what you are."

"There is no time!" Shay cried as another blast of pain hit her. "He's dying."

"What?" Mom said. "Why would you think that?"

"I feel it." Shay's hand flew to her mouth. "Oh my God. They're killing him. That's what it is—the devastation he felt, the misery, and now the pain."

Her mother's brow was furrowed in confusion. "Who's killing him? Why?"

"I can't believe it took me so long to realize this," Shay said. "It's Ernst. His family. They're killing him because of me! Because he loves me. He tried to bring a human into the family. It's just like it was with Sam. . . ."

"But you're not human anymore," Mom said.

"They *hated* me. They called me an abomination," Shay told her. "And then Martin showed up. It was just like before, when humans massacred their family in Greece. Martin was there to kill them all—except for the one specimen he took to run experiments on."

She leaped to her feet, then had to stand perfectly still for a moment to battle the nausea. *I've got to get to Gabriel.*

Except she didn't know where he was. The vampires wouldn't still be at the research facility, not now that Martin had discovered its location. Shay sank down onto the floor. Her mother crouched next to her. "What, baby?"

"I have no idea where he is," Shay said.

"What would you do if you did?" her mother asked, brushing Shay's hair away from her face. "I know you're stronger now, much stronger. But you're not strong enough to go up against Gabriel's whole family."

Shay pushed her mom's hand away. "So I'm just supposed to let him die?"

Her mother sighed. "Shay, it's not a matter of you *letting* him die or not die. You don't have any control over it. Like you said, you don't even know where he is."

"And you're happy about that!" Shay accused her.

A moment of hesitation told Shay all she needed to know.

"See, you can't even pretend you're not," Shay snapped. "You still don't think of him as a person—not even after what you found out about my father."

"I *am* happy about it," her mom said, anger creeping into her voice. "He took Sam from me. From *you*. Don't you think he deserves to die for that?"

"But they're doing the same thing to him that they did to Sam. If it was wrong then, it's wrong now," Shay protested. And as she said the words, she felt the deep truth of them. It wasn't right of Gabriel's family to kill him for falling in love with her.

"I can't be expected to care what happens to the creature who destroyed my life," her mother shot back.

"Creature! Creature?" Shay cried. "Is that how you thought of my father? Is that how you think of me?"

"Of course not. You're you. And Sam wasn't the same as those other ones. Look at how they treat one another. They say they're a family, but they go around murdering each other," Mom said. "Everything about that family is selfish and always has been! They took children just because—"

"You keep saying 'they.' Like all vampires are the same," Shay cut her off.

"No. You're different," her mother protested. "Your father was—"

"We're all different," Shay insisted. "Just like humans are all different. You can't lump us together. I thought you understood that when you were talking to Martin, but obviously, you don't. You're willing to let Gabriel die for loving me, because you think he's a creature, just some evil thing."

"Shay, why are we arguing about this? There's nothing we can do. What's going to happen is going to happen, no matter how either of us feels about it." Her mother sounded frustrated, but it was nothing compared to Shay's anger.

"Will you please just leave me alone? Please," Shay burst out. She couldn't stand to hear Mom say one more time how powerless Shay was. Gabriel's pain was still there, getting worse.

"I have nothing else to say anyway." Shay could tell from her mother's tone that she was hurt, but Shay didn't care. She was relieved when Mom left the room, shutting the door behind her with a gentle click.

Shay stretched out on her back on the carpet and closed her eyes. Gabriel's vertigo was so overwhelming that she had a hard time separating herself from it. She needed to think. There had to be some way she could help. She focused all her attention on the communion for a moment, trying to feel as close to Gabriel as she possibly could. If she couldn't find him, she could still be with him. She wasn't going to let him be alone as they drained the life from him.

She concentrated on the image of his face: his chestnut eyes that seemed to be able to see deep inside her; his beautiful lips, so perfectly full; the straight slash of his eyebrows; the sharp angles of his cheekbones.

Yeah, he was gorgeous, but that was just a tiny part of him. She thought about the way they could have philosophical discussions, how much he loved his family, how his hands felt as they moved over her body, and how the way he saw her had changed the way she saw herself. With Gabriel, she'd never been the sick girl, even when she could feel her body's deterioration accelerate.

I'm with you, Gabriel. You aren't alone, she thought.

The dizziness subsided for a brief moment, and a sense of comfort seeped through their communion.

And then pain again. Anguish. So strong, so awful . . .

Shay's eyes snapped open. The pain was coming from her right. She sat up, following the feeling, letting it draw her forward. "Gabriel?" she whispered.

Love. Guilt. Agony.

His emotions. And they were all coming from the same place, from the same direction. Shay closed her eyes and felt it, just as she would've been able to feel the warmth of the sun on her cheek.

"'I can sense where they are,'" Shay breathed, suddenly remembering what Gabriel had said back before they went to Tennessee. He was still recovering from drinking her blood. They'd been in a motel and he could barely move, so they had spent the whole night talking. He told her about a link to his family, how he knew if they were in trouble . . . and how he could sense where they were. They'd talked about so much that night—about him being a vampire, about her being the sick girl—that she'd almost forgotten about that detail.

"Mom!" she yelled. "Mom!"

Her mother burst through the door, eyes wild. "What? Are you okay?"

"The communion. It tells me how to find Gabriel," Shay blurted, her words falling over each other. "I can follow his emotions if they're strong enough. He told me that once, but I just now remembered."

Shay ran to her window and stared outside at the barren tree branches. That way. All of Gabriel's feelings came from that direction.

She could find him. She could help him. Shay hoped he was feeling her exhilaration as powerfully as she was feeling his physical weakness.

"Shay—"

"He's west. That way." Shay pointed out her window. "I don't know where exactly, but it's definitely west of here. I can follow it, follow his emotions like a . . . like a dog on a trail, I guess." She laughed at the image, giddy with relief.

"West." Mom's voice sounded skeptical.

"I need to borrow the car," Shay said. Earlier that night, she and her mother had abandoned the car she'd stolen in a not-great part of town. Keys in the ignition, fingerprints wiped off. Shay hoped the owner's insurance would pay up fast.

"You're not going anywhere," her mother said firmly. "I understand how you feel. But I'm not letting you put yourself in danger. Not after I just got you back." As if Shay were still a little girl. A little sick girl.

"I don't need your permission," Shay told her. "If you won't loan me the Mercedes, I'll find another car."

"Steal one, you mean," her mother snapped.

"If I have to," Shay shot back. "Stealing or letting someone die because he cares about me." She made scales with her hands, balancing them up and down. "Not hard to decide which matters more. So can I have the car or not?"

"No! It's almost dawn. You'll be going into your death sleep. If you're out on the road when that happens, you'll crash. Or the sun will . . ." Her mother shook her head. "You have to start thinking, Shay."

Shay frowned, wanting to fight. But Mom was right. The sun was coming. Shay had been so distracted by the communion that she hadn't noticed the growing pressure.

"I have to get to Gabriel," she said, even as she felt the beginnings of the death sleep pull at her.

"We'll talk about it tomorrow night," her mother promised. "Let's get you to the bed."

"Tomorrow night—" She didn't have the energy to speak. The death sleep consumed her. *Tomorrow night will be too late*, she thought as her vision went dark.

FOURTEEN

○ ○ ○ ○ ○ ○ ○ ○ ○ ○ ○ ○ ○ ○ ○ ○

THE GROUND TREMBLED underneath her. That was the first thing Shay became aware of as she awoke from her death sleep.

What was—

Gabriel! Memories of the last moments before dawn raced back into her mind, driving out everything else, any other questions. They were going to kill Gabriel. And there was no way she'd be able to get to him in time to save him.

Her eyes snapped open as she jerked into a sitting position. The ground still trembled, and she felt motion. Shay shook her head, disoriented. She was in a small, dark . . . not room. *Car.* She was in the backseat of a car with the windows blacked out and a heavy board separating her from the front seat.

Her vampire vision didn't give her much help, because there wasn't much to see, but Shay was pretty sure the car was her mom's immaculate Mercedes. She twisted around and pounded on the board with both fists. It cracked instantly, and Shay jerked her hands back. She really had to try to remember how powerful she was.

"Hang on, Shay. Give me a minute. I'm pulling over," her mother called. "No more knocking. We're going to need that board tomorrow night. I hope." She muttered the last two words, but Shay had no problem hearing them.

The car slowed, veered left, then came to a stop. Her mother yanked free the board that separated the front and back seats. "You did say west, right?" she asked, with a small smile. The smile widened to a grin in response to the expression on Shay's face.

Shay scrambled into the front seat next to her mother and gave her a smacking kiss on the cheek. "I love you, you know that?" she asked as her mother began to drive again.

"I actually do," Mom said. "There are some bags of blood in the mini-cooler."

Shay pulled one out and began to drink. "How did you—"

"I know my way around a hospital, remember?" her mother asked.

"But why?" Shay narrowed her eyes. "I didn't expect you to help."

Her mother sighed. "After you fell asleep, I couldn't stop thinking about something Sam told me once. About his mother, his vampire mother, Gret. She'd been dead for ages, but he never stopped missing her."

Shay's hand went to the locket around her neck. Gret's locket.

"Sam said that Gret always chose love and forgiveness, while his father—"

"Ernst," Shay said.

Mom nodded. "Ernst tended to choose anger. Sam lived his life trying to be like Gret. That's what he said." Shay's mom reached over and took her hand. "And you, you're just like your father. You think the way he did. The reason he was able to fall in love with me was because he didn't see all humans as being like the ones who had hurt him. He saw humans as individuals. And he died for it. I couldn't let that happen again."

Her mother's words gave her more strength than the blood entering her body. Mom understood. She really got it.

That joyful thought was followed by a deeply disturbing one. It was incredible that Mom had decided to help. But Gabriel's family hated her mother, maybe even more than they hated Shay. They saw her mom as the cause of Sam's death.

"Let's find a motel for you," Shay said. "I can take it from here, now that it's dark. I'll pick you up on my way home." *If I survive,* she silently added.

Her mother shook her head. "I'm getting you where you have to go."

Shay didn't have time for a big argument. "Okay, but that's it. You get me close, and I do the rest."

"By the way, I don't really know where we're going," her mother told her, not agreeing or disagreeing with Shay's statement. "I hope you do."

"Let's stop for a minute. I need to concentrate on Gabriel and see if I can feel the way. I'm still new at this vampire stuff. I'm not sure if my vampire GPS was telling me to go west for three miles or three hundred."

"We'll, I've been driving since about noon, so let's hope we weren't just supposed to head to the end of our block," her mom said. She pulled over on the shoulder of the highway.

Shay climbed out, wanting to smell the air, to see the moon. None of it would help her find Gabriel, but somehow she felt better being outside. "Please let this work," she murmured.

She stood facing the scrub trees that lined the edges of Interstate 80. She smelled raccoons in the woods, pine needles, and a lot of car exhaust. If she concentrated, she could hear voices from the houses in the development on the other side of the woods. She was tired. Exhausted, even though she'd just awoken.

I need Gabriel's feelings, not my own, she thought. *I've got to get to Gabriel.*

She bit her lip, hard, trying to block out the flood of sensations that filled her with every breath. Her own vampire senses were still a little overwhelming. And the emotions coming from Gabriel were weak.

"There!" she gasped. She'd hardly even registered the fact that she was feeling him. Gabriel's fatigue seeped through her, and she suddenly understood why she felt so tired—or rather, she realized that she didn't feel tired. He did.

He's almost dead.

Shay focused on the weakness, because that was Gabriel. She blocked out her own feelings and concentrated on him. Love. Still love. And sadness. "Resignation," she whispered. That was the word for it. Gabriel was resigned to dying.

"Fight it," she told him, as if he could hear. "It'll make it a hell of a lot easier to track your feelings if they're stronger."

She jogged back to the Mercedes and climbed inside.

"We're going the right way," she said shakily. "I feel him, and I think I can keep feeling him as we drive. I'm hoping I'll know if we start to go in the wrong direction. It's not as if I can get a picture on a map, I just have to follow the emotion. I don't know how far away we are."

Her mother nodded and pulled back out onto the road. They drove for a moment in silence. Outside, the highway whipped by in the dark, punctuated by a strip mall here and there. It reminded Shay of driving with Gabriel, back when he was holding her captive, driving through the night toward his family.

That wasn't a good memory. She'd hated him during that drive. Shay pushed the memory away. She didn't want to send negative emotions to Gabriel, not when he was so weak.

"So he's alive?" her mother asked after a moment.

"Yes." Gabriel wasn't in pain, at least not right now. That made Shay feel better. And he was still pulsing out love—love for her, she was sure of it—although she could feel panic shimmering around the edges. *I'm coming,* she thought. *I'll be there in time, I promise.*

"I guess they weren't killing him, then," Mom said. "Or he'd be dead."

"They don't do it quickly," Shay replied, not wanting to tell her mother too much about the horrible way Sam had died. She felt sure they were killing Gabriel the same way. "It's a ritual."

"Oh." Her mother began to knead the steering wheel with her fingernails. Shay knew she was thinking about Sam.

"How'd you even think to do all this?" she asked, trying to take Mom's mind off it. "The windows and the barrier?"

Her mother glanced at her in surprise, and then she laughed. "I used to date a vampire, remember?" she said. Shay heard her mother's heart beat a little faster, and the scent of blood grew a little stronger as her mother blushed. "Where do you think you were conceived, anyway?"

"Oh, that is just TMI," Shay cried, covering her ears in mock horror. But she laughed too. For so many years, when Shay was so sick that she could hardly ever make it to school, her mom had been pretty much her best friend. Shay had lost that feeling somewhere along the way. It had gotten buried in the resentment of her mother trying to control her—even if the control had been all about wanting to keep her alive longer. But now that best-friend feeling was back.

"So what's the plan, besides getting there?" her mother asked. She ripped open a bag of BBQ-flavored corn nuts and dumped some directly into her mouth.

"The plan is to stop the other vampires from killing Gabriel," Shay told her. "That's the only plan I've got."

Shay stared out into the darkness, her gaze reaching for miles. *I'm on the way*, she thought. And she wasn't a dying little girl, the way she'd been last time she'd faced his family. She was a vampire too.

A vampire who would be outnumbered four to one. Shay had no clue what she should do when they reached the vampires, but she was leaving with Gabriel. Either that, or they'd have to kill her.

◆ ◆ ◆

It was time. They were coming. To drink the rest of the life out of him. Gabriel hadn't cared before. He'd wanted it. He'd wanted the release and sweet oblivion of death because he didn't believe there was anything to live for.

But now . . . Shay. Something had changed in her emotions. There was worry, fear even. She'd been afraid on and off ever since she became a vampire, but this was different. She wasn't afraid of something that was happening in her life. She was afraid for *him*. Gabriel could tell the difference—there was a tinge of horror along with the worry, and a strong sense of urgency. She didn't hate him. She was worried about him.

It wasn't much, but it was enough to make Gabriel want, suddenly, to live.

Gabriel strained against the bindings that held him to the ground. His arms and legs trembled with the effort. There was no escaping. There was no hope for survival.

And they were coming in. Ernst leading the way into the scorched circle. *No Millie*, Gabriel realized. Fear for her rippled through him. What price would she have to pay for standing against Ernst on his behalf? He searched the family's communion for her. The mix of grief, anxiety, and fear he found didn't tell him anything other than that she lived. Were they holding her prisoner?

"Tonight this ends," Ernst announced, pulling Gabriel out of his thoughts. "I will drink until I feel his life force begin to flicker. Then we will all drink together, sharing in the moment of Gabriel's death."

"All?" Tamara asked. "I don't see Millie. She's still a part of this family, isn't she?"

So angry. Was she always this angry, and being with Richard just calmed her? Gabriel wondered. Ever since his death, Tamara had been filled with rage. Most of her fury was directed at him, but now it spewed toward Millie, too.

"If Millie doesn't drink tonight, she is no longer one of us," Ernst replied. "It will be a hard life for her on her own, but the decision is hers."

First Sam, then Richard, then me . . . now Millie, Gabriel thought. *The entire family will be gone before Ernst realizes the error of his ways.*

Gabriel's stomach clenched as he heard his father walk toward him. Ernst didn't immediately kneel down. Instead, he stood over Gabriel, staring at him. *What is he thinking?* Gabriel was simultaneously frustrated by and grateful for the fact that Ernst's connection to the communion had been severed. He was curious about what Ernst was feeling, but he also didn't want to spend the last hours of his life awash in the hatred of his father.

Ernst continued to stare at him, looking down into Gabriel's face. Gabriel forced himself to hold his father's gaze as the seconds ticked away, away, away. "What are you wai—," Tamara began, but Luis shushed her before she could finish.

Why the hesitation? Gabriel knew how deeply Ernst believed that any threat to the family must be eliminated. He'd believed it just as passionately once, fervently enough to take Sam's life.

Finally, Ernst dropped to his knees, landing heavily. "Gabriel," he said in a whisper. Then, fast as a snake strike, his eyeteeth bit into Gabriel's throat. Gabriel's blood went molten as it sped through his veins into Ernst's waiting mouth.

Memories of his life flickered through Gabriel's mind, and Ernst was a huge part of almost all of them. Many of the memories were good, but now they brought only pain. Gabriel loved Ernst, even now, even after what Ernst had done to Shay, even after Ernst had handed down a death sentence to him. And Ernst was killing him.

Gabriel was hyper-aware of each vein, each artery, each capillary. They were all throbbing. It was as if they were trying to cling to his blood. Trying uselessly.

I'm dissolving, Gabriel thought woozily. The ground began to do a slow spin underneath him, increasing his dizziness. Then he was free. He'd slid out of his body and was now hovering near the wooden beams of the ceiling.

He could see his body below him, bound to the dirt floor of the cellar. The body spasmed as Ernst continued to drink. Gabriel couldn't see Ernst's face—it was still buried in the throat of his body. His body. That thing down there. It didn't feel like it belonged to him anymore.

Gabriel wondered if he could just leave it behind. Float up, and up, and up, out of the room—and to Shay. All he wanted was to be with Shay.

Ernst raised his lips. A crimson streak ran from one corner of his mouth. "It's time. Luis, Tamara, join me in taking the last of his lifeblood."

"Slow down," Shay told her mom. "Gabriel's close."

And he was dying. There was almost nothing left of him in their communion. But love was still there, his love for her. Shay didn't want to think about what it meant. She wasn't trying to save Gabriel out of love. She was doing it because it was the right thing to do.

But she was following his love for her. Following it right to him.

Quickly, she finished the remaining blood from the cooler. She would need all her strength and power now.

A sudden spur of pain hit her, making Shay want to yell at her mother to go faster. But that wouldn't help. They had been winding their way along narrow country roads for the past hour, pulled this way and that by Shay's communion. She had stopped doubting it now, though. She was certain they were going toward Gabriel. His presence in her mind grew stronger with each mile they covered.

Shay's mother brought the Mercedes to a creep on the curving dirt road lined with pine trees. The road was so narrow, and the tree branches so long, that it was like driving through a tunnel. Even during the day, Shay couldn't imagine that much light made its way down.

As they rounded the corner, Shay put her hand on her mom's arm. "Stop. That has to be it." About three hundred feet away was an old wooden farmhouse. The feelings she was getting from Gabriel emanated from inside. She was sure of it. "Wait here while I go check it out." Shay climbed out of the car. So did her mother.

"Mom, no!" Shay whispered.

"You don't have a plan, not a real one. Which means you might need me," her mother said.

"But you're not—"

"I'm not letting you go in there alone is what I'm not," Mom replied. "I told you, I'm not losing you. I just got you back."

This was insane. What was her mother going to do against even one vampire? She had no way to fight or even protect herself. She didn't realize how much they hated her. She—

Shay realized that her mother had started walking toward the house. She quickly caught up to her and took her arm. But the soft sound of a footstep on pine needles caught her attention. Shay whirled toward it. Someone was out here with them!

"Please wait here for just one second, Mom. Just please, okay?" Shay begged. Then she darted between two of the pine trees and into the woods. With her sharp eyes, the darkness wasn't a problem, but she didn't see anyone, not even in the distance. She took a tentative step forward. *Crack.*

The sound of a twig snapping was loud in the quiet of the woods. She looked up and saw Millie perched on one of the branches of a nearby tree. Their eyes locked, then Millie leaped toward her, the motion more like flying than jumping. She landed a few feet in front of Shay.

This is good, Shay told herself. *I won't have to fight them all together.* She crouched down, tightening her hands into fists. God, she had all this strength, but no experience. She'd never been in a fight. Wasn't there something about where you were supposed to put your thumb when you made a fist? Kaz used to tell her about it . . . but was it on the inside or the outside? No time.

Shay hurled herself at Millie, aiming for her knees. That should knock her to the ground.

Instead, Millie grabbed Shay before Shay even managed to touch her and spun her around, locking her hands behind her back.

"I'm going to Gabriel. You can't stop me," Shay threatened as Millie held her powerless.

"Fine. I'll get some blood. If you manage to save him—and, honestly, I don't think it's possible—he'll need it," Millie answered calmly. She released Shay's hands.

Shay turned to face her, stunned. "Why would you help me?"

"I don't want him to die," Millie said simply. "I don't want to lose another brother just because he fell in love with someone Ernst doesn't approve of." Her body stiffened, her eyes taking on a faraway look. "You've got to hurry if you're going to do this at all."

Shay realized that almost nothing was coming through the communion from Gabriel. Was he dead? "Where?"

"Cellar," Millie told her. "Luis, Tamara, and Ernst. I don't know how you're—"

Shay didn't wait for her to finish. She raced toward the house, veering back over to the road because it was even faster.

"Shay!" she heard her mother cry.

"You stay there," Shay barked at her.

She charged up the porch steps. The door was locked. Not a problem. She stepped back a few paces, then kicked it next to the lock, just as she'd done back at the lab in Tennessee. It worked better this time—she only had to do it once, and she was in.

Shay scanned the room. No stairs. Probably in the kitchen. She found it easily, and—yes!—a door opened to a set of wooden stairs. She clambered down them, taking them three and four at a time, with no idea of what to do when she reached the bottom.

She skidded to a stop when she reached the earthen floor, what she saw freezing her in place. Gabriel, naked, staked to the ground. Ernst drinking from his throat. Luis drinking from his left arm. Tamara drinking from his belly.

"Stop!" she shrieked. All three feeding vampires lifted their heads. For the first time, Shay had a good view of Gabriel's face. His beautiful eyes were open, but they weren't chestnut brown anymore. They'd turned almost entirely purple, and they were glazed, staring blankly up at the ceiling. A small smile played about the corners of his lips. She couldn't tell if he was alive or already dead.

"You shouldn't have come here," Ernst told her. Tamara and Luis rose to their feet. Ernst stayed in his position at Gabriel's side. "What did you think would happen, you foolish little girl?"

"I don't care," Shay snarled. "I don't want to be alive without him, and I'm not going to stand here and watch you kill him." *Yeah, good plan*, she thought as Ernst sneered. But if she and Mom had delayed even a few minutes longer to gather hawthorn or other weapons, they would have been too late.

"Then we'll kill you, too. Richard wouldn't be dead if it wasn't for you," Tamara growled. She seemed eager for more blood.

"No one is killing anyone."

Shay turned to see her mother on the stairs, and her blood ran cold with fear.

The other vampires stiffened, wary. Luis took a step back, away from the human. But Shay's mother ignored them all, her eyes only on Ernst. Shay had never seen her so focused.

"You're Ernst," her mom said as she took her place at Shay's side. "Sam's father. Sam described you well. You—and Gret."

Ernst let out a hiss at the name of his dead love. He rose to his feet and strode toward Shay's mother. Instinctively, Shay moved in front of her, but her mom stepped to the side. She didn't cower from Ernst. She went toward him.

"You have blood on your face," she snapped. "Gabriel's blood. He's your son, and so was Sam. You're stained with your own child's blood."

Ernst gaped at her, stopping in his tracks.

"Gret would hate you for that." Shay's mother lifted her chin and glared at him. "You're killing her children."

"Don't you speak of her! You didn't know her. You can't say what she would feel," Ernst bellowed, his voice tight with anger.

"I didn't have to know her, because Sam did. He told me everything. We told each other everything, before you murdered him," Shay's mom retorted. "I know why you started the family. I know why Gret chose to end her life. How can you kill someone for falling in love with a human when you—"

Ernst let out a growl, his eyes narrowing dangerously.

"When you did the same thing," she continued, raising her voice. "Gret was human when you fell in love with her. She was human when you got her pregnant."

"That's not true!" Tamara burst out. "Ernst would never . . ." Her voice trailed off. Shay knew that Tamara could see the truth on Ernst's face. Just as Shay could. He looked stricken.

"What is she talking about, Ernst?" Luis asked. "You've always said there should be no secrets among any of us in the family."

Shay realized she was holding her breath. Everyone stared at Ernst, even her mother. Shay had never seen Mom so strong before. This small human woman staring down an old and powerful vampire.

Time seemed to stand still.

And then Ernst deflated. His furious expression collapsed into one of grief, and his cold eyes filled with tears. Suddenly, he looked ancient, old and tired. "Gret . . . she lost the baby," he said.

She got to him, Shay thought. *Mom managed to get under his skin.*

"She's telling the truth? There really was a baby?" Luis said, his voice shaking. "A halfblood?"

"An abomination," Tamara put in, staring at Shay.

"It was . . . it was gruesome. There was so much blood," Ernst went on. "The baby was dead. I knew it instantly, though Gret kept calling and calling for it. She was getting weaker, paler. I could see her life draining away."

"So you changed her," Luis said. "Just the way Gabriel changed—" He didn't say Shay's name, just gestured to her.

"Yes," Ernst answered. "I didn't even choose to do it, not exactly. I simply acted. There was no choice to be made."

"But she didn't want it," Shay's mother said. "Sam told me she was haunted, always, until she finally went out into the sun."

"She mourned so deeply for the baby. She . . . she blamed me for giving her life, because it separated them. She would rather have died, so they could move on to heaven together," Ernst said.

He's been thinking about this for centuries, Shay realized. *I think he's almost glad that Mom is calling him on it.*

"I gave her children the only way I knew how," Ernst continued. "We took orphans and raised them in our family. Gret loved me . . . she loved Sam. He was our first son."

Tamara's lip curled with revulsion. "You were in love with a *human.*" It didn't seem as if she had heard anything else.

"Yet you killed Sam," Shay said. "For doing the same thing you did. You killed your own son."

Ernst fell back from her as if she had struck him. "After Gret sought the sun, I needed family more than ever. It was all that mattered to me, that I not lose anyone else I loved."

"You were trying to keep us safe," Luis said, but his eyes went to

Gabriel and his voice shook with emotion. *He doesn't know who is right anymore,* Shay thought.

"By killing his own children? That isn't keeping the family safe," Shay's mother protested. She took another step toward Ernst. "You've twisted your grief into fear and hatred. Gret loved Sam. You murdered him."

Ernst gave a wrenching sob. "You're right. Gret would hate what I've done to Gabriel, what I did to Sam—" His voice broke on the name. "Love was the most important thing to her. She fought to stay with me for as long as she could, out of that love. But her love for the baby was stronger. She wanted to die, to be with our little girl."

"You separated me from my father the same way," Shay said. "By death. I'll never know him. And if you've killed Gabriel, too . . .'"

She turned her back on Ernst. He didn't seem like a threat to her mother anymore. He seemed broken. Her eyes went to Gabriel. So still. That same small smile on his face. She left Ernst behind and went to him, kneeling to remove the chains from his wrists. No one objected. Tamara and Luis were still staring at Ernst.

"You're okay," she whispered. "I'm here." But Gabriel didn't respond.

"Richard was your son too," Tamara said to Ernst. "Have you forgotten his death?"

"He died to save me. It should have been the other way around." Ernst sounded defeated. Devastated. Shay paid no attention. She freed one of Gabriel's hands and took a moment to stroke his cheek before she moved on to the next binding. She didn't notice that

Millie had arrived with the blood until Millie pressed the bag into her hands.

"Is he already . . . ?"

"No." Shay ripped it open with her teeth, then gently parted Gabriel's lips and poured the thick red liquid into his mouth. Most of it spilled back out, staining his pale cheeks. Shay pushed down her fear and tried again.

Gabriel's violet eyes didn't even blink.

Millie put one hand on Shay's shoulder. "I don't feel him anymore."

Shay focused on their communion with every molecule of her being. He was there. Just a whisper of a whisper of him, but there. "I do."

I feel him because of his love, she realized. *He loves me.*

She took some of the blood in her mouth, then leaned down and kissed him, letting the blood run from her body to his. It was as close as she could get to letting him feed from her.

"Shay. It's too late," her mother said. Shay looked up and saw Mom, Ernst, and Luis standing near her. Tamara hovered in the background. She took a step toward them, then backed up.

"He's still here. I can feel him," Shay insisted.

"No. He's gone. I killed him," Ernst said, his face ashen.

Shay shook her head. She gazed at Gabriel's face. There was no flicker of life. No recognition. "Come back to me. I love you, Gabriel. I love you," she told him, realizing it was true. No matter what he'd done, she loved him.

But his face remained expressionless, his body motionless.

Shay swallowed down the lump in her throat. How could she lose him now, when she'd finally figured out how she felt? She wanted to have a life with him, but instead, she faced an eternity of life without him.

Millie let out a sob.

Shay felt numb for a moment. She'd done everything she could, but Gabriel had suffered the same fate as her father. Dying for love. And Gabriel would never even know that she'd come back, that she loved him. He would die thinking she detested him.

"Gabriel," she whispered, leaning down to his ear. There was something Gabriel needed even more than her love. "Can you still hear me? I understand how afraid you were for your family. I know that's why you told Ernst about Sam and my mom. And I forgive you. I forgive you, and I love you so much." She kissed him again.

Tears fell from her eyelashes down onto Gabriel. Tears of absolute joy. He was kissing her back. The movement of his lips was faint, but Gabriel was definitely alive. "Drink," she murmured against his mouth. She pulled away ever so slightly. "I need you to drink all of this." She tipped the blood from the bag into his mouth, and this time his throat spasmed.

"He's taking it," Ernst said. His voice sounded . . . reverent. As if he'd witnessed a miracle.

"And now what?" Tamara demanded, arms crossed. Her voice sounded harsh in the hushed room. "Is she going to bring Richard back from the dead too? And what about that woman?" She jerked her chin toward Shay's mom. "She's the one who started this all. Without her, Richard wouldn't be dead. We'd all still be a family, Richard, Sam, Gabriel, all of us."

"She didn't kill Richard. Gabriel didn't kill Richard. Shay didn't either."

The words stunned Shay. It was the first time Ernst had spoken her name.

"That man did. Martin," Ernst continued, still staring at Gabriel.

"I'm sorry. I'm the one who told him about your kind," Shay's mother said. "I wanted to save Shay. I didn't know what kind of man Martin really was." She turned to Tamara. "I'm sorry."

Tamara hissed in reply. Lightning fast, Luis reached out and grabbed her by the arm. Tamara spun toward him, fighting to free herself.

"You won't attack the human," Luis told her, holding tight. "There will be no more killing here tonight."

Tamara stopped struggling, but her eyes went back to Shay's mother, and they were filled with fury. Luis didn't release her arm, and Shay felt a burst of gratitude toward him.

"That bag is gone," Millie said, pulling Shay's attention back to Gabriel.

As Gabriel drained the bag, Millie handed Shay another one. Gabriel still hadn't registered her presence. She wasn't even sure he saw the room around him. But he was coming back to her with every swallow of the blood.

Gabriel's eyelids fluttered, then closed for a moment. When they opened, he looked at Shay, his eyes clear and filled with love for her. "Shay. I hoped when I died I would get to see you again."

"You aren't dead," Shay told him. "Neither am I."

"I'm sorry," he said weakly. "About Sam. It's the biggest regret of my life."

"I know."

"That was my fault," Ernst put in. "I was the head of the family. I—"

"No." Gabriel tried to push himself into a seated position. Millie had undone the rest of the ties that bound him to the stakes. Still, he had to lie back down. He was too weak to hold himself upright. "I was an adult. I'd been an adult for hundreds of years. It was my responsibility to do what I believed." He reached up and squeezed Millie's hand. "The way you did," he told her.

With his free hand, he ran his fingers down the side of Shay's face, brushing away tears. "And you. You came back for me. After everything."

"I couldn't let the same thing happen again," she said. "Love isn't supposed to be so tragic."

He smiled at her. "You really are so much like Sam. He forgave me too—with his last breath, he told me that."

"My mom—," Shay began.

The sound of footsteps thundering down the stairs interrupted her.

Before Shay could even turn all the way around, Martin barged into the cellar. A trio of huge, unsavory-looking guys came down the steps behind him. Unlike Shay and her mother, they'd come prepared. They each held a tranq gun, and Shay was sure the guns were loaded with hawthorn.

FIFTEEN

○ ○ ○ ○ ○ ○ ○ ○ ○ ○ ○ ○ ○ ○

MARTIN MUST HAVE FOLLOWED ME *and Mom!* Shay thought. She threw her body on top of Gabriel's. Martin wasn't going to get him back. She would not let Gabriel be dragged back to that lab and used as a test subject again.

Pffft! A tranq dart flew over Shay's head, and almost immediately, Millie collapsed in a heap next to Shay and Gabriel. Shay scrambled over to her—positioning herself so that she blocked Gabriel, still so weak, as well as she could. She searched Millie's body for the dart, hoping if she pulled it out fast, Millie wouldn't be completely paralyzed.

Out of the corner of her eye, Shay saw Tamara leap onto the

back of one of Martin's goons and wrap her arm around his neck. *Jerk. Crack.* The man went limp, neck broken. Tamara gave a whoop of triumph.

"Martin, stop this!" Shay's mother screamed.

"Mom, run!" Shay yelled. She found the tranq dart embedded in Millie's thigh and pulled it free. "Just get out of here!"

Instead, her mother ran toward Martin. Tamara ran at him too. She reached him first, fangs bared. Before she could sink them into the flesh of his throat, a tranq dart hit her in the back. She swayed on her feet. Ernst grabbed her before she could topple. He turned to another stairway, one Shay hadn't noticed. In one bound, Ernst was up the steps, Tamara cradled in his arms. He kicked open the door, and a blast of night air hit Shay's vampire senses. Ernst disappeared outside with Tamara.

With vampire speed, Luis went after the goon that had shot Tamara. The third of Martin's men headed for Millie. "Got one down over here!" he shouted. "Taking it to the van."

Nobody's getting taken to the van, Shay thought. As the man leaned down to grab Millie, Shay backhanded him. He flew across the room and hit the wall with a dull thunk.

Shay stared at him for a moment, astonished by her own strength. She was a complete badass. *Pffft!* A tranq dart came whistling toward her. She twisted her body away from the sound, and a second later she heard the dart hit wood.

Ernst approached. Shay hadn't even seen him return to the cellar. There was too much going on, and everything was happening so quickly. He kept his body low to the ground as he scooped Millie up into his arms. "You save Gabriel," he told Shay. "Move fast."

"I can walk," Gabriel said, struggling to his feet. Shay saw tremors rippling through his naked body. A second later his knees buckled, and he would have fallen back to the ground if Shay hadn't wrapped her arm around his waist.

"Lean on me," she ordered. She and Gabriel had only taken two steps after Ernst when she heard Martin shout her name.

She jerked her head toward him. He held her mother pinned tightly against his chest. The third goon was on the ground behind him—dead or unconscious, Shay wasn't sure—and next to the goon lay Luis. The yellow tail of a tranq dart stuck out from his shoulder.

"Time to choose, Shay," Martin told her. "Mommy or the boyfriend." He brought a gun to her mother's head. Not a tranq. A real gun. One that shot bullets.

Shay's body went cold. She looked Martin in the eye, and she knew he'd do it. He would kill her mother.

Ernst had vanished up the steps with Millie. Shay was on her own.

Martin jerked his head toward the closest of the fallen goons. "Take that gun and tranq your vampire or I shoot her now."

"What we did was wrong, Martin," Shay's mother cried before Shay could answer, before she could even *decide* what to answer. "We treated him like an animal. I wanted to pretend he didn't have any emotions, that there was nothing human about him. But I was wrong. We were wrong. We need to let them all go."

"I wasn't wrong," Martin snapped. "What's it going to be, Shay?"

Everything slowed down as Shay stared at the gun to her mother's head. Mom's breathing had been fast and panicked. Now the moments between breaths stretched out . . . out . . . out.

Shay could smell Martin's sweat. A harsh chemical scent clung to him too. From the tranq guns? She wasn't sure.

She heard Ernst's movements outside. He was running, faster than any human ever could. But he wouldn't make it back in time.

Gabriel's body pressed against hers. His muscles tensed as he struggled to stand upright without her support. Shay wrapped her arm more tightly around him. He needed her strength whether he thought so or not.

Click. With that sound, everything felt like it was moving at normal speed again. Martin released the gun's safety. His finger twitched on the trigger.

"Take me!" Gabriel demanded, pulling away from Shay. "Just take me and let's end this."

"No!" Shay's mom reached down to a small metal cylinder hooked to Martin's belt. She stuck one finger through the metal loop at the top of the canister. With her other hand, she held the lever at the back of the canister down. "Enough."

Martin slowly lowered the gun, but he didn't let go of Shay's mother. He kept his face expressionless, but Shay could hear his heart thundering and his breath coming fast. The acrid scent of his sweat grew stronger. He was terrified.

"That's an incendiary grenade. If you pull that—," Martin began.

"If I pull it, the safety pin comes off. Then if I let go of the lever, there will be fifteen seconds until it explodes and sets this whole place on fire."

Shay stared at her mother in shock. When had she become a weapons expert?

Mom's head was lowered, her attention focused on the one finger she had positioned through the metal loop. "I was with you when you were planning Gabriel's capture, remember?"

"So you're going to kill us all?" Martin demanded. "Including Shay? She *can* burn. You know it's one of the few ways she can die."

"So now she's Shay again? You were calling her a monster just the other day," Shay's mom taunted him. "I'm not doing anything that would hurt her. She's a vampire now. In fifteen seconds she can easily get herself and Gabriel to safety. I'll only be killing the two of us."

"Mom, no!" Shay begged.

"Martin and I did some terrible things," her mother replied. "And I'm sorry for them." She looked at Shay, then moved her gaze to Gabriel. "Very sorry. Now you two get out of here."

"I'm not leaving you," Shay cried.

"I want you to have your life. That's what I want more than anything," Mom said.

Shay shook her head, tears blurring her vision.

"Gabriel is going to need your help to get out fast enough." Her mother used the metal loop to pull the safety pin free. "Shay. Go!"

Martin let out a high bleat of panic. He wrenched the grenade off his belt, jerking it away from Shay's mother. Her fingers slipped off the lever. Martin hurled the grenade as hard as he could, then turned and raced for the stairs.

"Run, Mom!" Shay screamed as she heard the grenade hit the far wall and fall to the floor. She hauled Gabriel toward the stairs.

Her mother raced ahead of her, but she was no match for Shay's vampire speed. Still holding Gabriel with one arm, Shay grabbed Mom and *threw* her to the top of the steps—and safety. She might be injured, but she'd be alive.

"Luis!" Gabriel managed to protest.

"I got him out." Ernst stood at the top of the stairs, blocking their exit.

Shay's heart gave a thump of fear—had Ernst changed his mind about letting Gabriel live?

Then Ernst gathered himself and leaped into the air, almost flying over their heads . . . and right into Martin. The velocity of Ernst's body knocked Martin back into the cellar, with Ernst sprawled on top of him.

Ernst twisted his head to look at Shay and Gabriel. "Go!" he shouted. And Shay understood. He was going to hold Martin there until the fire overtook them. He was going to sacrifice his life so she and Gabriel could escape.

"No!" Gabriel cried.

"Go!" Ernst ordered. "And know I love you!"

Shay wrapped both arms around Gabriel. "There's no time left," she shouted. She bent her knees and jumped for the top of the steps, pulling Gabriel with her.

They landed on soft pine needles outside, but Shay didn't linger. Still hauling Gabriel, she took off at a sprint, running faster than a sick girl could ever have dreamed. Her mother had already made it to the tree line.

The explosion came almost immediately.

Shay felt herself and Gabriel flung through the air. They landed in a heap twenty feet away. When they turned back to look at the farmhouse, it was an inferno. Shay prayed that Martin and Ernst were already dead. Escape was impossible.

Shay watched as the house collapsed into the cellar, then turned to Gabriel. His face was twisted with grief.

She didn't know what to say to comfort him. There wasn't anything *to* say. Instead, she held him tight as flying sparks lit up the night.

SIXTEEN

o o o o o o o o o o o o o o o

"I'M NOT SURE THIS IS SOMETHING you want to do," Gabriel said.

"Me either," Shay admitted. They were parked outside Olivia's house, where they'd been sitting for almost an hour. "But I'm going." Still, she didn't get out of the car. She wanted to explain to Olivia. Her best friend had truly come through for her, time after time, even though Shay knew she hadn't deserved it. She'd never appreciated Olivia enough. Now that she did, she was afraid it was too late.

How could she expect her friend to understand? As many times as she'd tried to figure out a way to describe everything that had happened, she hadn't come up with anything that felt even remotely right.

Olivia had seen Shay with her teeth planted in someone's throat. *How does she rationalize that to herself?* Shay wondered for the mil-lionth time. People with a full sanity tank didn't believe in vampires. Not unless they were forced to. Maybe Liv thought Shay was some kind of crazy serial killer. Or that she'd gone on a drug-induced frenzy. She *had* been pretty twitchy that night, and both Olivia and Kaz had noticed.

"So . . . you're going?" Gabriel prodded her.

"Yeah. Yes. Yep, I am," Shay said, so nervous, she was using three times as many words as she needed. She didn't reach for the door handle. "Really. In a couple of seconds. I just need something good first."

She turned toward Gabriel and threaded her fingers into his curly hair. "Come here." She gently tugged his head closer to hers. Not that he needed any urging to kiss her. Gabriel always wanted to kiss her. After everything that had happened, there were no bar-riers between them anymore. They'd gone through the most intense experience of their lives together, and they were bonded now, twined together forever.

There was something different about kissing someone you were in communion with, at least based on Shay's vast experience of hav-ing kissed a whole two other guys besides Gabriel. But in addition to the feel of Gabriel's lips, and the play of his tongue against hers, Shay was filled with his emotions, conscious every second of how much he loved her.

With a sigh, Shay forced herself to pull away from him. "Olivia," she said.

"Olivia," Gabriel repeated. "I could go with you."

"That would make it worse. Two vampires standing on her front porch, especially after what she saw me do . . . No, I've got to go alone." She kissed his cheek. "But thank you." Shay put her hand on the door handle, and this time she opened it. She walked directly to Olivia's front door and rang the bell before she had the chance to wimp out.

Olivia would be the one to answer the door. Or at least she was the only one home to do it. The scents that Shay was picking up from Olivia's parents and younger brother weren't fresh. They'd been gone for at least a couple of hours.

She's coming, Shay thought, hearing Olivia's soft footsteps. Her stomach gave a slow roll as the door swung open. Olivia's face paled as soon as she saw Shay, and Shay was intently aware of the change in her friend's blood flow. It was pretty easy to fight down her blood-lust, though. Mom had stolen more blood from the hospital, and Shay had fed right before they left.

Olivia started to slam the door, but her human reflexes were no match for Shay's vampire speed. Her human strength was no match for Shay's vampire power either. Shay easily caught the door and held it open, even though Olivia was using all her weight to push it shut.

"I just want to talk to you for one second," Shay said. "Please, Olivia. I'm still your friend. I'm still the person you've known forever, the person you love to boss around. I'm just me."

"You ripped that woman's throat out," Olivia accused, her voice sharp with panic. "There's nothing you can say. I saw you."

"I didn't rip it out. I didn't even really hurt her. I drank from her, that's all." *That's all.* Like the fact that Shay drank blood would reassure Olivia. "I . . . something happened to me, Olivia. Martin was giving me these transfusions and—"

"I'll call the cops." Olivia took her cell out of the front pocket of her hoodie. Shay could easily have snatched the phone away, but that wouldn't calm Olivia down and get her to really listen.

"Let me explain first," Shay begged.

"No. Leave now or I call," Olivia insisted.

"Please. I'm not going to hurt you. I can explain—"

Olivia tried to dial, but her fingers were trembling too much to hit the buttons with any accuracy. "I don't know what you are, but you're not Shay. Get away from me. Now!" Her voice rose with each word, until she was screaming, her eyes wide and bright with hysteria.

"Liv—," Shay tried again.

"Got it!" Olivia cried. "It's ringing. Go or I'm telling them to come get you."

Shay held up both hands. "Okay, I'm going."

"Don't ever come back," Olivia warned.

"I won't," Shay answered, tears stinging her eyes. She turned and ran back to the car. She jumped behind the wheel and slammed the door. Gabriel didn't ask what had happened as she drove back to her house. He didn't need to. He'd have been able to hear every word without a problem. And even if he couldn't, their communion would tell him that it had gone very, very badly.

She thinks I'm a monster. The word repeated itself over and over in Shay's head as she drove. *Monster, monster.*

"Most humans really are as scared and dangerous as Ernst thought they were," Gabriel said quietly. "You and your mother are the exceptions. Most people . . . well, they assume that we're evil. All of us."

"I know," Shay whispered. "I just didn't want to believe it."

He was silent for the rest of the drive, letting her cry.

"Do you think we need to be concerned that she'll send the police here?" Gabriel asked when Shay pulled into her driveway and turned off the car.

She kneaded the steering wheel with her fingers, a habit she'd picked up from her mom without even realizing it. She made herself let go. "I don't think so. I think she wants to forget it ever happened. And it's not as if the police would have an easy time believing I tore someone's throat out with my teeth. I'm still known around here as the sick girl."

"There's that," Gabriel agreed. "But we still have to leave. We shouldn't even stay another night. We've been here far too long already." Shay's mom had driven Shay, Gabriel, Tamara, Millie, and Luis home five days before, after the fire. They'd taken Martin's van, since he'd already rigged it to keep the sunlight out. Mom's Mercedes was too small to hold them all. They'd awoken at sunset in Shay's garage—weak and shaky, with Tamara, Millie, and Luis still paralyzed and hawthorn-sick.

"That's what they were talking about when we left," Shay commented. Tamara had been urging Luis to leave with her, just go, right then. Even after Shay's mother had saved her life, dragged her into the van, taken her to a safe place, and kept her out of the sun, Tamara was still filled with hatred and mistrust. The instant the hawthorn had begun to wear off, she'd wanted to leave.

"People are going to start asking questions about Martin soon," Gabriel said. "A man like that, who's been on the cover of *Time* magazine and everything, can't disappear without a huge investigation.

We need to be far away when that happens. We'll all get new identities, start a new life."

Shay sighed. She didn't need to be in communion with the other vampires to feel their confusion over what to do next. She felt the same confusion within herself.

"They're really getting into it now," Gabriel commented. For a moment they both listened to the argument going on inside. With their vampire senses, it was easy to hear the raised voices.

That was all he said, but Shay could feel his sadness—sadness and, underneath that, grief over Ernst's death. "Do you think . . . It doesn't sound like everyone wants to stay together. At least not Tamara," Shay said. "Will they break up the family?"

"Do you want the family to stay together?" Gabriel asked her.

Shay started to answer, then hesitated. "How can you have a private conversation when you live with other vampires?"

"Privacy isn't really a thing with us. With the communion, we're all connected anyway. Or we were," Gabriel replied. The communion only existed between him and Shay now. All the other family members had been hit with hawthorn darts during the attack at the farmhouse. "But right now they're probably too busy with their own conversation to listen to ours."

True. It was hard to talk to someone and listen in on a separate conversation at the same time. "I know how important your family is to you. It's just that when I look at Tamara and Luis, all I see is them draining the blood out of you."

"I did the same thing. To Sam. You know that," Gabriel said.

They hadn't talked about it since that night when he'd almost died in her arms. Shay fought down the image of Gabriel drinking from her father, putting him to death. "You thought it was to keep your family safe. And we've both forgiven you—my father and me," Shay reminded him. It was the truth. She believed it in her heart and her gut. She didn't think she would have made the same choice, but then she hadn't seen her family annihilated by a bunch of humans.

"That's the same reason Luis did it to me," Gabriel answered. "Tamara too."

"No, she wanted vengeance. She was furious. She wanted to kill you because she thinks you killed Richard. She's still seething, I can hear it in her voice." Shay almost started kneading the steering wheel again, but she stopped her hands in time.

"In a way, I did kill Richard," Gabriel told her.

"No, what you did was—," Shay began.

"I didn't save him," Gabriel interrupted. "I let him sacrifice himself, when if I'd simply left you in the basement and gone to help Ernst, we most certainly would have killed Martin before he could detonate his bomb."

"I know." Shay reached over and took his hand. "I'd be dead if you hadn't gotten me out of there, though. I hate that you had to make that choice." She could feel the weight of it in him, and he already carried so much guilt and regret.

"It wasn't a choice," Gabriel said, his dark eyes intent on her face. "I couldn't let you die. But that doesn't mean Tamara's wrong."

"It was Martin's fault," Shay said. "Not yours." But she tried to imagine how she'd feel if someone had let Gabriel die to save . . . anyone else's life. Even thinking about it opened a well of icy blackness in her chest. "And now he's dead," she added.

"And we're alive," Gabriel said.

"Yeah." It was hard to believe that they'd both survived that night. Her mother, too. Shay had so much to be thankful for, and yet . . .

"Thinking about Olivia?" Gabriel asked.

"Yeah," Shay said. "The way she—"

Shay didn't have time to finish before Tamara strode out of the house, her face hard with determination. Gabriel climbed out of the car and intercepted her. Shay followed him.

"We were just going to go in and talk to everybody about what we should do now," Gabriel told his sister.

"You do that," Tamara told him. "I'm gone." She tried to step around Gabriel, but he blocked her.

"Tam, we're still your family," Gabriel said. "We still—"

"The only reason I joined the family was Richard, and he's dead," Tamara said, her eyes, cold and hard, flicking over to Shay. "I'm leaving."

"Okay, fine. Do you know where you're going?" he asked. She hesitated. "Look, just stay with us until you figure things out. It's safer."

"Safer? Are you delusional?" Tamara snapped. "She brought all this on us." Tamara jerked her chin at Shay.

"And my mother and I saved your life," Shay reminded her.

"After you led the killer to us. After he killed Richard," Tamara shot back. She shoved her thick hair away from her face. "I understand that you saved me. It's the only reason you and that human woman are still alive." She turned back to Gabriel. "I won't be around them another second. Them or you."

This time when she started to circle around Gabriel, he let her. "Let's go talk to the others," he said to Shay.

"You okay?" Shay asked, even though she could feel through the communion that he wasn't. Worry, and anger, and anxiety, and guilt were pulsing out of him.

"You're with me. That's all that matters." *Liar*, Shay thought, but she smiled at him. Even though it wasn't all that mattered, it was the most important thing. To both of them.

When they walked into the house, they found Luis, Millie, and Shay's mother gathered in the living room. "We couldn't stop her," Luis said.

"It's her choice," Gabriel replied. "Now we have to figure out what the rest of us are going to do. I think we should leave for one of the other safe houses tonight. We can get to the ones farther west as long as we're willing to risk staying in motels along the way. If we arrive at night and check in, we should be safe enough during the death sleeps. Once we're at the safe house, we can regroup and make real plans."

"I want to come," Shay's mom declared. "There's nothing for me here anymore, and I'll be the one who has to explain what happened to Martin. It'll be easier for me to just disappear, frankly."

It's true, Shay realized. *It's not like she has friends here, not close ones, anyway. She's lived her whole life for me for so long. I'm all she has.*

"I'd like her to be with us," Shay told the others. "I know I don't really have the right to a vote or anything—"

"You have the same rights as any of us. You're part of the family," Gabriel said. "She's part of the family," he repeated, as though waiting to be contradicted. But Luis and Millie just nodded. "How do you feel about Emma joining us?"

"You could use me, you know," Shay's mom reminded them. "I can go out in the daytime and protect you during your death sleep. I can be your front person with other people. Humans. Human people," she finished awkwardly.

Shay saw Luis's mouth twist in a small smile.

"You've lost a father," Mom added in a rush. "I think you could use a mother. Even if some of you are hundreds of years older than I am."

Shay looked at Millie. She wasn't sure about Luis, but she thought Millie would say yes.

"I shouldn't have a say," Millie replied. "I'm not going with you," she added quickly, tears shimmering in her eyes.

"What?" Gabriel burst out.

"Mils, that's crazy," Luis said.

"I don't want to hide anymore," Millie explained. "I want to live in a city. A huge city. I want to do things. I want to do *everything*."

"You're not thinking of telling people the truth about yourself?" Gabriel gasped.

"It would be a horrible mistake," Shay's mom said. "They'd lock you away. They'd do unspeakable things. Just look at what Martin—"

Millie held up her hands. "I don't mean I'm going to walk around telling people I'm a vampire," she said. "I just don't want to be so isolated anymore. Since I was a child, I've been hidden in caves and labs and houses in the middle of nowhere. I have been alive for ages, but my life has been so . . . small. I want to know more people." She gave a teary smile at Gabriel and put her hand over Luis's. "Not that I don't love you guys."

Shay nodded. She knew what it was like to live a life with so many restraints, expected to be cautious all the time.

"It's way too risky," Gabriel began.

"It's her choice," Shay said, cutting him short. "And I understand why you'd want that," she added to Millie.

Gabriel didn't look happy, and Shay could feel more worry in her communion with him, but he didn't try to argue. He turned to Luis. "And you?"

"It's not going to be the same," Luis said.

"It's not," Gabriel agreed. "And I don't want it to be. I want our family to be a place where there's room for all kinds. I don't want us to be so ruled by fear that we're willing to kill each other to stay safe. Or what we believe is safe."

"I've been part of a family, your family, as long as I can remember," Luis said to Gabriel. "I don't have even one memory of another life. But I feel like my family doesn't exist anymore."

"In a way, it doesn't," Shay said, wondering if she had the right to speak. "You've lost your father and a brother. Your sisters are going their own way. It isn't the same family. That doesn't mean it won't still be yours. My family is different now too."

"We have a lot to figure out," Gabriel put in. "And we'll do it together. Together we'll figure out what our future can and should be."

"Okay. I'm with you," Luis said.

"Millie, you'll always have a home with us. You know that. Or you can just come visit for holidays," Shay's mother said. She gave a little laugh. "Do we celebrate holidays?"

"Like Gabriel said, we'll figure it out together." Shay was filled with a rush of anticipation and hope, the emotions so powerful, they made her a little giddy. She was about to start planning her future. Her *future*. She used to believe her future would be short, and filled with sickness.

But now she had an eternity, an eternity with Gabriel, and her world was full of time. Time, and love.